Jagged Road to Sainthood

Vista Townsend

JAGGED ROAD TO SAINTHOOD

Print Edition 2015 ISBN 978-0-990618-1-8

First Edition

Printed in the United States of America

Books By Vista Townsend

Science Fiction
Age of Quintessence series

Synthetic Genesis
Shadow Legacy
Vortex Crucible

Fantasy
Salt Legacy series

Masters of Souls

Historical Fiction

Jagged Road To Sainthood

Based on

Confessions
By Saint Augustine of Hippo

And

The Life of Saint Augustine
By Possidius, Bishop of Calama

Dedication

To God who is my soul's delight,

my parents who first showed me what it is means to live Christ-like,

my sister who is my best friend and critic,

and Monica my fellow Latin comrade.

Part I

"You have made us for yourself, and our heart is restless until it rests in you."

~Saint Augustine, *Confessions, 1.1*

Chapter One

A youth swept a broom across the mosaic floor of the Basilica Pacis, brushing away grime brought in by the constant flow of visitors. Triferus paid little attention to the geometric patterns of the tiles decorating the tomb underneath his feet. It was just one of several dozen, the names of saints blurring together, their heroic stories of sacrifice and triumph meaningless to him. He moved slowly, limping slightly with each step.

The large main chamber of the basilica was bare except for a wooden altar and pillars which separated the nave from the aisles. Log beams held up the tiled terracotta roof. The only seating found in the entire room was at the semicircular apse where a stone bench was built into the wall. There bishops and presbyters sat during services while the congregation stood. Sermons sometimes lasted over two hours, short compared to the lengthy debates given in the government forums which drew large crowds listening all day to lawyers' embellished speeches.

The morning liturgy was already over, but a few townspeople still entered the church. None spared a glance at Triferus, not that the youth cared. Dressed in a plain brown tunic, he looked like a servant, but the monks who oversaw the basilica hired none, seeing themselves as God's servants ready to do the humblest of duties. Triferus lodged at the nearby monastery which had taken him in, an injured refugee. After recovering his health, it had been expected for him to seek a new home, but he had nowhere to go. Who would hire a cripple when the city of Hippo Regius was crammed with desperate refugees willing to work long hours with little pay? The monks had taken pity on the youth and let him remain with them, at least for now. But unless he decided to take up the vocation of the cloth, he would need to leave when the war ended.

Sometimes Triferus considered becoming a monk. What else was he good for? No longer could he handle the backbreaking work of a farmer. No military officer would train him to wield a sword. He lacked the education for a scholar. But he could clean floors—perhaps his life's fate for what short time was left to him. Rarely did a day go by without the city walls being assaulted. At any moment a breach in the defenses could allow thousands of Vandal barbarians to pour into the city.

Stress from the constant, looming army took its toll on the city residents. They knew the war was going poorly. During services desperate people packed the sanctuary to pray for forgiveness, seek consolation, give penance, or beg for help. Daily monks were called upon to give last rites.

A woman dashed through the double doors, holding a limp toddler in her arms. She glanced franticly around.

Seeing Triferus holding the broom, she said, "I must have a priest, quick! My daughter is dying."

"This way." The teenager's face showed no emotion as he led her through a side door to the baptistery.

Bishop Possidius, thin from lack of proper food, was in the process of dunking an infant in the pool. Still standing in the water, he handed the silent, sickly baby back to her pale father and looked at the newcomers.

The mother dropped to her knees, cuddling her child. "Please, baptize her. Wash away her sins before it is too late."

The bishop looked down at the child then spoke gingerly to the worried mother, "I am sorry, but your child is dead."

"No! She still breathes. Look, her chest rises."

He examined the still body while the mother tried to hold back sobs. "Again I am sorry, but it is too late. The soul is gone."

The mother bent over her child, weeping. "She was fine last night. Just a little cough." As the weary priest walked up stone steps out of the pool, she grabbed the hem of his wet, black robe. "You must do something! What sins has my child done to condemn her? She has always been a good girl."

Possidius offered what hope he could. "God will be merciful to young children in purgatory." He motioned for another priest to take the limp child. "We will see to her burial."

"But she will remain outside the church. Always." With tears streaming down her face, the mother reluctantly let go of her daughter.

The bishop offered more words of comfort while Triferus grimly watched. Three months ago the youth would have felt pity for the woman's plight, but that was before his own happy, innocent life had been ripped from him. Now only cold detachment filled him. Everywhere was death and suffering. The only way to survive was to forget everything, focus only on daily activities such as chores or where the next meal would come from. He walked back into the sanctuary and continued sweeping.

But his mind betrayed him. As the broom brushed across tiles, he thought about his mother whom he had watched do this same chore thousands of times. The image of her face the last time he saw her flashed in front of him. Her limp, defiled body, blood draining from a slashed throat. His young sister, holding their mother's hand, herself dying from a deep knife wound. Triferus dropped the broom and fled from the basilica, but the memories clung to him.

He had been tilling land with his father when they saw smoke rising from the village. Triferus had been guiding the ox through a field which belonged to their landlord while his father broke apart large clumps of sod with a wooden hoe. They abandoned the ox, still in harness, and rushed back towards their hut on the outskirts of the village—but they were too late. A raiding party was sweeping through the hamlet, killing all who opposed them. Triferus's father heard the screams of his wife and rushed into their house. He was disemboweled with a swipe of a sword before he had moved two steps inside. Standing right behind his father, Triferus was paralyzed by shock as he watched his father slowly fall to the dirt floor. The hesitation saved him. A blade aiming for his head missed. Another soldier slashed the tendons of his right leg. Triferus lost his balance and his head smashed against a table.

He awoke later, weak from blood lost. Triferus crawled to his bloody sister and held her limp hand. She gave a brief smile of recognition, even as her eyes began to dim. Fighting against tears, Treferus sung her favorite psalm from church, holding back his tears until she was gone. He held her body tight, weeping, expecting any moment to follow his family into the next world.

An elderly man who lived a few huts away on the same planation shuffled in. His tormented eyes swept over the bloody bodies of the family he had worked alongside harvesting crops with for many years. Seeing Triferus alive, the grieved man tied a tourniquet to the teenager's leg and gave him water to drink. Then he left, looking for others to help. That night Triferus slept on the dirt floor of the hut by his dead family. In the morning the neighbor returned with several men to bury the dead. They carried Triferus outside and sat him under a shade tree. Still in shock, Triferus silently watched the graves being dug, his mind unable to accept that the safe, blissful world of his youth was gone forever. His family had only been tenants, a step barely above slavery. They had to obey the commands of their master who owned their house and the land they farmed. Their master had been a fair man, providing decent food for his workers during the starving times of winter. Now there was no master to save him. The man had been murdered along with so many others from the village.

Rumors had circulated for weeks that a vast army further north was advancing across the providence. Since the village was not near a major trade route, the inhabitants had thought the soldiers would bypass them unnoticed. They had been wrong. Most of huts of the planation looked the same as they had the day before, for the inhabitants were too poor to have kept the raider's attention for long. It was the nearby village which took the blunt of the raid. Several homes and businesses had been burnt, along with the church. The raiders, dressed as local soldiers, had struck in the middle of the day when many men would have been out in the fields. The raiders plundered quickly, terrorizing the residents while looting for supplies. Livestock stolen. Grain bins emptied. Several women and children taken away as slaves. Any who tried to challenge the raiders were slaughtered. The elderly priest had first been tortured to reveal where the church's valuables were kept then murdered in front of captive townspeople.

The raiders left as quickly as they came, leaving behind the weak, elderly, and injured. Villagers who had managed to hide during the raid slowly reappeared, helping were they could. Fearing another attack, the survivors gathered what they could and fled toward the largest walled city—Hippo Regius, the royal port where the Numidian kings had once lived before North Africa had become a Roman providence.

Triferus joined the exodus, limping with a crutch. Family and friends kept close together, carrying their supplies. Triferus had no relatives left alive, and his few friends were kept busy attending to their own families' needs. As they continued north, the flagstone road became crowded with refugees from other towns, and Triferus lost sight of his fellow villagers. That night as he slept alone under a stunted bush beside the road, his pack was stolen along with his remaining food and water. The next morning he desperately searched for it, asking nearby refugees if they had seen it. They either shook their heads or ignored him.

He continued along the road, hoping to find someone who knew him, but he only saw the tense faces of strangers. Despair clung to Triferus as he limped under the hot sun by day or shivered in the cold by night. Never before had he felt so completely alone, forsaken by all who knew him. Triferus became weaker, his mind barely holding to reality. Pleasant memories of his youth, memories of working beside his father in the fields, kept him going for a while. Finally, he collapsed beside the road, awaiting death. Exhausted, he even longed for it, wishing for rest from the torment of losing his family, of the nightmarish images of seeing their lifeless bodies.

For a second time death did not come.

Instead, a cart stopped. A middle-age priest wearing a black robe directed several monks to examine Triferus. Seeing him still alive, the priest tended his infected leg wound and gave him water. Triferus thirstily gulped the water, uncertain if he dreamed. Then the monks placed him in the wagon beside other injured refugees. Over the following days Triferus mainly slept, but he remembered blurred images. Waking up next to a copse of an elderly man who had died during the night. Passing a regiment of Roman troops withdrawing east away from the advancing Vandal army, their heavy sandals thumping on the cobblestone. Desperate people hailing the monks, pleading for prayers. Nights surrounded by endless weeping of refugees mourning the loss of homes and friends. Triferus cried too, at times cursing those who had killed his family.

One night when his grief was strongest, he remembered hearing the songs of the monks, their strong voices singing of faith in the midst of destruction. Nearby people joined in. The harmony of the voices in the dark sent chills down Triferus's body, stopping his tears. Later when the priest came to check his injuries, Triferus finally felt like talking.

"Why do the Vandals attack us? What did we do to them?"

"We invited them here," said the priest, cleaning out the latest maggots from Triferus's wound then wrapping it back in the same dirty cloth. The priest had already used up all his medicinal supplies days ago. "Or at least General Boniface did, thinking by allying with his former enemies he could defeat a greater enemy. But King Genseric turned against Boniface, and now we all pay for the general's foolishness. What is your name, son?"

"Triferus." The youth gritted his teeth against the throbbing pain in his leg.

"I am Possidius, Bishop of Calama."

"Was your city attacked?"

"Not at the time we left. The Vandals have a special hatred for us Catholics. Many of them are Arian heretics. They kill any of us they find."

"Then we all die." Despair filled the teenager, his vision blurring from the pain.

"That is God's decision. He has given us a place of refuge. I have a friend in Hippo Regius who will take us in." He patted the youth's shoulder. "Rest now."

Over the next few days, Triferus became sicker as a fever raged through him, his infected leg throbbing. By the time they reached Hippo Regius, Triferus was barely conscious. He stared at the vast stone wall which had protected the ancient city for over a thousand years. He dozed, only semi-aware of passing through the crowded streets. Arriving at the monastery, the monks carried him and the other injured inside. Over the following days, some died while others recovered. The survivors left, seeking acquaintances in the city. But Triferus had nowhere to go, no family to seek out. The villagers of his hometown might be anywhere. As Triferus's strength returned, he began helping the monks with chores.

By then, the mighty Roman army had withdrawn to Hippo Regius without engaging the Vandals. Thousands of refugees poured into the royal city like rats before a raging flood, bringing news that city after city had fallen before the invaders. Then one day the fertile plains of corn surrounding Hippo Regius were darkened by eighty thousands Vandals setting up camp, preparing for a long siege. Their ships blockaded the port, cutting the city off from the outside world. Now three months had passed. Food had become scarce, disease rampant, death common.

Triferus wandered about outdoors, needing something to take his thoughts off his missing family and his fear of the barbarian army which lay beyond the city wall. Numerous stone buildings besides the basilica were nestled close together across the insula including the monastery with its offices, a secretarium where councils of bishops met, a sizeable library, and a vegetable garden. In the middle of the grounds was a small, elegant chapel dedicated to the martyrs. The insula took up nearly two acres in the heart of Hippo Regius. To the west a large park separated the church grounds from villas of wealthy citizens. The original church had been small, but over the course of several centuries, land had been donated and the church reconstructed into a modest cathedral.

Several richly dressed visitors gathered around a monk who read a scroll aloud. Near the library two presbyters from different dioceses debated over a theology issue which meant nothing to Triferus. From the chapel of the martyrs, a psalm was chanted by several monks practicing for the evening service. Triferus stopped and listened to the melody, letting the peaceful rhythm clear his mind.

"Beauty stirs the soul," said an elderly bishop leaning against the doorway to the chapel, a faraway look in his peaceful eyes. "The skies turn grey and threatening when our lives have no music in them. Our hearts become lonely and our souls lose their courage."

"The sky always threatens now." Triferus thought of the fiery arrows and stones which Vandals shot over the walls, destroying homes near the edge of the city.

"We must tune our hearts to brave music, giving us the sense of comradeship with heroes and saints of every age."

"What need have I for saints? They are dead. Along with my family."

"So young to lose so much." The elderly priest looked kindly at the fifteen year old. "We remember the saints to quicken our spirits so we may be able to encourage the souls of all who journey with us on this road of life."

Triferus looked away, trying to hide a rush of anger. He did not wish to offend the holy man, but he was sick of apt answers which changed nothing. A fit of deep coughing struck the priest, and he held on to the door to keep his balance.

The youth stepped forward, wondering how he could help. Possidius, now dressed in a dry robe, hurried over. He held the elderly man until the spasm ended.

"Augustine, you should be in bed."

"Music drew me from my sickbed, old friend."

"You need rest now."

Possidius guided his mentor to the dormitory. Even with his lame leg, Triferus kept pace with them, opening doors as needed. Though the elderly priest was the chief bishop of Hippo Regius, his small bedroom was like the others, simply furnished with a narrow bed and chest containing clothing. On a small table rested several scrolls and an oil lamp. Light streamed in through a small window.

As Augustine lay on a thin mattress, he said, "Could you bring me a copy of Genesis? And Ambrose's *Hexaemeron*, if it has been returned now."

"Of course."

Triferus followed Possidius to the library. From floor to ceiling were shelves of wooden boxes filled with scrolls organized by authors. Possidius easily navigated through the large collection, passing both Christian and secular texts. He handed Triferus several scrolls. Two boys moved among the shelves, retrieving text to practice their reading. Routinely during services they read scriptures in strong, steady voices which carried across the congregation. Triferus watched them enviously as they browsed through the scrolls.

Possidius spied the look. "Can you read?"

Triferus glanced down at the parchments in his hand. "Some. I finished primary then helped my father on the farm we rent."

"Perhaps it is time to continue your education."

"Tenants have no time for such luxury."

"There is no master here demanding crops to be harvested on time. Choose anything you wish. We keep a well-stocked library."

"Your writings are beyond my understanding. I have tried listening to readings of monks but they make little sense to me."

"Ah, it can be challenging to know how we are supposed to interpret verses. I have seen too many debates on that, occasionally being a participant myself. Perhaps a narrative will be more to your liking. Something with substance. A true story."

The bishop moved to another wall of wooden boxes. "This section contains works by Augustine. My friend is a prolific writer. Here is a collection of his sermons." Possidius glanced at scrolls in the wooden bins. "Ah, he even keeps copies of old letters. Needs better organizing, I see. This large section contains copies of his many books, theology mainly." Possidius bent down and pulled out a thick scroll. "Perhaps this will interest you. It is widely circulated, read in Rome and even by some of our Greek speaking comrades in the Eastern Empire."

"What is it about?" asked Triferus, taking the book.

"Augustine wrote his life's story shortly after he was appointed bishop over thirty years ago. It does not go heavily into theology accept at the end. I will take Augustine the books he wanted. Go ahead and practice your reading. If you run into something you do not understand, just ask me or another priest. We take great joy in explaining text."

"I noticed."

Possidius let a small smile slip, remembering his own youth. Then he continued perusing through the scrolls.

Triferus left the library and sought out a quiet spot away from clergy and visitors. Anyone reading a book at the insula often drew listeners who paid rap attention if the text was interesting, interrupting the reader as questions arose. Triferus wanted no one to hear his awkward reading, especially if the book was popular. He unrolled the first section and began speaking the words aloud, keeping his voice low.

Chapter Two

Villas dotted lush plains of wheat fields and olive groves. Two-story homes of wealthy landowners were surrounded by paddock for their horses, fishponds, and cypresses trees. Roads crisscrossed the region, connecting small, conventional towns to the thriving cities of North Africa. At Thagaste, a wedding procession left the church and headed out of town to the groom's estate. As the guests marched, they joked and laughed, singing merrily to music from lyres and tambourines.

The young bride, wearing an embellished dress, kept her grim face hidden behind a saffron veil. She walked near her elderly nurse while her mother and younger sister joined the celebration. Monnica felt no merriment. At fifteen, she was already three years passed the legal age for marriage. She had been tutored for years for this day, but still it frightened her. What kind of man would her husband Patricius be? He was not even a Christian but believed in pagan gods. Her parents liked his political position on the town council and his generosity in giving money. He liked her dowry of gold jewelry and silver coins.

The procession reached the small estate which was to be her new home. Patricius only owned thirty acres, its fields and orchid worked by tenants. His mother Lepida, a widow, welcomed the bride into the villa with a short, jubilant speech. Patricius grinned at his bride. In his mid-thirties, he was brawny and tan from a life often spent outdoors. He took Monnica's timid hand and led her inside. The guest lingered for a while, reclining on couches and snacking on lavish dishes prepared by slaves. Jokes abound about the consummation and children, causing Monnica to be grateful for the veil which hid her blushing face. As the sun began to set, many guests headed home, but a few who had a long distance to travel stayed the night.

Monnica remained calm until Atia, who had kept near her all day, rose to leave. The bride held tightly to the nurse's hand. Atia had been there her whole life, teaching her to read, disciplining her when she went astray, passing on her deep love for God. As a slave, Atia was highly respected in her master's house, having raised Monnica's father and now his children. The elderly slave squeezed her ward's hand reassuringly and then left with the family.

Fear plagued the bride. She was alone in a strange household. The jokes and revelry continued from the guests lodging overnight. Lepida comically told of her own wedding night, causing listeners to laugh at her misadventures. Patricius sat beside his wife, letting his strong, lean body brush against her. She kept still, closing her eyes and praying for courage.

When he took her hand and led her to his bedchamber, her heart throbbed in fright. He pulled back her veil and studied her. Lush, black hair and olive skin showed her Berber ancestry. Her race had controlled the North African providence of Numinia for countless centuries until one of their jaded princes had joined with the Romans, aiding in the conquering of his own nation. For over half a millennium Rome had firmly ruled the providence. People of every race could be found in the thriving cities, but in small communities such as Thagaste the Berbers still made up the majority of the population.

Patricius ran his fingers through Monnica's long hair then touched her heavy gold earrings—her dowry for the wedding. "You are more beautiful than Venus."

"Do not say that." Monnica flinched, realizing she had just commanded her husband. "I mean, please do not compare me to a goddess. It is sacrilegious."

The groom laughed. His muscular, Roman profile had caught the eye of many when he strolled about town. His bronze skin hinted he had at least one Berber ancestor. "You may find my speech boorish, but I know how to turn a girl into a woman. Venus will indeed be envious of you." He blew out the lamp and reached for his young, nervous bride in the darkness.

The next morning Monnica had to endure more jests as the household prepared for the wedding banquet. Lepida ordered her five slaves to aid a professional chief hired to cook for the wedding. Monnica helped wherever she could by rearrange the pillows on the couches where the guests would dine and washing walls so that the mosaic pictures shone brightly in the sunlight coming in through windows. Patricius joked that her labor was unnecessary as that was why they had slaves, but he was pleased his bride was not spoilt. Lepida kept a sharp eye on her daughter-in-law, fussing that the pillows were not aligned correctly.

As her family and friends arrived, Monnica became a cheerful host, putting up with their jokes. Musicians played flutes, drums, and kitharas as slaves brought in trays loaded with fruits cut into fanciful shapes and meats covered in spicy sauces. Patricius drunk the wine heavily, but Monnica only took sips. Atia had trained her well in childhood to avoid indulgencing. Monnica was happy as long as her family was near, but when they left, loneness filled her. She considered begging her father to give her Atia, but knew her younger sister still needed the nurse's care.

The next morning Monnica rose early and helped the slaves clean. She listened to their conversations, learning their relationships. Agorix guarded the strongbox at night where the family's money was kept. He was mated to Magia, the cook who prepared the normal household meals. They had six children over the years but two had died young and two sold. Only their daughters Statilia and Turia, both beautiful maidens in their twenties, remained. Ruso, a strapping twenty-five-year-old, was a talented horseman who often accompanied his master on hunts. He had been sold into slavery at the age of five when his parents could no longer afford to feed their many children.

Monnica skipped breakfast. When her mother-in-law awoke, she asked permission to attend the morning liturgy in Thagaste. Lepida agreed as long as Monnica did not go alone. Selecting Turia, Monnica walked to town with the slave following several steps behind. Most of the town's buildings were Roman in design, white-washed stone with red terracotta roofs. On the outskirts of Thagaste was a race track for chariots. Nearby was a small arena only big enough for animal fights. A colonnade courtyard surrounded the forum where civic functions were conducted including court cases and tax collecting. Several temples to ancient Punic deities were visited daily by Berbers holding tightly to traditional beliefs.

Monnica climbed the steps to the only Christian church in town. Simple in design, the stone church had wooden beams to support the clay-tiled roof, no glass in the windows, no seats in the sanctuary. Worshipers stood throughout the services.

Turia paused at the doorway, reluctant to enter.

Monnica smiled reassuring, "You may worship with me if you wish."

"I prefer to visit the shrine of Tellus Matar, the Mother Goddess." Turia kept her eyes downcast as she spoke.

"You have at least an hour. Do as you please."

Monnica entered and found her family standing among the small congregation. During the service she felt protected and loved, with her mother to the right, Atia on her left, her father and sister nearby. After the sermon ended, the priest asked the unbaptized to leave. The church door was then shut and the sacrament of Eucharist given. Monnica moved forward with the others to take a bite of bread representing Jesus' tormented body and drink wine from the cup symbolizing blood lost during the crucifixion.

When the service ended, Monnica stepped outside but did not see Turia. She began walking through town towards the shrine of Tellus Matar. Reaching the small temple, she only saw a priestess and several worshipers. Feeling uneasy, she walked inside, frowning at the statue of the stone goddess and incense burning on the altar. Still not finding the slave, she hurried outside and continued to search. As Monnica passed the forum, a group of young men who knew her older brother called her name. They asked her how his studies in Madauros were going and had a wife been chosen for him yet. After briefing chatting, she parted from them. Near the public bathhouse, she finally spotted Turia talking with several brawny slaves taking a rest from hauling wood to heat the water.

Angrily Monnica marched up. "You were supposed to meet me at the church."

Keeping eyes downcast, Turia said, "You said, 'Do as you please.' I pleased to visit my brother."

Casting a glance at the male slaves studying her, Monnica stammered, "Oh…it…is time to return to the villa." She could not bring herself to call it home yet.

As she walked away with Turia trailing, one of the wood carriers said to another, "She is decent looking, but her breasts are too small. How long until Patricius bores of her?"

"A month tops," said Turia's brother.

Monnica quickened her steps. Arriving back at the villa, Turia began setting the table for lunch. Monnica began to help, noting the frown on the slave's lips.

Turia set clay cups on the table. "Your help is not needed, mistress. I know how to do my job."

"I did not mean to imply differently."

Lepida swooped in. "Good, you are back. We have been invited to a dinner party next week by Romanianus. Patricius, can we afford a new palla for your wife?"

"I think it can be budgeted." The new husband greeted Monnica with a deep kiss, causing her to blush in embarrassment when he pulled away.

Turia slammed down an amphora of wine. It tipped over, sending red liquid across the table. Patricius snapped at her, "Watch what you are doing!"

"Sorry, it slipped." Turia scurried to clean up the mess.

As the week progressed, Monnica tried to find her place within the household. She helped Lepida with household duties and shopped for food in the market when coming back from church services. Lepida was friendly yet critical of everything Monnica did. The wool was spun incorrectly. The vegetables purchased from the market were of poor quality. The meat too old. The honey tainted. Monnica remained silent when criticized, determined to do a better job.

She sensed loathing from Turia and her sister with their occasional sly comments and actions, but they did not directly challenge her. Monnica pondered her own actions, wondering if she had done anything to cause strife. She had always gotten along well with the slaves in her father's household.

The night of the party arrived. Turia and Statilia helped their mistresses dress in long stolas secured by clasps on their shoulders. Monnica's new palla was put on next, the bright blue veil showing up vividly against the white dress. Lepida nodded in approval after she adjusted her daughter-in-law's hair arrangement. Ruso styled his master's toga, skillfully arranging its many folds. Patricius greeted his wife and mother in the atrium then they walked to their neighbor's large villa. Romanianus was the richest man in Thagaste, owning more land by far than anyone else in the region. He spared no expense hosting lavish banquets for his guests, which included the entire city council of Thagaste.

As the youngest adult at the dinner, Monnica felt out of place. Several of the wives were friendly, recounting stories of their first days of marriage. The party lasted late into the night with many guests becoming drunk, including Patricius. As they walked home in the dark, Patricius sung love ballads loudly. When they arrived at their villa, the slaves helped them dress into simpler clothing. Then Monnica headed to Patricius's bedchamber.

Ruso blocked her path. He was well-built like his master but rarely showed emotions. "You cannot enter tonight, mistress. He already sleeps."

Perplexed, Monnica returned to her bedroom. The next morning she was up early spinning wool into string when she spotted Turia leaving Patricius's bedchamber. The teenager frowned. Only Ruso should have access. When her husband finally came out, he greeted her with a kiss and complained of a hangover. Despite the pain, he headed into town to be a witness at the forum for a friend suing a neighbor. That night after supper, he did not invite her to his bed. She stayed in her room but watched through the crack of her slightly opened door. Shortly later, Turia headed into her master's chamber and did not leave till early morning.

Monnica was devastated, her thoughts irrational. What had she done wrong to turn her husband away? They had barely been married a week. Had she not worked hard enough? Perhaps she should have worn more jewelry at the party. Found higher quality vegetables at the market. Was her palla the wrong color?

Monnica barely spoke during breakfast. Patricius was cheerful, bragging how his friend had won the court case the day before. Lepida noticed her daughter-in-law's sober face. After her son left to hassle his tenants, she questioned Monnica.

"Are you well, daughter?"

"Yes."

"You skipped attending church this morning."

"I did not feel like praying." Actually, she had prayed all night, but she could not bring herself to walk into the church where her blissful family would ask about her marital life.

Lepida sat beside her daughter-in-law. "What has upset you?"

"Why does my husband not call me to his chamber? How have I displeased him?"

The matron sighed. "Nothing. Your body is still developing its curves. Even then, he will continue to call his slaves. All husbands do."

"Not in my father's household. Such a thing is forbidden by our God."

"Perhaps such rules are followed in a Christian household but not here. Nor in most of the empire. Besides, you will be grateful when you are older. When you tire of your husband's attention, just send a slave."

"I would never do that." Monnica stood. "I feel like praying after all."

The teenager left the villa with Magia in tow. The middle-age slave walked slowly, carrying a basket for shopping. Monnica walked quickly, soon leaving the other behind. The morning service was already over when she reached the church. She entered and knelt at the altar. Her prayers turned into tears as she poured out her sorrow.

The priest noticed her grief. "Daughter, what troubles you?"

"I am too ashamed to say, Father."

"I have never seen you so distraught before. Is anyone sick?"

"No." Monnica wavered, needing someone to talk to who could understand. "It is my husband. He has turned from me to a slave." She burst into fresh tears. "What have I done that God punishes me?"

"I am grieved to hear that. Blame not yourself. It will bring little comfort, but I know other wives who also deal with this. It is a common problem among the pagans. I offer you what advice I can. Until Patricius turns his life over to God, his habits will not change. He must first see God's love through you. Only then, when he gives himself to God can he become the proper husband you deserve."

Monnica listened closely, drying her eyes. "I will do as you say. My ministry will be husband's household. I will live a virtuous life so I may be a witness to them."

She returned to the villa determined to live up to her pledge. Over the following weeks she aided her mother-in-law with household chores and listened to her husband recount his daily adventures when he returned home in the evenings. Many days he was cheerful, but other times he ranted, especially when money ran tight. Nights when Patricius sought the companionship of the voluptuous slave girls, Monnica kept her grief to herself. Twice a day she walked to Thagaste for liturgies. Sometimes Magia accompanied her, but more often it was one of the cook's daughters. Monnica tried to show kindness to them, for it was not their fault that their master called them to his bed. Yet they resented her, obeying when commanded but gossiping behind her back.

Lepida began hearing tales that Monnica flirted with slaves at the bathhouse and married men at church. One day when they were alone, Lepida questioned her daughter-in-law.

Monnica was shocked by the accusations. "I would never dishonor my husband or God in such a despicable way. I am always with others who will prove my innocence. Who has made this charge against me?"

"Both Tunia and Statilia. They claim to have seen you do so."

"How can they say I flirt in church when they have never been inside? But my parents do attend. Ask them if I have ever dishonored them. You yourself often accompanied me to the bathhouse. Have you seen my eye even once turn towards another man?"

Lepida studied her daughter-in-law, seeing the sincerely in the teenager's eyes. "You have done much for me here. I could not ask for a harder working daughter. I cannot perceive a flaw in your character, but I have known Tunia and Statilia to lie before. I will put an end to this gossip before the sun sets."

When Patricius arrived home, he bragged about winning a bet at the races. Seeing him in a good mood, Lepida beckoned him to a room out of the slaves hearing and told him about the accusations.

Patricius dismissed the complaint. "Slaves' gossip. Worry not about it, Mother."

"It is your place as the *dominus* to keep them in line. You sleep with them more than your own wife, and they begin to believe they are better than her. If you do not discipline them now, Turia will think herself the *domina* when I die."

Patricius sighed. "I will do as you ask."

After dinner, he called the entire household to the atrium. With whip in hand, he addressed the slaves. "There is malicious gossip being spread about my wife. For every lie I hear about her, that slave will pay with lashes. Tunia and Statilia, disrobe."

The sisters stared at him, shocked.

"Both of you have gossiped about my wife. Three lashes each."

Trembling, the slaves turned their backs and dropped their clothing. Patricius's whip cut across their backs. Statilia whimpered, crying out in pain with each lash. Tunia refused to make a sound. Their parents watched without protest. Ruso's face was as stoic as his master, showing no emotion. Lepida watched with approval while Monnica flinched with each strike. After it was over with, Monnica filled a bowl with water to wash the blood from their backs, but Lepida stopped her.

"They have a mother who will tend to them. Go, comfort your husband. Perhaps your God will bless you with a son soon."

Chapter Three

In unison boys stood in a line chanting their multiplication table. Most stood straight, faces expressionless, but a few glanced warily as their teacher walked slowly behind them, listening carefully for mistakes. Suddenly his cane smashed against a boy. The child whimpered, struggling to remember what eight times four was. Older students sat on stools in pairs, practicing reciting a long passage in Greek to each other. The instructor sent the younger group back to their stools to practice writing the Latin alphabet on wax tablets. Then he called older boys up one by one to recite their required passage.

"Please, God, make him skip me. Please," Augustine silently pleaded. He could handle anything in his native tongue of Latin. Passages from the *Aeneid* with the wooden horse full of armed soldiers, the burning of Troy, and the ghost of Creusa stirred his imagination. He had spent hours memorizing the classic, but the *Iliad* he loathed, despite it also described the battle of Troy. Why did Homer have to write in Greek? And why did he, a Roman citizen of the West Empire, have to learn literature from the Greek speaking East Empire?

Frets and prayers did not save him. Too soon his name was called. He walked to the front of the one room school and began reciting, feeling the glare of his stern teacher and hearing the cane tapping in the man's hand. Several verses went by fairly smooth, then his tongue stuttered on a long word. Down came the cane across his back.

"Again, from the beginning of the prayer," barked the teacher.

Augustine trembled in dread as the Greek words tumbled out, "Thus did he pray, and Apollo heard his prayer. He came down furious from the summits of Olympus, with his bow and his quiver upon his shoulder, and the arrows rattled on his back with the rage that trembled within him. He sat himself down away from the ships with a face as dark as night, and his silver bow rang death as he shot his arrow in the midst of them. First he smote their mules and their hounds, but presently he aimed his shafts at the people themselves, and all day long the pyres of the dead were burning. For five whole days…"

The cane smashed across the boy's back again. "It was nine days he shot at the people. Nine. Start again."

Augustine tried to remain focused but the fear of the dreaded cane hindered his memory. He managed to make it to the end with only one more smack. Relieved the trial was over, Augustine went back to his stool and picked up his stylus to begin writing the passage on his wax tablet. When he ran out of room, he used the blunt end of the stylus to smooth the wax and then the sharper end to press letters into the malleable surface. Parchment was too expense to waste on school exercises.

Finally the teacher dismissed the boys. Eagerly they packed their writing tools into satchels and headed out the door. Many were greeted by guardian slaves appointed by their parents to watch over them when away from home. These slaves often hung outdoors near the school while classes were in session. The more ambitious ones watched the class through windows, learning the same lessons as the students. Other wandered off to explore the town, arriving back at the school before dismissal. Agorix, now in his late forties, preferred to lounge around, playing games such as dice and knucklebones with other slaves. Augustine greeted his guardian, and they began walking towards the church to meet his mother for afternoon prayers.

Thinking quickly, the boy held out his satchel to Agorix. "Father said he wanted me to purchase a new stylus. Mine is cracked. How about you buy it for me? The money is in the bag. If you get a good deal, there may be a semis or two left over for you. I will walk the rest of the way to church myself."

Agorix grinned, revealing several missing teeth. "I'm sure I can scratch up a bargain."

Augustine slowly strolled towards the church, waiting until Agorix had disappeared into a shop. Then he dashed down side streets, avoiding any path his mother may be traveling. Soon he reached the edge of town and headed towards the race track. Near it boys had gathered in a field for a ball game. Some were young slaves whose masters were too involved betting on races to notice their absence or they had wandered off from errands their mistresses had sent them on. Others were sons of tenants too poor to send their kids to school. Augustine felt a stab of jealousy at their freedom. To go where you wished without constantly having a guardian.

"I beat you here today," greeted Didius, a boy about Augustine's age who had also ditched his chaperone.

"Do you have such speed with the ball as you do when hiding from your own slave?"

Didius tossed a leather ball at Augustine. "Let's find out."

They joined the game, selecting opposite teams. Eagerly they kicked the ball across the field, pushing and shoving others in their way. In the heat of the excitement, social classes vanished. It mattered not if it was slave or patrician who scored a goal, the whole team still rejoiced. If someone on the opposite side broke a rule, Augustine was quick to yell foul. If a team member or himself cheated, he heatedly defended the action. All that mattered was winning.

Still, Augustine kept an eye on the sun. As it dipped closer to the horizon, he left the field and hurried back through the streets of Thagaste to the church. Timing had to be just right. He stopped in the alleyway by the church and smoothed down his black hair and brushed dirt off his white tunic. He waited until the doors opened and the congregation began to exit. Spotting his mother leading his younger sister and brother, he walked up to her.

Monnica frown. "Augustine, you missed liturgy again."

In his politest voice, the boy said, "I apology, Mother, but Father asked me to buy a new stylus today. I hurried ahead of Agorix hoping to hear at least the final prayer, but, alas, I was too late."

His mother studied him. Monnica was now *domina* of the household for Lepida had died several years before. "What did you learn in school today?"

"We recited from the *Iliad*. Shall I show you?" He began quoting Greek, knowing she would not understand a word of it.

She smiled, proud of his accomplishment. "You have an excellent memory, son. Your teacher said you are the brightest in class."

"Really?" Augustine was shocked. If he was the best why then was he beaten so often?

"Tomorrow you will be here on time for evening prayers."

"Tomorrow is a holiday."

"God does not take holidays."

Agorix arrived with Augustine's satchel and new stylus. Monnica examined it, approved of the purchase, and led the family homeward. Augustine noticed that Agorix was munching on a pomegranate just purchased in the market. Once they reached the villa, the kids headed to the garden to play while dinner was prepared.

"Who won the game?" asked Perpetua, three years younger than Augustine. Like all the siblings, she had inherited the olive skin and dark hair of their mother.

"What game?"

"Or was it a play this time? I saw you break your stylus on purpose yesterday. I know you well enough to know where you went. I will not tell, if you share all the details."

Augustine grinned. "We won. I scored ten points myself." They settled on a stone bench in the garden, talking while their three-year-old brother Navigius played with rocks on the ground.

Their father arrived in time for dinner, announcing that Romanianus was back from Rome and was hosting wild animal fights. Both Augustine and Perpetua begged to attend.

"Tomorrow is a holiday. No school. Please, Father, can we go?"

"Sure," Patricius winked at his son. "You can me help choose bets."

Monnica cut in. "Perpetua stays. The circus is no place for a proper young lady. It is time to begin lessons in spinning wool."

The girl groaned. "Boys have all the fun."

Augustine only briefly felt pity for her before thoughts of animal fights filled his imagination. It was all he talked about the rest of the evening. The next morning he accompanied his father to the small amphitheater packed with spectators. The boy excitedly watched wild animals slaughtering each other in the sandy pit. If the animals showed hesitation to fight, slaves podded them with long sticks. A lean wolf tore apart a young bear. A tiger and lion ripped into each other. The mangled tiger finally limped away victorious. Before each round Patricius asked Augustine which animal the boy predicted to win. Then the father placed a small bet accordingly. The boy felt pride that his father had listened to him whenever his choice won, but he also knew deep disappointment whenever he backed a losing contender. Patricius spent more time socializing than he did actually watching the fights, entertaining his friends with raunchy jokes. He introduced his son to acquaintances by claiming his son was the best in the school. Sometimes he had the boy recite lessons.

One man said, "Sounds sophisticated. So what did he actually say?"

Patricius laughed. "How do I know? It is all Greek to me."

Father and son ate lunch at a *coupona*, a restaurant where fresh dishes of food where displayed on a counter and customers choose what they wanted. After selecting roasted chicken and vegetables, they sat at a table where Patricius's friends discussed the fights. A pretty waitress filled their cups with wine. Augustine delightedly sipped the wine, grateful his mom was not here to stop him. The men's jokes became more lewd as they began flirting with the waitress. Augustine became uncomfortable as he watched his father caress her arm.

"Father, can we go to a play this afternoon?"

20

"Sure," said Patricius, winking at the laughing waitress. "Maybe we can watch Jupiter seduce another chaste maiden." He pulled some coins out of his pocket and tossed them to Augustine. "Go ahead and enjoy yourself. Meet me at the bathhouse later, but do not tell your mother I let you go off alone."

Augustine quickly took the sestertii and left, wishing he could forget that look his father had given the waitress. At the theater, he watched the actors reenact the story of Apollo pursuing the nymph Daphne. Just as the god was about to embrace the virtuous nymph, she prayed to her father who changed her into a laurel tree. Augustine usually enjoyed plays, but this one caused him to reflect about his parents. His mother often told him he had another father, God, who he should emulate. Then there was Patricius who behaved like Apollo, chasing women without caring how they were affected.

Leaving the theater, he ran into Didius. The boys headed to the ball field and played the rest of the afternoon until a thunderstorm ended their game. Augustine used the excuse of rain to avoid meeting his father as he took the long way home, walking through ripening wheat fields. His tunic was soaked when he reached the villa. Monnica lectured him while a slave dressed him in dry clothes.

He sought solitude, standing under the roof and watching rain falling into the garden. Perpetua found him and begged for details about the animal fights.

"Not now. I am not in the mood."

"All I did today was go to church and spin wool—which is much harder than it looks. You got to have fun. Now share with me, or I will tell Father you broke your own stylus."

Augustine studied his sister, her innocent eyes craving excitement. "I will tell you a story instead." He recited from the *Aeneid* the ill-fated love story of Dido and Aeneas. After the murder of her husband, Dido fled with followers to a new land and founded the city of Carthage. Struck by Cupid's arrow, she fell in love with shipwrecked Aeneas. They married but then he abandoned her to follow his destiny to establish Rome. In grief she committed suicide by stabbing herself with a sword.

As he spoke, Augustine summarized most of the story but he quoted Dido's suicide speech. "As long as Fate and the gods allowed, receive my spirit and set me free of pain. I have lived a life. I have journeyed through the course that Fortune charted for me. And now I pass to the world below, my ghost in all its glory." As Augustine finished the tale, tears ran down his cheeks as he thought about the nymph in the play and the betrayal of his own father to his mother.

"You are a good speaker because you feel things so deeply," said Perpetua, wondering about her brother's tears. "You could win poetry contests. Will you tell me about the animal fights tomorrow?"

"Yes, tomorrow."

But the Fates did not smile on the boy. He developed a fever overnight, and woke up to coughing, his chest burning. Monnica tended him, bathing his hot forehead, giving him water, and forcing him to eat. By the next day, he threw up anything he ate, his body hot then cold. Breathing became difficult, causing Augustine to fear death had come for him. Remembering sermons from church, he begged his mother to be baptized so he could avoid hell, confessing to her his crime of ditching Agorix and sneaking off to ball games.

Monnica had been eager for her son's salvation, but not this way. Still, she hurried to the church to make arrangements. Patricius paced back and forth across the atrium, passing the household shrine of the goddess Tellus Mater. Incense rose from the small altar, but still his firstborn faded away. The boy's wheezing became worse as he struggled for air. Patricius entered his son's room and watched Magia hold the child down as his whole body convulsed.

"This is how my youngest died," said the slave, her face pale.

Unable to watch, Patricius walked outside and continued his pacing. Near the garden, in despair, he dropped to his knees and prayed to his wife's God, begging for his son's life. Shortly later Monnica returned with the priest. They crowded into the boy's small bedroom, watching him sleep peacefully.

Magia touched his forehead. "His fever suddenly broke and the coughing stopped. He breathes normal now."

"It is a miracle," said Monnica, holding her child's hand.

"Do you wish to baptize him when he awakes?" asked the priest.

Patricius answered, "He will just soil his soul again."

"How about you, councilman?" The priest fixed firm eyes on Patricius.

"Uh…no. But perhaps I will stop by for liturgies if I finish my business in time."

"You are always welcomed."

Monnica closed her eyes, silently thanking God for both her son's life and the change of heart in her husband, however small it may be.

Chapter Four

Women carrying empty clay jars chatted while standing in a loose line around the town's deep well. The wives could send their slaves, but many preferred to come themselves to fetch water—and enjoy gossiping with neighbors. While Monnica listened to a heated discussion about the price of wool, a newcomer stepped in line behind her. The girl kept her face shadowed by a dull-blue pallas covering her hair.

Monnica turned to Arria. "They say wool prices are down again."

The sixteen year old, only married five months, kept her eyes downcast. "There will not be much profit this year."

Noticing a dark bruise on the other's cheek, Monnica frowned. Should she speak or be silent? It was not the first time she had spotted such marks on others.

Paulina, a spirited mother of six, also noticed the bruise. "Men and their boorish manners. I have wanted to take a broom to mine many times. Did so once. But he hit harder. I could barely walk for a week. Still have a bit of a limp after all these years."

Arria ducked her head and pulled the veil down further. "It was my fault. I forgot my place and criticized how much money he lost on a bet."

"When it comes to money, women have far more sense. Some husbands would bet their children on a race if it was legal. Here is a trick which works well for me. I tell my husband that an item cost more than it really does. Then I pocket the rest."

"I could never lie to mine."

"Why not? You think they tell you the truth about their doings? What does your merchant husband really do when he travels? Who do you think keeps the brothels employed in the cities?"

Arria looked down at the empty jar in her hand and said nothing.

Monnica tried to cheer her up. "Not all men are like that. There are many fine Christians."

Paulina laughed. "Like your husband? Mine still speaks of the time Patricius lost a bet to him and refused to pay. When my husband insisted, Patricius cried foul, claiming the cock fight was fixed. Then he stripped off his tunic and challenged mine to a wrestling match, winner take all. Few men in town can outmatch your husband's temper."

"Yet I have never once been hit by him." Monnica smiled as if jesting, but spoke from her heart. "If women would not wag their tongues, nagging their husbands until at wit's end, then the men would resort less to their fists." She turned to Arria. "I suggest waiting until your husband is relaxed, then speak about your concerns in a gentle manner, never directly criticizing him."

Arria nodded. "I will try that."

Paulina snorted. "Men are arrogant enough as it, believing they rule the world. But it is us who cooks their meals and mend their clothes. If it was not for us women serving their every need, they would not last a month. And it is our place to remind them of that every so often."

"From the day I first heard the marriage contract read to me, I saw myself bound as a legal servant whose place is to serve my husband."

"Be a slave to my own husband? I am freeborn. Slaves bend to my will. If my husband tries to order me about like a dog, he will have a force to reckon with."

Monnica sighed then poured water from the well's bucket into her clay jar. As she turned towards home, she smiled encouragingly at Arria who brightened a bit. Perhaps the young wife would take her advice and avoid further conflict with her husband.

Reaching her house, Monnica passed the water over to Magia then began sweeping and straightening the pillows on the couches. Perpetua joined her mother in cleaning. Every few minutes one or the other glanced out a window to stare down the road. Late evening they spotted four travelers, dusty from a full day's walk, nearing the villa. The travelers had not reached the yard before Monnica, followed by her daughter, rushed out and jubilantly hugged Augustine. Patricius smiled proudly, while Agorix and Ruso continued on into the villa with packs.

"You have grown another inch," said Monnica. "As tall as your father now. Did they feed you well in Madaura?"

"Language is our food, poetry our wine," said the handsome sixteen year old, grinning at his mother.

"Fine son we have." Patricius thumped Augustine on the back. "Graduated the grammaticus top of his class, our tuition well spent. His professor said our son has a very promising future. Now I am ready to rest my wearied feet."

As the family moved inside, Perpetua quizzed her brother with questions about Madaura, a city located twenty miles away. For the last four years he had lived in a dorm at the esteemed grammataicus, studying language and literature, coming home on long holidays and summer vacations. Always he was accompanied by Agorix or Ruso.

"What is there to tell that I have not said before? Madaura's race track, theater, and bathhouses are still far larger than ours. The forum outshines ours with its many statues of gods."

"Tell me the plot of every play you have seen since your last visit, every poem you recited. Did you win this year?"

"First place."

Perpetua clapped in delight. "Recite it for us now."

"I apologize, but I am weary from walking all day. Where is this food whose aroma drives me delirious?"

Turia and Statila set the table by the garden while their mother finished cooking. As Augustine moved to the table, he spied his nine-year-old brother silently watching him. The child nodded a greeting then took a seat. Chatter was nonstop as Augustine spun tales of his adventures. The meal finished, Augustine recited the section from the *Aeneid* which had earned him a laurel wreath. While he spoke, his sister played a lyre to enhance the mood. Several months had passed since he had recited the passage, but easily came back the poetic words of Juno expressing rage and grief when she realized she had not the power to keep the Trojans from Italy.

"Defeated, am I? Give up the fight? Powerless now to keep that Trojan king from Italy? Ah, but of course—the Fates bar my way." Looking at his parents' proud faces, Augustine poured emotions into the words. "But I who walk in majesty, I the Queen of the Gods, the sister and wife of Jove—I must wage a war year after year on just one race of men! Who will revere the power of Juno after this—lay gifts on my altar, lift his hands in prayer?"

When he finished, the household burst into applause, including the slaves who had gathered. Only young Navigius was unimpressed. He sat with arms crossed, a frown on his lips. More poetry and music followed. Patricius grabbed Monnica and twirled her in a dance step.

She lightly shoved him away. "The sun has set, and there is much work waiting for tomorrow."

"Then let it wait," said her husband. "We shall throw a dinner party. I have no need to pay for entertainers, for my children shall provide it."

Monnica frowned. "Perhaps it would be best to wait until after the final crops of the season?"

Jovialness left Patricius. "Crops, yes. My tenants are lazy, letting rain ruin half my hay. I shall increase their rent if they lose the wheat harvest. My donkey can press more oil from a single olive than they can from an entire bushel." As he continued to rant, his family drifted away in different directions, the joy of the homecoming drained.

Shortly after breakfast the next morning, Patricius called Augustine into his small office. On the desk lay a feather pen and tiny clay pot holding ink next to a stack of invoices and bills written on parchments.

"Son, it is time to talk about your future. As you know, I have big plans for you. No farmer's life for you. With a voice like yours, the Fates have chosen you for public speaking—a lawyer who will draw crowds from miles around to hear your eloquence in the forum."

"I am eager, Father, to continue my studies." Augustine had enjoyed the excitement of Madaura, but longed for freedom away from spying paedagogus and his parents. At sixteen he was now a legal adult, eager to embrace all the pleasures it offered.

"I may have the smallest estate of the town council, but by Jove, I will send you to the best rhetorical school in the providence. That will give them a reason to finally envy me."

"Then it is to Carthage I will go?"

"Yes, but there will be a bit of a delay." Patricius sighed and settled in a chair, running a hand through his short, gray hair. "The obligations of being on the council plus putting you through grammaticus has depleted my coffer. I even had to turn down a request for your sister's hand because I cannot afford a dowry. Was a good offer too, from a goldsmith. But do not worry, son. I will secure the money with a few years of good harvests or perhaps I can woo a patron."

Augustine felt disappointment yet relieved for a respite. At Madaura he had developed a deep love for literature and a craving for praise which drove him to always strive to be the best. Now there would be no teachers with their canes, no lengthy passages to memorize, no math problems to solve. Endless hours to do as he pleased.

Over the following weeks, Augustine explored Thagaste with no chaperone, hanging out with friends from his childhood, a few which had also finished grammaticus. To oblige his mother, he usually attended morning liturgies then rambled the rest of the day, playing ballgames, attending plays and races paid with the small allowance his father gave him. Evenings he entertained his sister and mother with poetry. His younger brother also listened, but had little to say to him.

One rainy day, Augustine found Navigius sitting alone, watching the drops fall off the eaves. With a book in hand, Augustine sat down and began reading.

The boy interrupted, "Turia had a miscarriage again while you were gone."

"She is a bit old for motherhood." Uneasy, Augustine lay down the scroll. "Who was the father?"

"Who do you think?"

"But Father is a catechumen."

"Do you think going to church a few times a week would change him?" Navigius shuffled his feet. "He loves you more than the rest of us, including Mother."

"No, his pride is what he loves most."

"You are blessed to be leaving here soon. I have accepted I do not have your oracle skills. Father will never pay for my schooling beyond primary, but I do not mind. I am tired of school anyway."

Trying to connect with his brother, Augustine said, "You have a talent for breeding the best livestock. Father has not forgotten at the market last year how you spied that raggedly mare for sell that everyone else kept passing by. You claimed she would birth a fine foal, though she was yet not showing. Father brought her cheaply. And you were right. She birthed a high quality foal."

"Thanks," said Navigius, allowing a brief smile at the compliment. "Her owner's son had mentioned to me a month before that one of Romanianus' stallions had broken loose and spent time in their pasture."

To raise money, Patricius daily harassed his tenants, demanding they work harder, nitpicking everything they did. He made rounds to the influential residents of Thagaste, seeking to strengthen contacts. Unable to purchase new clothing, he only wore his toga when invited to occasional dinner parties. Monnica, on the other hand, spent much of her time helping at the church, visiting the homes of plebeians to give food to the sick and cheer-up the elderly. When arguments arose, disputers sometimes sought out Monnica to serve as peacemaker to avoid public lawsuits at the forum.

Augustine continued to enjoy his new freedom. As they strolled through the streets, his friends bragged of sexual exploits. Not wanting to appear different, he claimed to have had experience at Madaura, though in truth he had never even kissed a girl. He secretly wished his parents would go ahead and arrange a marriage for him, but they were too concerned about furthering his education.

One day while at the baths, desire burned in him as he observed a beautiful half-clad maiden enjoying the warm pool he shared with a dozen others. Seeing the tassels of her silken hair falling across her ample breasts, Augustine's body stirred. His father, sitting beside him, noticed and grinned. To celebrate his son reaching manhood, Patricius took the youth to a tavern and drank till he could barely stand. Augustine, who only had one cup, guided his drunken father home in the dark. Monnica met them at the door of the villa, frowning as her husband sung loudly to the moon goddess.

"Woman, be proud of your son. Tellus Mater will bless us with grandchildren soon."

Monnica looked anxiously at her son then helped Patricius to bed. The next day she gave Augustine a long lecture about fornication. Above all else, she warned him not to commit adultery. The youth listened politely, but demised her words as soon as he was out of her sight. It was his peers' opinions that matter most.

A few evenings later, Augustine was ambling down a county lane with several friends. They jested, each trying to oust the others.

Didius propped against a fence, studying a pear orchid beyond. "When I was a boy, I once picked a pear here, but the slaves ran me off."

Lucan, whose father was also on the council, grinned. "How about we steal them? Strip the trees bare."

Augustine looked at the dozen trees owned by Romanianus. The patrician had occasionally invited his parents to dinner parties. Augustine had nothing against the man but he wanted to avoid his companions' scorn. "How can we harvest the fruit without being caught?"

"We will come after dark, of course. Who would suspect us, sons of outstanding citizens, as thieves?"

The others youths laughed and began making plans. After the sun set, the gang returned with sacks. Giggling at the mischief, they picked all they could find in the semi-darkness of a full moon. Then they strolled down the lane, eating pears while telling stories about wooing their supposed lovers. They tossed cores over their shoulders as they talked, feeling a giddy bond of brotherhood in their crime. Tired of carrying the heavy sacks, they dumped the remaining fruit in a pig pen then drifted away to their homes, not caring that the slave in charge of the orchid may be beaten for the missing fruit or that the pig owners blamed for the theft.

A month later, Patricius told Augustine to dress in his best tunic for tomorrow they were to visit Romanianus. The next morning they walked to the luxurious villa which dwarfed theirs with its many bedrooms, swimming pool, two banquet halls, a well-stocked library, ball court, heated baths, and decorative gardens. But father and son saw none of these today. They entered the villa through the vestibule and stood in the large atrium with other visitors all coming to pay homage. Some sought advice, others business deals or handouts. Romanianus sat on a decorated throne in the middle of the chamber, his feet resting on a footstool. A drape partly separated him from the rest of the room, and his most trusted slave hovered nearby, telling clients when to step forward.

When his turn came, Augustine felt nervous, fearing his part in the stolen pears may be known. His father was confident, having participated in many such meetings as both patron and client.

"Greetings, Romanianus. The last games you hosted were fabulous. I won eighteen sestertii on that tiger fight. Brought my son along today. He is a fine boy, the brightest in all of Thagaste, next to yours of course. He is to study in Carthage as soon as I can secure the finances. Go ahead, Augustine, quote him something."

The youth recited the first passage he could think of from the *Iliad*. Stern-face, Romanianus folded his hands, listening carefully. He had become the *dominus* of his family rather young after his father had died in a hunting accident. At only thirty-five, he was highly educated, well-traveled, and the most powerful man in the surrounding district.

"Your Greek lacks the correct diction. How well do you know your Virgil?"

Augustine quoted a section from the story of Dido, feeling as if he stood in front of one of his teachers again, but this time if he failed, the results would be far harsher than a caning.

"Your memory is good." Romanianus leaned forward on his cushioned throne, studying the youth. "What symbolism was Virgil implying by Aeneas's abandonment leading to Dido's suicide?"

Pretending to be confident, Augustine said, "Virgil was explaining the reason why Carthaginians and Romans were enemies for centuries, leading to the Punic Wars and the Romans completely destroying Carthage. A century later, Julius Caesar rebuilt it. Due to its ideal location, Carthage has grown to become the second largest city in our Empire with a population of half a million, second only to Rome."

"You know your history and geography." Romanianus continued to quiz Augustine for several more minutes. Pleased with the results, he said, "Like me, you are from a small town but with big dreams. Determined and ambitious. I foresee you becoming a great lawyer."

Augustine swallowed, "That is my hope, sir."

"But I have also seen many promising youths flounder, throwing their education away on frivolous entertainment. Carthage is nothing like Thagaste or

Madauros, which together would not equal one district in the great city. Are you motivated enough to remain focused among great distractions?"

"Yes, sir. I am driven to always be the best. Ask any of my teachers."

Romanianus smiled. "I already have. Your primary teacher still talks fondly of you. Patricius, I will contribute half the funds needed to further his education, provided he does not waste this opportunity."

The father beamed. "My son will make both of us proud."

"I expect that. And Patricius, for the upcoming council meeting, do I have your pledge to vote with me?"

"Of course. I am in complete agreement with your opinions."

As father and son walked out of the villa, Augustine felt a rush of excitement. Finally, he could pursue his passion for literature while experiencing the excitement of city life. And be far away from his parents. Patricius bragged the entire walk home, dreaming of the fame his son would win. It would be the last pleasant memory Augustine would have of his father.

Weeks later a sudden sickness lain Patricius on his deathbed. As he realized his life was slipping away, he asked to be baptized. Monnica cried tears of joy as the priest did so. Days later, her tears turned to grief as her husband was buried in the ground. Augustine felt no grief, only anger at his father for his many infidelities. He also felt irritated with his mother for putting up with it. He expected her to sell Statilia and Turia, but she kept them, treating them with kindness. When they began attending church with her, he felt rage against them too. How could mistress and slaves live in harmony as if nothing had happened?

Despite his anger, Augustine kept his frustrations to himself. Monnica treated the tenants on her estate with respect, and they responded by working harder for her than for her husband. Within a year, the money was secured for Augustine's education.

Chapter Five

Augustine was seventeen when he travelled with Romanianus's entourage to Carthage. They covered the two hundred miles by horseback, paved roads allowing for quick travel. Romanianus had business contacts to meet, but he took time to ensure Augustine had an excellent teacher and a small apartment to be shared with several second year students. Then the youth was left alone in the vast city.

Augustine stood alone in middle of the main room of the apartment, taking in his new home. Unwashed clothing and dirty dishes were scattered about the main room. The floor was stained from unwiped spills and dropped food crushed underfoot. Was there even a broom in the apartment? His mother would never have allowed her home to become such a mess.

The latrine pot sat on the floor just a few feet across from the small stove made from thin iron bars. Accustomed to running water, Augustine grimaced, realizing water would have to be daily fetched and carried up two flights of stairs. Wooden panels divided the three bedrooms from the rest of the untidy apartment. Augustine placed his belongs in the only empty bedroom, glad he at least had a proper bed and a chest to store his items.

Midafternoon two youths walked in, chatting about a race they had attended. Seeing their new roommate had arrived, they introduced themselves. Rogelius had grown up in Carthage, his speech urbane as he bragged about his knowledge of the city. Probus was from a large town about two days travel away. Whenever possible he liked to slip facts about his favorite gladiators into conversations. Both youths were from well-to-do families who expected them to become famous lawyers.

Wanting to impress his roommates, Augustine rambled through supper about his favorite poetry. Finding out they were also fans of Virgil helped him to relax. But as they began talking about philosophers, Augustine realized he was not as well-read as them. After the meal of undercooked soup was finished, the others left Augustine to clean the dishes as they settled into chairs to read by lamp light.

The next day, feeling both nervous and excited, he followed his roommates to the city's forum for his first lesson. Unlike Thagaste, Carthage's forum was a huge complex of connecting basilicas, temples, courtyards, and porticoes. Among the marble pillars and statues where shops and restaurants selling high-end merchandise. People from all racial and social classes mingled, gathering in small groups to discuss the latest news, debate an issue, or watch an entertainer. While the majority was men, some women mingled among the crowds. Proper ladies kept their hair covered and servants in tow. Prostitutes openly flirted, their hair styled in elaborate braids mimicking the upper-class.

The main floor of one of the public buildings had been designated for education. Thick curtains covered wooden panels dividing the large chamber into classes. Teachers rented the spaces, each competing against other instructors for renown in order to attract wealthy parents who hopefully would send their sons to them. Tuition was paid by the parents to the teachers when the school year ended. The more students they taught, the higher their pay.

Augustine and his roommates navigated the curtained corridor to their class in the middle of the huge chamber. As Augustine sat on a wooden stool waiting for the lesson to begin, he glanced up at the embellished ceiling high over his head. Their stern teacher Pulcher scrutinized his students, politely welcoming the newcomers. When ready to begin, he stood in front of the youths. Immediately they quieted.

"Before Agememnon left for Troy, he was warned by a prophet that it was against the will of the gods for him to set sail unless he sacrificed his daughter Iphigenia. You must choose a side and defend it. Rogelius, you speak first."

The second year student stood confidently in front of his peers. "Agememnon bore the weight of responsibility for his soldiers' lives and the duty of bringing back Helen. By asking him to sacrifice his daughter, the gods were testing him to see where his loyalty lay. The gods were pleased with his decision to slay his daughter and blessed him, giving him victory over Troy. By placing duty over family, he showed the heart of a true warrior."

"A strong opening which needs development," said Pulcher. "Who will counter his argument?"

Wanting to make a good impression, Augustine volunteered and walked to the front of the room, hoping he appeared calm. "Duty is, of course, important, but so is love. Agememnon showed no love when he claimed to be taking his daughter to her wedding ceremony yet killed her instead. Love did not motivate him when he stole a comrade's beautiful slave, leading to strife between the allies then later forced the doomed prophetess Cassandra to become his concubine.

Nor did he show love to the gods when he ordered their temples desecrated after Troy was captured. In the end, he only earned the gods' wrath and his wife's revenge, leading to his murder when he returned home. If he had spared Iphigenia's life because of love, the gods may have been pleased to bless a warrior who would not be overcome by arrogance. Instead, it was ultimately his downfall."

"Interesting twist. You dramatic pauses need to be longer. Probus, counter his statement."

For the rest of the morning, the debates continued. Pulcher choose topics which required students to pull from their knowledge of Roman law, history, philosophy, and religion. For lunch, students headed to nearby vendors to purchase food. As Augustine bought stew, he watched Rogelius and Probus along with several others surround a shy freshman who had difficulty speaking in class. They teased the youth till he broke down in tears and ran off. The others laughed relentlessly.

Spying Augustine watching, Rogelius said, "Good job today, roommate. No leeks for brains. Most country boys break easily. Looks like we will not need to find a replacement for you so soon."

Augustine tried to appear confident, knowing the others were still measuring him. "This is not my first time in a city. I finished top at Madauros."

"Top? Then you will enjoy a little extra practice before class resumes." Rogelius began walking back to the basilica were the classrooms were located.

The other youths snickered and followed. Augustine tagged along, wanting to be part of their group but not trusting them. Arriving at the maze of curtained partitions, they peeked into classrooms. Finding one empty, Probus took out a small clay jar holding liquamen, a popular fish sauce known for its strong odor. The youths began smearing the sauce on stools pupils would set on after lunch. Augustine watched but did not join in on the prank.

Studying their handiwork, Probus said, "We are not called the Wreakers for nothing. Next room."

The youths entered another class. They picked up all the stools and carried them across the hallway into another class. Rogelius explained that the two teachers were rivalries and would blame each other. He then rifled through scrolls left on a small table, pocketing one of them. They had barely walked out into the corridor, when students and teachers began returning from lunch. Trying to hide their mirth, the Wreakers headed to their own class, bursting into laughter when they heard cursing from upset people in other rooms.

The Wreakers had left their own class untouched. Pulcher entered, his eyes sweeping over his sober students. After giving them one more round of debates, he led them on a field trip to another basilica where court cases were in process. The vast chamber was divided into rooms by heavy curtains. At the front of each room was a platform on which sat a magistrate and centumvirs which judged the cases. To the side sat stenographers recording the dialog. The defendants and prosecutors sat on wooden benches while the audience, made up of people from all walks of life, stood closely together listening to the speeches. Famous lawyers arguing cases dealing with aristocrats drew the largest crowds, but even simple cases were well attended.

Pulcher led his students to a room where a murder trial was already underway. The defendant's lawyer was deep into a speech listing evidence to prove his client's innocence. As the young man spoke, he cited Roman law and history while quoting famous writers. When he misquoted Cicero, several in the audience jeered, causing the lawyer to stutter, leading to more insults from the crowd. As the lawyer finished his speech, a group directly behind his bench clapped enthusiastically while the rest of the crowd only gave light applause. Then the prosecutor gave his closing speech. This lawyer was older and more polished, smoothly weaving humor and famous quotes into his recital of the evidence while referring to Roman justice and pride. When he finished, the whole crowd burst into applause, including Pulcher's students. Before the verdict was given, Pulcher led his students back to class.

"Who do you predict will win the case?"

Augustine answered, "The evidence for the defendant's innocents was strong while the prosecutor gave weak cause of guilt. The man should go free."

Pulcher turned his attention to Rogelius. "Explain who will win."

"The man will be executed or sent to the mines. His lawyer was unable to win the crowd, only his paid laudiceni clapped. The prosecutor spoke eloquently, earning the crowds approval. The centumvirs will side with him."

"Correct. Rare is the lawyer who loses the crowd and wins the case. That, students, is why you are here. To learn eloquence, how to turn a well-spoken phrase, to have the audience drinking deeply your every syllable. Honeyed words spiced with symbolism and rhetoric. But word choice is not enough. You must know when to move, how to entertain, and when to convince. Phrasing, tone, and pitch must be perfect. Only then will you win the crowd. He who controls the mob has power that even emperors fear. Do you have the gift of Mark Antony? Can you twist a mob rooting for your enemies into a malleable weapon preforming your will? The day you can do that, you become a demigod, a son of Apollo."

Augustine listened closely, dreaming of the day he would stand before a crowd hanging onto his every word, his magnificent speeches saving the lives of desperate people. Everyone admiring him. But he had much to learn first. Over the following weeks he worked hard to overcome his country diction in order to pronounce words like cultured Romans. New books and authors were introduced, widening Augustine's gasp of literature, history, and philosophy. Keeping his promise to Romanianus, Augustine stayed focused on his studies, quickly rising to the top of his class. The other students noticed, and the Wreakers often invited Augustine to hang with them after classes were over. Wanting to feel part of a group, Augustine kept silent when they teased shy freshmen or vandalized other classes.

On holidays, he joined the Wreakers as they prowled the city. There was much to see. Two massive man-made marinas protected the hundreds of ships bringing cargo from across the known world. The Antonine Baths, the largest outside Rome, was built by the sea and offered splendid vistas for the thousands of visitors enjoying the heated pools, saunas, gymnasiums, swimming pool, and gardens. A giant amphitheater where animal and gladiator fights took place was modeled after the Coliseum in Rome. Then there were the race tracks, theaters, and markets. Hundreds of temples and shrines were dedicated to Greek, Roman, and Punic gods—the largest being those for the triad Jupiter, his wife Juno, and Minerva. Mingled among them were Jewish synagogues and Christian churches. Most streets were narrow with insula apartments rising up several floors, but there were also large avenues lined with trees.

Augustine drank in the sights, eager to experience everything. Above all, he wanted to fall in love, to experience the ecstatic emotions the poets wrote so lofty about. He was in love with the emotion of love, but did not know how to go about wooing a girlfriend. No longer did he care to wait until his mom secured a marriage for him five or ten years later. Plays amplified his desire. The splendid performances at the large theaters held Augustine in rapt attention as choirs of boys sung and male actors played out depraved stories of gods and heroes, reenacting seductions, rapes, suicides, and murders. The greater the tragedy, the tighter the audience was bond to the story, both men and women weeping openly for the grief of fictional characters.

After watching a particularly tragic story of two lovers parted by selfish parents, Augustine felt melancholy as he ambled down the narrow street with Rogelius and two other classmates. A plaza opened up in front of them, revealing the large temple of Tellus Mater, the Great Mother. They wandered into the temple, passing eunuchs wearing pomaded hair and women's dresses. Entering the main chamber, Augustine stared in fascination at the lofty statue of Tellus Mater, goddess of earth and fertility. Berbers held her in high esteem. Her temples had spread from Asia Minor to Africa then Rome, with many lesser earth goddesses slowly merging their identity with hers. Back home, Augustine's father had kept a small household idol of her, but this stature was huge and lifelike. The beautiful goddess sat in a chariot pulled by lions. Her elegant hands held a tambour. Her crown was shaped like a city battlement. Around the base of the stature twirled eunuchs clapping bronze cymbals.

In a corner of the temple a small crowd had formed around several priestesses standing by an altar. Curious, the youths moved closer. A man knelt in front of the stone altar, praying fervently. The priestesses' chants fused with the man's deep voice. In the midst of a thick cloud of incense, he stood as a priestess handed him a sharp blade.

Sweating, the man raised it and cried, "In the name of the Great Mother, I offer my seed so that all Romans' virility will be blessed and increased." With quick slices of the blade, the man mutilated himself by cutting off his manhood.

Augustine and two youths jumped backwards, shocked.

Rogelius laughed at them. "Where do you think eunuchs come from?" After they had walked away from the crowd and bloody altar, he added, "I never have figured out why the ultimate act of devotion to the fertility goddess is giving up your fertility. Guess I will never be one of the chosen."

Trying to appear unperturbed, Augustine said, "At least we do not sacrifice our firstborn, like the original Carthaginians to Saturn."

"Which meant less Carthaginians for our soldiers to kill when we invaded." Rogelius glanced at several temple prostitutes eyeing the youths. "Any of you have a sestertii I could borrow?"

"Just a few semis," said Probus.

"Not enough. Religious whores do not come cheap."

"How about a brothel? We could afford them."

"Speak for yourself," said the other youth. "I am down to my last sestertii for the month. Perhaps we could pick up some free action at the baths."

"Not near here," complained Rogelius. "The Antonine Baths separate the women. We would have to walk too far to another bath."

Augustine had remained quiet, feeling a sickening of his stomach as he thought of his father. He needed to find an excuse to leave the group without earning their scorn.

Rogelius noticed Augustine's pale face and grinned wickedly. "I know the perfect spot for a good Catholic like you."

Augustine grimaced. Rogelius knew that he sometimes went to prayers at one of the smaller churches. Seeing the other youths looking at him, Augustine said, "Lead on."

Without explaining where they were going, Rogelius led them towards the harbor. He easily navigated the narrow, crowed streets. The boys paused occasionally to admire the more lavishly dressed maidens. Slaves guarding entrances into insula apartments glared dangerously at the loitering youths until they moved onward. It was the duty of the door guards to ensure that only residents and their guests entered the buildings belonging to their masters.

The sun was sinking into the sea when the boys reached the harbor. Hundreds of ships were docked in the artificially created harbor, its two marinas protected by a strong seawall. Slaves unloaded merchandise shipped from as far away as Britannic. Rogelius finally stopped in front of a stone basilica, simple in design but large enough to hold hundreds of worshipers.

"A church?" complained Probus. "Christian maidens are notorious for being celibate. They might as well be the virgin priestesses of Vesta with our luck."

Rogelius just grinned. "How well do you really know Christians? This is the Shrine of Cyprian, built over the spot where Cyprian was beheaded, supposedly the first Christian martyr in Africa. And tonight, dear friends, is one of their vigils. They stay up all night getting drunk. What location could be more perfect for us? Watch and learn."

The youths entered the crowded church filled with worshipers standing close together, rhythmic swaying as they chanted psalms. As the sun disappeared, candles were lit and bottles of wine passed around. Like a lion testing its prey, Rogelius skillfully wove threw the packed congregation, brushing up against beautiful maidens, seeking those who would respond. Not wanting to be left out, the other youths copied him.

Augustine felt shy at first, only accidently bumping against others. But as the night progressed more worshipers came, and people stood shoulder to shoulder in the dim light, their bodies swinging to the chanting. Becoming more confident and slightly buzzed from the wine, Augustine began brushing against women's hips and bosoms. Many took no notice, presuming it was an accident. Some instinctively pulled back, and Augustine would mutter an apology before moving on.

Then Augustine saw her—a nymph in a candlelit sea. Her body swaying, her voice angelic, her blonde hair unbound. Augustine felt lust as he never had before. He moved to her side, squeezing in between a middle-age woman and the maiden. Neither paid any attention to him as they continued to sing. Augustine let his hip rub against the maiden as she swayed. He expected her to pull away, but she ignored him. Feeling bold, he slid his fingers down her arm. This time she glanced at him. Augustine smiled back. She frowned and looked away. Not ready to give up, he continued to bump against her as the crowd swayed in rhythm.

She could have moved away or fussed at him. Instead, she stared start ahead, face blank. No longer did she sing. Gently he moved his fingers down her arm, touching her hand. When she did not pull away, he intertwined their fingers, their bodies swaying in unison. They stood, connected, for several minutes until a cup of wine was passed. Augustine took a deep sip then passed it to her, brushing her hands. A burly man on the other side of her noticed and stared menacing at Augustine. Reluctantly the youth slipped away, but he did not go far.

He continued to watch the nymph. Was her guardian a husband or father? The burly man turned, scrutinizing the crowd. Seeing Augustine still staring, he moved toward the youth. Augustine melted away into the throng, eventually reaching the back wall where the Wreckers had gathered. Grinning, they headed outside into the dark night, bragging about their adventures.

For the next few weeks, all Augustine could think about was the maiden. Who was she? How could he find her again in such a large city? He began to neglect his studies. Instead, he spent his afternoons wandering down random streets in the hope of spying her. He visited the Shrine of Cyprian several times, but there were only a handful of visitors. It would be months before another vigil was scheduled. He gave up hope of finding her again, moping about, finding isolated spots to quote to himself monologs of depressed heroes who grieved lost love.

Then one day, by random chance, he spied her. She was leaving a church after evening prayers. Through the narrow, crowded streets he followed her until she disappeared into a small butcher shop. He waited, expecting her to come back out, but when she did not, he moved closer. Then he spotted the burly butcher— the same man she had stood beside at the vigil. Augustine felt anger and jealousy, but he dared not enter the shop. Instead he sought out Rogelius.

The next day his roommate approached the small shop, pretending to be interested in a haunch of pork hanging from a hook. Augustine watched from a distance, trying to catch glimpses through passersby. Finally Rogelius return.

"Well? Was she there? Who is he?"

Rogelius smirked. "You sure know how to pick them. A beauty I would love to pluck."

Augustine's hand tightened into a fist. "You will not touch her."

"Relax." Rogelius laughed. "You spotted her first. But she is going to be a tough one to woo. Her father is a freed slave. By his looks, he might have been a gladiator or warrior from a northern tribe. Could split you in half with one slice of his hatchet. Sure she is worth it?"

"I would face the whole fleet of Greece for her."

"Then we come back tomorrow and try to speak to her alone to seek a rendezvous."

Augustine feared that Rogelius might try to take her for himself. "Thank you for your help, but I can handle it myself now that I know he is only her father."

"Are you sure?"

"I have wooed many a maiden back home. I can handle her."

Despite his bragging, Augustine was nervous. The next day he attended evening liturgy at the church he had spotted her coming out of. She was there with a woman and several young children, probably her mother and siblings. Augustine almost gave up hope of speaking to her, but after the service, she went in the opposite direction of her family, basket in hand, to shop. Augustine moved between the booths and stalls, wanting to get closer to her but afraid to speak. What if she wanted nothing to do with him?

She turned a street corner, and he lost sight of her. Quickening his pace, he rounded the corner, almost running into her. She had been waiting for him.

"Why are you following me?"

"Uh…um…you are the most beautiful goddess I have ever seen. Tell me which temple is yours so I may worship you."

The maiden laughed. "You are the boy at the vigil, the one who held my hand."

"You did not pull away."

She gave a half-smile then turned her back as she continued down the street. Encouraged, he kept close, asking her name when she paused to look at vegetables at a stall.

"Galla." She picked up a turnip, testing its firmness.

"Which means 'from Gaul.' You are of Gothic descent?"

She shrugged. "Perhaps. You sound educated. No one in my family can read."

"I am Augustine from Thagaste. I am a rhetoric student. Someday I will be a famous lawyer."

The maiden turned her attention from the cabbage to him. "Then you are wasting your time talking to me. I am just a freed slave. My father only brought my freedom last year. He is still saving for my younger sister and brother."

"I do not mind that you were a slave. You are far more beautiful than most free-born women I know."

Her eyes narrowed. "Have you known many women?"

"Uh, my mother and sister. You are the first my heart has leaped for. Since the moment I first saw you, my every thought has been captive to you. Free me from my cell."

The girl looked away, blushing. "You speak boldly."

Augustine quoted from the *Aeneid*, "What could wound the Queen of the gods with all her power? Why did she force a man, so famous for his devotions, to brave such rounds of hardship, bear such trials?"

"You speak eloquently."

"My lips have won renown, now they seek to win your love."

Again the girl blushed. She quickly purchased the cabbage. "I must return home."

"Will you speak with me again tomorrow?"

She gave a shy yes then hurried away, leaving Augustine ecstatic. He could think of nothing else the rest of the day, dreaming about her through the night. The next morning, he could barely concentrate on his lessons, giving poor speeches when called upon. The sun moved too slowly across the sky, the evening seeming as if it would never arrive. He was at the church early, heart throbbing as he watched her enter with her family. After the service, she parted again from her mother to shop. Augustine kept near her, reciting poetry and cracking jokes. She played coy, keeping her eyes on vegetables, but smiling at the attention.

Weeks went by as they repeated the routine. When a holiday due near, Augustine asked if she would spend the day with him. They met by a marble statue of Venus then explored the city. Streets were packed with people enjoying the day off from work. Hand in hand, the couple wove through the crowds, avoiding dirty water occasionally tossed from apartments high overhead. The streets were lined with shops, vendors loudly calling out their sales. When Galla admired a beaded necklace, Augustine brought it for her.

Eventually they reached the plaza in front of the Tellus Mater's temple. Spectators formed a ring around a parade of temple prostitutes dressed in bright pallas, their stolas leaving shoulders bare, wigs dyed in outlandish colors. Drums thundered, cymbals clashed, and horns wailed. Among the whirling prostitutes moved the concentrated eunuch priests, dressed also in colorful stolas and wigs, faces powered. While some danced, others gashed themselves, blood running down their arms. Occasionally dancers grabbed someone from the crowd to join them. The steps became more sensual as dancers wiggled hips, bending bodies erotically. The spectators became buoyant, shouting out lewd comments.

Galla turned away from the dancers, her face blushing deep red. Seeing her discomfort, Augustine tore his eyes from the dancers and guided her away from the temple. He brought her a meal at a coupona. They sat at a table munching on leeks and mutton, chatting while lightly flirting. Occasionally waitresses disappeared upstairs with diners who paid for a bonus with their meals.

"My mother asked me to carry some cloth to my older sister. Her husband's apartment is near here."

"Lead the way."

Augustine held her hand as they walked through the streets and entered an insula. The slave guarding the entrance recognized Galla and waved her and Augustine in. The couple climbed up flights of stairs, the higher levels had dirty floors with graffiti on the walls. The richest inhabits lived on the second floor where escape was easier in case of fire. Galla pushed open a door on the fourth floor. The apartment had been subdivided into tiny living areas by wooden dividers, each an abode for renters. No one was home.

"My sister must be out enjoying the holiday." Galla placed the wool cloth on a table and moved to the glassless window. "You can see the Hill of Juno from here."

Augustine moved beside her and placed an arm around her waist. This was the first time they had been alone without the ever-present mob of pedestrians. "The only vista worth seeing is you."

The maiden smiled. "You say the nicest things to me when I am only worthy to fasten your shoes."

The youth leaned closer and whispered from the *Aeneid*, "She with all her eyes and heart embraced him, fondling him at times upon her breast, oblivious of how great a god sat there to her undoing."

Galla blushed and stared downward at the window sill. Augustine stroked her blonde hair then moved his hand to her cheek. He turned her face to him and kissed her soft lips. He pressed harder and she yielded, her arms wrapping around him.

He whispered, "Which is your sister's bedroom?"

"I will show you."

She took his hand and led him down the narrow, darkened corridor where he attained his long desired prize.

Part II

"Grant me chastity and continuance,
but not yet."

~Saint Augustine, *Confessions, 8.17*

Chapter Six

The fading light of the sun vanishing behind the church made it difficult for Triferus to continue reading. He rolled up the scroll, pondering the story. Some words had been difficult for him, but he had understood most of what he read. Strange to fathom that the elderly bishop he had briefly chatted with at the chapel was the youth from the story. The old man had once been in love? Priests were not allowed such emotions, that Triferus was certain. What had happened to the girl? She was not here at the monastery. Perhaps she lived at the nunnery several streets away.

Triferus sighed, wondering if a girl would ever look at him with longing. Back home there had been several maidens he had watched from afar but had rarely spoken with. When his parents thought the time was right, they would have arranged a marriage, hopefully after asking his opinion. With no land or education, Triferus could only expect a tenant's daughter as his bride, poor like himself. But that was when he had a strong body to work the land. Now he had nothing to offer. And no parents to make an arrangement.

A deep ache for his lost family filled Triferus. Three months and he still felt lost and empty. The life he had enjoyed ripped savagely from him. Sometimes he envied his dead family. Their lives had ended abruptly while he lingered in misery, hunger and despair his constant companions. The monks shared the produce from their garden, but with dozens of clergy who had taken refuge at the monastery and countless beggars visiting daily, their limited food was never enough.

Evening liturgy was to begin soon. Triferus hobbled to the sanctuary packed with worshipers. He kept near the back, leaning against a wall, invisible in the throng. As the congregation chanted a song, Triferus remained silent. He had not sung since his sister's death when he had held her hand, humming her favorite hymn as life bleed from her body. Why had he not died that night?

Heraclius, the priest who Augustine had chosen to be his successor as bishop, spoke about faith. With a firm voice of authority, he confided to his listeners that he shared their fears of the future, understood their terror. In times of trouble he encouraged them to look to God for help. Triferus listened, feeling jabs of angry. Have faith? When his family was dead and the countryside ravaged? City after city falling to the butchers. Why did an all-powerful God not stop this?

At the closing of the sermon, those not baptized where dismissed. Triferus received the sacrament of communion along with others, drinking the watery wine. He did so not because he cared, but he simply did not want to draw attention to himself if he refused. He had been baptized last Easter, an idealist youth who trusted the teachings of the village priest completely. Where had faith gotten that cleric? Torture and death.

After most of the congregation left, Triferus headed to the kitchen and grabbed a bowl of lentil soup consisting of more water than substance. He passed the large dining table filled with conversing priests. Carved into the wood was the inscription, "Who injures the name of an absent friend may not at this table as guest attend."

When Triferus had first seen the words, he had asked Possidius their meaning. "Ah, Augustine had them inscribed long ago. He loves hospitality and discussion, rather than eating and drinking. Our meals here are always simple, but the conversations insightful. If a visitor begins to gossip, Augustine reminds him of that inscription. If the visitor persists, Augustine leaves with his meal unfinished. The guilt of causing a holy man to go hungry keeps anyone from committing the offense twice."

Tonight Triferus bypassed the crowded table and found a quiet corner to eat, preferring solitude. He sipped the lentil soup slowly, trying to make the meal last as long as possible, wishing for bread. With the wheat fields cut off from the city, it was a rare commodity now. Conversations around him briefly held his attention. Several young monks excitedly talked about a rich man who had converted, giving half his possessions to the poor. Two presbyters debated the meaning of the Trinity, both using quotes from Augustine to try to prove their point. At the table, the bishops talked in deep, concerned voices, worrying about the dioceses they had left behind. What had become of their churches and congregations? How many priests who had stayed behind were still alive?

At the head of the table, Augustine listened wearily, the burden of lost lives weighing heavily on him. The bishop broke his silence by saying, "I would have you know that in this time of our misfortune, I asked this of God: either that he may be pleased to free this city which is surrounded by our foe, or if something else seems good in his sight that he make his servants brave for enduring his will, or at least that he may take me from this world unto himself."

The other bishops were quiet for a moment, absorbing his words. Then Heraclius said, "Let us add our prayers to yours, brother, that we will continue to have the ability to endure whatever God chooses for us to face."

The priests bowed their heads in prayer, many weeping, including Augustine. Bothered by the sight, Triferus quickly finished the last of his watery soup then slipped quietly out of the room. Still hungry, he navigated the dark hallways to his bedchamber. With supplies short, oil for lamps was limited to major rooms where people congregated. In the darkness, Triferus unwound his bedroll and lay on the floor near a wall, out of the way so his roommates would not trip over him in the dark when they entered. He shared the small cell with several young monks who had fled just before their towns were burned.

The morning began as tedious as countless others. Dreary light filtered in through the cracks around the wooden shutter. The coldness of the stone floor seeped through Triferus's thin bedroll. His two roommates where already gone, probably kneeling in morning prayers somewhere. Triferus rolled up his blanket and hobbled to the kitchen for a breakfast of porridge. Then he grabbed a broom and began sweeping. He had nothing more important to do.

Mid-morning he was cleaning the forum of the monastery when a tall, formidable man entered. From his clothing, Triferus could tell the visitor was a soldier of high rank.

Seeing Triferus staring, the man said, "I have come to visit Bishop Augustine."

"He is not receiving visitors…at least that is what Possi…Bishop Possidius said." Triferus tried to speak formally. "His illness became worst during the night."

The soldier's face saddened. "It grieves me to hear of his reclining health. Yet I still need to speak with him. If he is awake, tell him General Boniface needs an urgent word with him."

"Boniface?" Triferus felt rage kindle in him. This was the man who had boldly invited the Vandals from Spain, thinking he could control them. It was his fault that half of North Africa lay in ruin. Triferus clenched his fists. "I will ask if he wishes to see you."

As he limped to Augustine's cell, his thoughts were in chaos. How dare Boniface show his face on consecrated ground! Triferus paused outside Augustine's bedroom, considering not knocking at all. General or not, Boniface should not have the audacity to disturb a sick, elderly bishop. Just as Triferus was about to turn around, the door opened as Possidius stepped into the hallway carrying a tray of half-eaten porridge.

"Uh, General Boniface is here. He wants to talk with Augustine, even though he knows the bishop is sick."

Possidius looked grave. "If he is here, the reason will be dire. Take this tray to the kitchen. I will see if Augustine can meet his visitor."

Triferus shuffled his way down the hallway, hoping Boniface would be sent away. To his disappointment when he returned, he found that Augustine had arisen and Possidius was helping him walk to his study. Triferus was then sent to fetch the general.

Barely able to hide his disgust of being in the same room as Boniface, Triferus said through clenched teeth, "Bishop Augustine will see you now." He led the soldier down the hall to the study. After watching the man enter, Triferus kept nearby, sweeping the corridor three times till the door reopened for Boniface and Possidius.

Walking down the hallway, Boniface said. "He looks worse than I have ever seen him. Surely God will not take him when our need is greatest?"

Possidius sighed. "Only God knows the number of our days. I do pray he will be with us for many years yet."

Once the general was showed out, Possidius returned to help Augustine back to his cell. The elderly bishop moved slowly, his body weak, his mind weary. Even so, he continued to give instructions as he was helped into bed. "I wish to spend my remaining days in prayer. Let no one disrupt me except for physicians or to bring my meals. And have copes of several of David's shortest Psalms copied for me. Hang them on the wall where I might read them."

"It will be done as you say."

Back in the hall, Triferus said, "How dare the general disturb him. He is a heartless monster."

Possidius rebuked the youth. "You know not about what you speak. Boniface carries the weight for the protection of our entire providence on his shoulders, just as Augustine carries the weight of all its souls. Do you think either man carries such a burden lightly?"

"He invited the Vandals here. It is because of his pride I lost my family, my home, my entire village."

"A mistake he is risking his life to correct. As our Lord says, 'He who has not sin can cast the first stone.' Be not quick, Triferus, in judging others."

"I have never shed blood like him. He is a hideous man which deserves the abyss of hell."

Anguish lined Possidius's eyes. "No one deserves hell, not even the Vandals. Look carefully to your own heart. Hatred destroys the hater, eroding the joys of life."

"My life ended three months ago." Triferus fled away as quick as his lame leg allowed.

Triferus wandered about the church grounds, fiery thoughts smoldering on the kindle of his grief. How dare Possidius defend the general! Why would Augustine, sick as he was, even talk to Boniface? The general should not even be allowed on church grounds. Triferus tried to avoid others as he rambled about, a difficult task as there were clergy and visitors everywhere. Growing tired, his lame leg throbbing, Triferus sought solitude. If he looked like he was studying, perhaps no one would ask him questions. In his bedroom he found the scroll he had been reading the day before.

He went outside in the sunshine and sat on the steps of the church near some bushes, ignoring passersby. In a low voice he continued the story of Augustine.

Chapter Seven

Augustine waited near the theater, searching the crowds. Every moment he spent apart from Galla felt like an eternity. They met most evenings at the church, but there was only a short time for flirting before she left to join her family. It was the holidays that he lived for when they both had the whole day off. They explored many places in the city, but their path always led to her sister's apartment in early afternoons when it would be empty.

Seeing blonde hair in the crowd, Augustine moved away from the wall to join her. "Ready for the play?"

"I was wondering if we could skip. I do not feel like being around a crowd today. Perhaps a quiet garden."

They headed to the Hill of Juno. Nearing the huge marble temple honoring the goddess, they entered a decorative portico, a roofed courtyard surrounded by columns and statues of gods and heroes. Alcoves were hidden among the flowers and life-like statues. Sitting on an isolated stone bench, Augustine pulled Galla to him and kissed her. She remained stiff, nervous.

"What is wrong, my nymph?"

She twisted her hands, nervous. "How much do you love me?"

"With every breath of my lungs, every beat of my heart. Your alluring lips are my wine, your body my substance." He tried to kiss her again but she pulled back.

"I am pregnant."

He froze, caught off guard. "Are you sure?"

Galla nodded, her eyes large with anxiety. Augustine pulled away from her and stared across the flowery courtyard, rubbing a hand through his short black hair. His long silence terrified her, causing her to burst into tears.

"I will do whatever you ask. Just do not send me away. My father cannot afford to support another child. Do you…want me to…expose it?" Unwanted infants were often abandoned either by the rocks near the sea or at designated spots about the city. Slavers took the healthiest infants, leaving the others to die.

"No, my mother would never forgive me for such a barbaric act." Augustine sighed, uncertain how he should feel. Fatherhood was supposed to await him in a distant future after a proper marriage. Not now while he was still in school, living on a limited budget. How could he afford to support a family? When he looked into Galla's fearful eyes, he knew he must find a way. "It is of my blood so I will take care of it..." He touched her wet cheeks, wiping away tears. "...and you. Move in with me."

"You must ask my father."

"I will do so today."

He pulled her close and held her, feeling her body slowly relax. She trusted him with her future, and he vowed to himself not to fail her—despite his lack of money. Surely his mother would not withhold his allowance but Romanianus might. He would have to be very careful how he phrased his next letter to his patron.

The couple stood and walked back through the city, talking little. They reached the butcher shop and stopped before the counter. Around them skinned animals hung from hooks. Her muscular father skillfully sliced a lamb with a hatchet. He paused in his work and looked between his daughter and Augustine. A dark scar ran across his cheek, another deep scar ran down half the length of one arm. Augustine felt tongue-tied. He was being trained to speak in front of the most esteemed men of the city, but he was speechless before a freed slave.

"Do you wish to buy something?"

"Your daughter."

The man's eyes darkened, his hand tightening on the weapon. "She is not for sale."

"I mean, I seek permission to make her part of my household. I am a rhetorical student with a promising future. I can support her."

The father studied Galla clasping the youth's hand. "I bought your freedom just last year. Do you wish to throw it away so quickly for this patrician?"

The maiden firmly meet her father's eyes. "I love him. He will take good care of me and our child."

"You are pregnant?" The butcher brought his hatchet down, cleanly severing the lamb's head. "He will never marry you. You know imperial law forbids marriage between freed slaves and patricians. You would live in sin with this boy?"

Galla's lips quavered. "Yes, Father. He will one day be a famous lawyer. You should hear him speak."

51

"I have already and am not impressed." He glared at Augustine then turned to his daughter. "If you are certain, then go say goodbye to your mother. She is preparing dinner."

After squeezing Augustine's hand, Galla stepped behind the counter and climbed narrow stairs up to the loft where her family lived. Her father stared menacing at Augustine.

Trying to befriend him, Augustine said, "At least this saves you the cost of a dowry."

"And you the cost of a slave. I know your kind, playing on the dreams of the impoverished, turning innocent girls into harlots to serve your pleasure."

"I am not like that. My love is true. I will take excellent care of Galla and the child."

The butcher picked up the bloody hatchet and leaned across the counter. "You better, boy, or there will be a reckoning."

Galla came down the stairs carrying all her belongs in a leather satchel. Behind the maiden came her teary-eyed mother and siblings. She hugged everyone, including her father. Then she trustfully took Augustine's hand. He led her in the direction of the forum, carrying the heavy bag for her. A few blocks away from the public buildings, he entered an apartment building and introduced Galla to the door guard so she would be permitted entry when he was not with her. Just inside the entrance was a large barrel holding urine from the apartment's inhabitants. Once a day slaves from a fullone would collect the rank liquid, using its alkali acid for washing laundry. Augustine led Galla up to the third floor. When they entered the apartment, two youths paused in their debated over the meaning of a book to stare at the maiden, their eyes feasting on her shapely body and blonde hair.

Rogelius grinned. "It is about time you brought your pet home."

Augustine stepped in front of her. "This is Galla. She is mine. If anyone touches her I will cast him into the streets."

"You do not have such authority, as we began renting this place before you."

Probus leered, "Come now. You will not share with your fellow brothers? She is prettier than most temple whores."

"She carries my child." He looked each roommate firmly in the eyes. "She is off limits."

The youths quieted. Then Rogelius stood and placed a hand over his heart. "She will be safe with us, I swear by Jove. But you will confuse the poor child. Will it come out Gaul or Berber?"

"Perhaps like a striped zebra," said Probus.

The joke lightened the tension in the room. The classmates returned to arguing symbolism while Augustine led his new concubine to his bedroom. The partitioned area had a bed, a desk cluttered with parchments, and a locked chest holding personal items.

He sat her bag on the floor. "I know it is not much."

"It is twice the size of my sister's room." Admiringly she touched the thick feather mattress supported on a wooden bed frame with crisscrossed leather straps. "It's more than I have ever had. My family sleeps on the floor."

"Try it out." Augustine sat on the bed and pulled her to him. "When I graduate, I will take you to my villa. From our second floor you can look out over miles of wheat fields and olive groves, the sun bathing the countryside in golden light. Hear the beating of livestock and crowing roosters, not the relentless pounding of feet and grinding wheels on flagstone. That is where our child will be raised."

"You make it sound so wonderful. I have never been outside Carthage."

"You will love Thagaste."

The next morning he awoke when Galla rose from the bed. As he watched her dress in a pale stola, he admired her gorgeous body and began pondering the meaning of beauty. Her perfectness was equal to any expensive statue he had seen in temples and forums. "You are a goddess come to life."

"You are a trained flatterer." Still, she smiled at the compliment.

He tenderly grabbed her arm and pulled her back into bed, kissing her deeply. After a few minutes she pulled away. "I must prepare breakfast."

Augustine sighed, reluctant to relinquish her warm body. "You will find we keep little food here, perhaps because my roommates and I do not trust each other."

"May I have money then so I can buy us something?"

Augustine arose, found his money pouch on the floor beside his tunic, and gave her a few coins.

"Should I also cook for the others?"

He was about to say no, when an idea occurred to him. He quickly dressed then caught up with his roommates who were picking up their satchels to head to class. "How would you like to have real meals every day, not food grabbed from stalls?" He had their immediate attention. "Each of you can contribute a little money, and Galla will turn it into a proper feast."

"Her father is a butcher," said Rogelius, already licking his lips at the thought. "Could she get us discounts on meat? Would be nice to have it more than once a week."

"Can she buy pork?" wondered Probus. "I have never tasted it, but my cousin says it is delicious."

Galla smiled with the realization she could earn at least a little respect from them. "Yes, I can get pork and beef and fish. I can cook dishes with sauces and spices which only the richest usually eat. My grandmother was a cook for a city official, and I inherited some of her recipes."

The youths eagerly opened their pouches and handed her money. Galla was good on her word. That night on a small wood-burning stove she cooked pork feet smothered in a spicy fish sauce, cut decorative designs into fresh radishes, and glazed rolls in honey. The youths bragged they were eating like senators and handed more coins over to her for future meals.

While Augustine and his roommates were at school, Galla cleaned the entire apartment, scrubbing away years of grime, turning the bachelors' pad into a well-kept suite. With his girl won, Augustine focused harder at his studies. When he won a poetry contest, it was the personal physician to Emperor Valentinian who placed the laurel wreath on his head. The victory allowed him to befriend a few officials who invited him to dinner parties hosted at their villas. When he returned home, Galla would question him in detail about the dishes served then try to copy the recipes if she could buy the ingredients.

Augustine wrote to both his mother and Romanianus, going into great detail about his successes at school, only mentioning in passing that he had taken a concubine and was expecting a child. Many weeks passed before a merchant traveling from Thagaste brought the responses. He broke the seal from his patron first. Romanianus congratulated him on both the poetry victory and the upcoming child, offering a few tips in dealing with newborns. His mother expressed her disappointment in him along with a reminder to attend church.

With Galla by his side, Augustine strolled through the many shops of Carthage. Her favorites were jewelry, though the most she could do was stare at the handcrafted silver and gold. Needing textbooks, Augustine looked for bargains he could afford. One day he came across a scroll which changed his outlook on life. The ancient book was *Hortensius* by Cicero, a distinguished orator and lawyer. During the last days of the Republic, Cicero had championed a return to traditional government and values. Mark Antony eventually ordered his assassination, but the philosopher's works continued to be widely read.

A hunger awakened in Augustine when he read, "Not to study one particular sect but to love and seek and pursue and hold fast and strongly embrace wisdom itself, wherever found." This wisdom Augustine wanted above all else. He began spending hours searching through bookshops for rare text written by renowned authors, but their prices were beyond his meager allowance. Still, there was a rush of excitement each time he unwound a scroll and read the words of the ancient philosophers. What wisdom did these men of renowned share? What truths did they whisper beyond their graves?

He tried reading books that Catholics considered holy, but he found their writing style unpleasing, far below his standards. What did Hebrew writers from a backwards providence have to say compared to esteemed Cicero who had dined with Caesars? Rarely did he now attend liturgies, but Galla continued to go every day.

Other books besides philosophy beckoned him. Astrologers claimed people's fate could be predicted based upon the alignment of stars when a person was born. Augustine brought several of their texts and attempted to read the horoscopes of his roommates. When his predictions turned out to be more wrong than right, he visited astrologers, seeking to understand their mysterious art better.

The superficial conversations of the Wreakers began to bore him, leading him to seek more cultured companions. One afternoon he searched through the bins of a bookshop. Galla was several stalls away, buying vegetables. Augustine picked up a scroll on astrology. The text intrigued him, and he debated if he could spare the money for it and still buy a required book for class.

A dark-skinned man nearby noticed the title of the book Augustine held. "Are you a student of the stars?"

"I dabble in it, but wisdom is my true pursuit."

The young man smiled as he offered a challenge. "Then answer me this, why do twins born at the same time often have different fates? I have seen this with my own eyes more than once."

The question fascinated Augustine. "A well-thought out question which I must ponder before I can give an answer. I am Augustine, a rhetorical student."

"I am Nebridius, a wisdom seeker like you." The man wore a pileus hat. Some freed men chose to wear it as a reminder of the day it was placed on their shaved heads when they were granted manumission.

As Augustine chatted with Nebridius, he discovered the man had a keen mind and was well-read, though he had never officially attended school. They talked for several minutes until Galla arrived with a laden basket of vegetables. Augustine instinctively volunteered to carry the basket. Her swollen belly showed that the birth of her child was not far off.

Spotting the hat of Nebridius, she smiled. "I always wished for one of those, but I only have my parchment as proof of my freedom—even though I cannot read it."

Seeing Augustine's tenderness towards his concubine, Nebridius became more relaxed. "My father was our master's most trustworthy slave. I served as paedagogue to his son, drinking in the knowledge the boy took for granted. Upon our master's death, he willed freedom to my entire family, giving my father a few acres along with a suitable amount of gold. My father invested wisely, and using his master's contacts, now owns one hundred acres right outside the city."

"You father is an example of what one can accomplish through shrewdness," said Augustine.

Nebridius nodded, liking what he saw in Augustine. "I visit Carthage often to listen to philosophical lectures at the forum. Been in a few debates myself. Never liked it when someone gives too short an answer to a great question."

"One of the reasons I became a rhetorical student. I wanted to truly understand wisdom."

"In my search, I have discovered that too many claim to know wisdom but only spout nonsense."

Augustine laughed. "Aye. I have met many of them myself. I enjoy waiting until a fool has finished his idiotic banter then slice through it with logic and wit."

Galla leaned proudly against her lover. "Augustine wins most debates in his class."

Wishing to continue the conversation, Nebridius said, "My father is hosting a dinner party next holiday. I invite both of you to come as my guests."

Having never been to a formal party, Galla excitedly talked about it all the way home. Then she became worried her clothing was too shabby. Augustine gave her money for a new stola but worried about funds becoming too low. Still it was worth the price to see Galla beaming in a new, white dress highlighted with an old palla she had dyed bright blue. She wore the beaded necklace Augustine had brought her on their first date. Attempting to mimic fashion of the upper-class, she styled her hair into small braids which twisted around each other.

The trip to the villa would have taken several hours walk, but Nebridius had thoughtfully provided a litter to spare Galla the hardship of traveling when so near birth. As slaves carried the litter through the crowded streets, Galla peeked through its veil, delighted to watch crowds part before them. When the fertile countryside spread out before her, she oohed in delight. Never had she seen ripen fields stretching as far as the eye could see, dotted with homesteads. Augustine smiled at her happiness then continued reading a book Nebridius had mentioned in their conversation the week before.

Eventually the slaves turned off the main road and traveled down a path between ripening fields where slaves weeded crops. They passed into shade cast by olive trees. Beyond the grove was a large, elegant villa surrounded by trimmed hedges. Among carefully tended flowerbeds, brick paths weaved between large marble statues of famous heroes. The foundation for a new wing to the villa was being laid by hard working men hauling dirt to flatten the area.

Nebridius greeted the couple when they stepped out of the litter by introducing his parents and young sisters. Other guests arrived, several of which were also freedmen. During the banquet, guests lay on couches as slaves brought in course after scrumptious course of lavish food. Due to her pregnancy, Galla sat at a nearby table. So she would not be alone, the *domina* of the family joined her. Nebridius' mother was uneducated like Galla, and they quickly became friends, trading cooking and housekeeping tips. The men and educated wives discussed politics, literature, and philosophy.

Nebridius and Augustine stayed up late into the night debating with several other men. The two learned they approached topics in similar fashions, often having the same opinions. When they did disagree, each laid out their beliefs logically, earning the respect of the other.

By the time Augustine found his guestroom, Galla was already asleep in a large, lush bed. In the dancing lamplight, the braided curls of her hair seemed to be transformed into real gold. He bent and kissed her. She sighed, half-opening her eyes.

"I did not mean to wake you."

"I was only dozing, waiting for you." She wrapped her arms around him as he lay beside her. "This place feels like a dream I wish to never wake from. Never have I known such luxury, been treated so kindly."

"Nebridius and his family are welcoming." Augustine stroked her hair. "He is a like-minded scholar. I have invited him to share our apartment whenever he visits Carthage. We have extra rooms now that Rogelius and Probus have recently moved out to begin their careers."

She flinched and touched her stomach. "Our son kicks."

Augustine touched her abdomen, waiting. Soon he was rewarded with the thump of invisible feet. "He is eager to see the world."

"Just like his father."

Augustine wondered what his son would be like. Smart like himself, eager to learn about everything? Or perhaps it was a daughter who would be as beautiful as her mother. While he had originally cared little about becoming a father, he now was eager to introduce his child to the world he loved: plays and feasts, sports events and races, poetry and books. There was so much he wanted to share.

The next day a litter carried them back into the city. A week later Nebridius moved in, bringing with him a chest full of scrolls—his greatest treasure. For hours he and Augustine would peruse them, debating their meanings. Galla waddled about, fixing them meals and cleaning up afterwards. Nebridius would stay for a week or two then journey back to his parents' estate for a few days. When he returned, he brought fresh vegetables from his family's garden along with another scroll from their private library.

The night Galla gave birth, Nebridius was the one calming Augustine as the young father paced about the apartment while Galla screamed from their bedroom. Worried, Augustine entered to check on her. Groaning, Galla sat on the birthing stool, hands clenching its arm-rests, her face sweaty. Seeing him, the midwife ordered him away, muttering about hindering men.

"Relax, friend," said Nebridius, pouring Augustine another cup of cheap wine.

"Why must the price for new life be so excessive?" Augustine gulped the red wine, remembering stories of woman who died during childbirth.

"Galla is strong. She will come through just fine."

When cries of an infant filled the air, Augustine dropped his cup and rushed into the bedroom. As customary, the midwife placed the wet, squirming baby on the floor, awaiting the father's verdict. If a man believed the child was not his or disappointed that it was handicapped or a female, he could turn his back, refusing to accept the newborn into the family. On such occasions, midwives took the unwanted babies away, exposing them by either abandoning them on rocks by the sea or at other designated spots about the city.

"It's a boy," said the weary midwife, wiping her hands clean on her apron.

"My son." Without hesitation, Augustine scooped up the infant and held him high in the air, accepting the boy. His voice trembled in awe as he beheld the tiny feet and fingers. "He is perfect." The new father placed the infant in Galla's outstretched arms. "What shall we name our son?"

Despite her exhaustion, she smiled as she beheld her child. "Adeodatus, for he is a gift from God."

Chapter Eight

Augustine pressed against a wall along with others to avoid the guards surrounding a litter. Perhaps behind the expensive veil was a renowned senator or a high priestess of a triad temple. The litter passed and people began walking again. Augustine watched the passersby, rich and poor of many races, jostling and bumping against each other in the crowded streets. Most women kept their pallas pulled over their heads to form hoods. The richer ones were escorted by slaves.

When the crowd thinned, Augustine continued his stroll, heading towards his favorite bookshop. The scent of fresh bread drifted in the warm spring breeze. A primary teacher stood at the edge the street, surrounded by children sitting on the ground reciting the alphabet above the din of traffic. Rent was high in Carthage and primary teachers were paid little, leading them to resort to outdoor classrooms. Many were former slaves who had received a rudimentary education as a paedagogue while watching their master's kids. Some teachers only accepted male students, but others opened up their classes to females, happy to take any parent's money. No females received an education beyond primary accept by private tutors in rich families.

At nineteen, Augustine was enjoying life. He continued to outperform other rhetoric students, earning attention from several lawyers at the forum. Invitations to dinners were increasing. Galla sometimes complained about being left home, but he would silence her by saying their conversations would bore her. Besides, who would look after Adeodatus? Depending on the generosity of the host, he sometimes brought leftovers home which cheered her up. When Nebridius was in Carthage, the two visited the forum and debated with other scholars about countless topics. The greater the controversy of the subject, the more Augustine found himself drawn to it.

Today, he was alone. Entering a familiar bookshop, he began inspecting the cluttered bins, looking for rare scrolls. The shopkeeper approached, his fingertips black from writing with ink.

"How did you enjoy Apuleius's *On the God of Socrates*?"

"I appreciate you sharing a book by a native of Madaurus, but I must admit I found several faults. Daemons as intermediaries between gods and humans seemed extravagant. How could one tell if they are good or evil?"

The middle-age bookseller smiled. "You are a philosopher seeking truth."

"I seek wisdom, wherever it may be found."

"Then I have something for you to see. A book like no other, one which holds both truth and wisdom hidden from all but the hungriest of seekers."

The man led Augustine behind the counter into a backroom. He unlocked a chest and pulled out a large package wrapped in cloth. Gingerly he unwrapped the object to reveal a book of wonders. As the bookseller flipped its pages, Augustine drew closer, staring speechless at the large parchments stitched together tightly on the left. He had seen a few handbooks bound this way, but all were tiny, just collections of poems or a thesis. This was voluminous with colorful pictures drawn in the margins.

"A rarity like this is far beyond my price range."

"Ah, this book cannot be brought. If caught with this you might be killed, or at least severely punished."

"Yet you show it to me?"

"I have been observing you for a long time now, seeing which books you like, questioning you to judge your thoughts. You see easily through false arguments while hungering for knowledge. Tell me, where does evil come from?"

Still staring at the wondrous book, Augustine replied by rote. "The Greeks say it was when the first woman Pandora opened a jar and released all evils upon mankind. The Christians claim it was when the woman Eve ate fruit from a forbidden tree."

"Do you believe such tales? How can opening a jar or eating an apple create evil? Long before jars or fruit existed there was good and evil. The larger region is light, the realm of the spirit and soul. Darkness exists in the material world, forming a wedge which cuts into the light by using our ignorance and polluted bodies. Human souls become caught by the Darkness, forgetting our real nature and our mission. By eliminating vices and dark desires we can reach enlightenment."

Augustine frowned. "Which religion says this?"

The bookseller patted the manuscript reverently. "This is holy scripture written by the prophet Mani from Persia. We are called the Manichean, and we can be found everywhere. Laws may press us to be silent, but several of my brethren boldly speak in public about our beliefs. I invite you to come to one of our secret meetings. It may change your life, seeker of wisdom."

Intrigued, Augustine could not turn the offer down. Several nights later he arrived at the designated villa, entering through a side door after giving a password to a slave. He was led to the cellar where cushions and blankets were spread out. Already men and woman sat on them, discussing religion while slaves brought refreshments. The bookseller greeted Augustine then introduced him to the others. Plebeians and patricians mixed together, chatting easily. Women spoke their thoughts without fear of reprimands. Augustine was impressed by names of the attendees, including a few prominent politicians. He settled on a cushion as an elder read a passage from the treasured book then explained its meaning. Questions were encouraged. Augustine listened spell-bound, eager to understand the wisdom contained in its sacred text.

He learned that five years earlier Theodosius I had decreed a death sentence for all Manicheans, but only in certain regions had that punishment being carried out. In Carthage, several bold Elect regularly lectured about their Manichean beliefs at the forum, drawing curious crowds. Other followers kept their beliefs private to avoid persecution but provided financial support to the Elect. The secretive meetings allowed Manicheans to know who their fellow believers where. When opportunity offered, those in high public positions promoted their fellow Manicheans, even if the other candidates were more qualified.

One meeting was not enough for Augustine. He came back often, sometimes bringing Nebridius with him. While Augustine was mesmerized, his friend remained skeptical. As one meeting broke up, Augustine and Nebridius lingered to chat with the elders.

"You attacked Genesis tonight by putting Jewish animal sacrifices in the same category as pagan offerings," pointed out Nebridius.

The elder was relaxed, eager to speak, his face pale from his special diet of fruit and vegetables. "Many religions believe by killing animals and sometimes people, these barbaric actions appease their gods. But doing so only pleases Darkness. We refrain from meat because the particles of life which lay within all life rouse the demon of Darkness within men. Plants contain light particles which, when consumed by the Perfect, our elders, set the light free."

Nebridius frowned, unable to accept such ideas, but Augustine nodded in agreement.

"Let me go about it a different way. Manicheans believe all killing is wrong. The original Carthaginians sacrifice their own children to Saturn. In the Torah, Abraham was willing to kill his son to please Yahweh. The Christians believed that Yahweh sent his only son Jesus to be sacrificed. In the end, all these religions are the same. Shedding blood brings pleasure to the gods."

Augustine leaded forward. "I have always wondered why the Catholic Church places such strong emphasis on the execution of Jesus."

The elder laughed. "How could a real god be killed? Would a god actually choose to leave paradise and walk among us? Would he have nails and hair which needs to be trimmed? God is far holier and more pure than such mundane nonsense. God is spirit, not flesh, both male and female at the same time. He cannot be touched or seen. It is the material substance which is foul and misshaped. By us choosing to practice the twelve virtues and the luminaries labors, we can live a pure life, becoming perfect, the Elect."

"What if someone cannot follow all these commands?" Augustine worried. He wanted to be part of the Elect, but their rules were extremely strict. So many pleasures banned.

"There is still hope. You can be a Hearer, helping the Elders liberate the soul from matter, the light-spark of God from the enslaving darkness by refraining from meat, wine, and sex. Serve the Elders, picking fruits for us to consume to release their particles."

Augustine and Nebridius discussed the meeting as they walked back to the apartment using a lantern as their only light through the narrow unlit streets.

Nebridius stepped over a drunkard passed out on the cobblestone. "I do not see how Manichean have anything better to offer over any other religion."

"Do you not see? We are not at fault for our own sins. We are born with the corruption of evil within us. It is the Darkness's fault that we are depraved. But purity is possible."

"By eating fruit?" As they passed a brothel, several prostitutes beckoned them, but the men ignored them. "How long could you keep to their strict rules?"

"I could forgo the wine and meat."

"But sex?"

Augustine paused, wistful. "That is the one thing I cannot give up. One bare leg from Galla and my vows would melt away." Both men laughed then quieted as they passed a band of night watchmen, the one in front holding high a lantern to light the armed guards' way.

"I will know such appeal soon when I wed."

"So the details are settled?"

"Yes, her parents and my father finally agreed, though he was grumpy with the dowry they offered. Her family received little from their master upon manumission. He finally relented after my mother reminded him that he once owned nothing himself."

"You are marrying a pauper's daughter. Is she worth it?"

A dreamy look came over Nebridius' face. "Yes. A thousand times yes."

Augustine laughed. "Good, as you will be fettered to her the rest of your life."

"You choose as I did, beauty before wealth."

"Unlike you I am bound but not fettered."

Nebridius presumed his friend would forget about the forbidden sect, but Augustine kept attending the meetings, drawing deeper into their mysteries, certain that truth was contained in their wondrous, mystical books. Perhaps it was the exoticness of the eastern religion that drew him or that it was prohibited by law. Why did the emperor fear Mani? If there was no truth in Mani's words, then simply ignoring the sect was enough. There were countless legal gods and strange philosophies across the empire. Why was Mani's teachings singled out from the rest?

He invited Galla to attend a meeting, explaining that freed slaves were treated equal with the others. She left Adeodatus with her older sister. The secrecy of the meeting disturbed her. Women, like the men, were encouraged to ask questions following the reading of the secret text, but the discussions were beyond her grasp. She did catch on that Manicheans scornfully viewed the ancient Jewish heroes like Abraham, Moses, and David who had multiple wives.

When they were back at their apartment, Galla questioned Augustine about it, but he pushed her objections aside. "Do you wish for me to take many lovers?"

"No, of course not. But they claim the patriarchs were in the wrong. Yet these men were chosen by God."

Augustine began to playfully undress his concubine. "God choose Abraham who married his own sister? Choose Moses who committed murder then ran away, a coward? Choose David, both a murderer and adulterer? Why would a holy God choose such tarnished vessels as his ambassadors to the world?"

"God chooses who he wills." She slipped from his touch to check on her sleeping son. "Who are we to questioned God?"

"I dare to question. If he has a voice, let him speak to me. I am listening."

"Then go to church with me tomorrow."

"I grew up being forced to attend services with my mother. I have heard countless sermons. There is nothing new for a priest to tell me." He wrapped his arms around her slender waist and kissed her neck.

"Manicheans are declared heretics by the Church and Roman law. You should stay away from them."

"Do not worry your pretty head about it." Augustine drew her towards the bed. "I am the philosopher. You are the cook."

As the second year at the rhetoric drew to a close, Augustine pondered his future. He had been expected to begin working as an assistant to a lawyer. That life no longer appealed to him. He only wanted to continue his pursuit of wisdom, not twisting lies to persuade a crowd. If he had been wealthy, he would had spent the rest of his life happily surrounded by books, reading the day away and writing about his own theories. But his funding was soon to end and he needed a job. After much contemplating, he decided to become a teacher. He could combine his passion for literature with work that paid, passing on his love for wisdom to his students.

When he told Galla, she just stared at him while her son silently nursed in her arms. After taking a long moment to recover, she sputtered. "But teachers make little money. We could not even afford this apartment."

Augustine smiled reassuringly. "We will be in Thagaste living with my mother. And I will not be a primary teacher but grammaticus. There are none at Thagaste, and our brightest boys must travel to Madaura. It will be easy for me to find students while charging a decently high price. Families will be eager to pay, for it will still be far cheaper having their sons educated locally than sent away."

"What about your benefactor? Will he not be angry that he wasted his money supporting you?"

"Am I his slave that he commands me to do his bidden? In gratitude for his help, I will volunteer to educate his son for half price."

Galla placed Adeodatus on her shoulder to burp him. "Do as you wish." She had already learned that once his mind was set, he would not heed her misgivings.

Augustine walked over and sat on the bed beside Galla. "I do this for you and our son. You will love Thagaste. We shall live in a proper villa with running water and fields for Adeodatus to run in. Slaves to help with chores."

"I would not know what to do with myself if I am not cooking."

"If you wish to cook, you may, using fresh vegetables from our well-tended gardens."

Already the pangs of being separated from her family pulled at Galla. Once they left Carthage, would she see her parents or siblings again? Despite how she felt, Galla said, "I will go wherever you go."

Augustine picked up his satchel to head to class. "One other thing. Mani discourages us to produce offspring because it creates more corrupt matter. We can have no more children. You will need to chart your monthly flow for us to avoid intercourse during your most fertile time. And you will need to start using contraception."

She frowned, her eyes narrowing. "Anything else you wish to share with me this morning?"

"No, that is all. I promise you will love Thagaste." He bent and kissed her. "I look forward to supper tonight. Always I have a ravish appetite for your succulent dishes. Just do not serve meat."

He headed out the door, eager to battle classmates with words, leaving Galla alone with the baby. As she changed her son's dirty cloth, she wondered what had happened to the romantic youth with dreams of grander who she had fallen in love with a year ago. Settling to be a grammaticus teacher when he had the talent to be a renowned lawyer? And this nonsense about not having more children. She hoped his interest in Manichean would soon fade.

Adeodatus waved his small fists in the air, legs kicking. Galla smiled and kissed her son on the forehead. "Time to head to the market to buy your father his vegetables. Don't worry, I will give you meat when you are older. Now for morning prayers."

She scooped up her son and headed toward church, determined Adeodatus would grow up to be a proper Catholic.

Chapter Nine

A merchant wagon rolled through the paved streets of Thagaste, heading towards the market. Surrounded by crates and baskets, Galla slept with her head against her lover, her arms cuddling their infant son. Augustine watched familiar buildings pass by. He was home. Part of him was excited about dreams of the future, overseeing his own school, passing on prodigious knowledge to the next generation. But he still had his mother and Romanianus to contend with—Monnica he dreaded worse than his patron.

The wagon stopped. The market had many booths selling a wide-variety of items, including vegetables from nearby farms. The aroma of cooking meat from several vendors made Augustine's stomach growl. It had been many hours since their last meal of dried fruit. He reminisced of his youth when he had often explored the market with his friends, buying snacks when he had a few coins.

Augustine awakened Galla, and they climbed out of the wagon. While Augustine paid the merchant they had traveled with, Galla surveyed the small town, impressed by its wider, less crowded streets. The white plastered buildings with red terracotta roofs were shorter but tidier than the tall, graffiti-speckled apartments of Carthage. Little sewage or trash was tossed on the cobblestone streets.

"There is so much more space here."

"Wait till you see the countryside." Augustine picked up several of their bags, leaving the rest for slaves to fetch later.

He led the way out of the market. Several people recognized Augustine and called out greetings. The return of a dead councilman's son was noteworthy in the small town, and he was stopped repeatedly by both well-wishers and the curious. Augustine kept conversations short, saying Galla was tired.

Didius, one of Augustine's old school mates, fell in step beside him and volunteered to carry a bag. He had attended grammaticus in Madaura with Augustine, but his family could not afford to continue his education further. "Carthage has done wonders for you. Who would have guessed you would earn such a beautiful wife."

"Concubine."

"Oh," Didius glanced at Galla holding her sleepy son. "How has your mother dealt with that?"

"It is my choice, not hers. Tell me about the great events of Thagaste which has happened in my absence."

"The usual deaths, births, and marriages. Much to gossip about but little has changed. Your sister's upcoming wedding is stirring some attention. Your mother rejected three proposals before accepting a patrician two villages away who owns twenty-five acres. That was after she refused a man who owed sixty. Rumors say she could not afford the dowry."

"She wrote me about that. She refuses to give Perpetua away to anyone who is not a faithful church-going Catholic."

Didius nodded. "I think she chose well. He is reputed to be of fine character, though not as well educated as you or I. Soon you will be blessed with many nephews. During your studies do you happen upon books by Cicero? I found his *Hortensius* fascinating."

"As did I. He wrote that the function of wisdom is to…"

"…discriminate between good and evil." He enjoyed Augustine's surprised stare. "I may not have the funds to attend a tertiary, but I still continue my studies on my own."

"I am delighted to discover that another appreciates Cicero as I do." Augustine realized his childhood acquaintance had changed considerable in the last two years. In their youth, they had only spoken about superficial topics, but now both had matured, their minds broadened. "I have taken his words to heart, 'There is nothing worse than a hasty judgment, and nothing could be more unworthy of the dignity and integrity of a philosopher than uncritically to adopt a false opinion or to maintain as certain some theory which has not been fully explored and understood.' I no longer believe something because others claim it is true. I must probe and examine until I find the truth."

"You understand me." Didus smiled in delight. "I too feel frustrated with those who believe blindly but lack understanding about what they claim to believe in."

"In Carthage I have had the opportunity to read the works of great men, writers of philosophy, science, and religions. Tell me, have you heard of Mani?"

"Vaguely. Is he not a creator of a forbidden religion?"

"Yes. I have much to share about him if you are not afraid to look beyond what is taught at services or spoken by the masses."

"I fear not truth, only the lack of understanding."

The two men remained in deep conversation as they strolled out of Thagaste into the countryside of lush fields of ripen wheat. Galla silently followed behind, understanding little of the topics they discussed. Adeodatus awoke and stared at the green world around him. He reached out, trying to grab birds flying in the sky, his young mind unable to grasp that they lay beyond him.

When they neared the villa, Monnica and Perpetua rushed out to embrace Augustine. His sister had bloomed into a beautiful maiden well-trained to begin running her own household. He noted that his mother had a few more wrinkles, her hands callus from her many labors. Without Monnica saying a word, he knew she was disappointed that he had taken a lover he could never marry. Still, she hugged him, beaming that he had returned.

Galla watched the greetings nervously, holding Adeodatus tightly. Upon Patricious' death, Monnica had become the *paterfamilias* of the family, having legal authority over the lives of her family. She had the power to send her son's lover away and could deny her grandson's birthright as an heir. The estate had flourished under Monnica's management, and she treated both slaves and tenants kindly. As a former councilmembers' wife, she continued to be active in the community, settling minor disputes, and giving alms to the poor.

Monnica turned to Galla and smiled. "Welcome to my home. May I hold him?" Monnica cooed over the baby, rocking him gently. "He has his father's eyes. The same as Patricius. And his mother's blond hair. How handsome you will be when you grow up, my grandson. Adeodatus, gift from God. A name well chosen."

Didus handed the bag he was carrying to a slave. "I must take my leave. Augustine, once you are settled in, come by for a visit. I would enjoy continuing our discussion."

"I look forward to it." Augustine was relieved to have already discovered on his first day a likeminded friend.

The evening was spent in lively discussion with Augustine answering the many questions his mother and sister peppered him with. At one point, Perpetua pulled out her lye, playing while Augustine quoted poetry. Monnica beamed in delight, the slaves pausing in their work to listen. Navigius sat quietly, arms folded. Now twelve, he had finished his primary education but money was lacking for sending him to a grammaticus. Childhood at an end, he had begun taking up the duties of his father, overseeing farm work. Galla sat in a corner, rocking her son, feeling like an outsider.

The next morning Augustine rose early to visit Romanianus. Best to face him immediately and hope to win his approval. While he was gone, Galla roamed about the villa, uncertain what to do. The slaves tended to household chores while Monnica and Perpetua dyed old cloth to be made into new outfits. Galla attended morning prayers with them, but she felt uncomfortable walking beside the *domina*. Unconsciously, she kept her eyes downcast as if she was still a slave and Monnica the mistress.

Augustine arrived home in a cheerful mood. His carefully worded proposal to Romanianus had gone smoothly, and he had received his patron's blessing to start a school. Now he had to deal with his mother. He waited until late evening to approach her. Monnica was in the herb garden with Galla, discussing which plants would be best to season the food for supper.

"Hold these for us." Monnica handed fleshly cut thyme and basil to Augustine then pointed to the parsley. "They must grow more before we pull the largest leaves."

Galla knelt in the rich soul and smelled deeply of the plants. Here she felt as peace for the first time since leaving Carthage. "I have bought herbs many times in markets but never grown them myself. The fresher they are, the better the favor."

"I will teach you how to garden. My son tells me you are a skilled cook."

"She is one of the best I have met, Mother," said Augustine.

Galla smiled at the compliment. "May I cook supper tonight to show you?"

Monnica nodded. "Yes, I look forward to sampling your dishes."

Augustine carried the herbs to the kitchen where Galla began to cook, delighted in using an actual oven instead of a charcoal brazier. She placed chicken on the iron bars and ground the herbs, making her own sauce, determined to make a meal that would please the *domina*.

Monnica took her grandson from Statilia. Age had stolen the slave's beauty but had mellowed her fiery disposition.

"Mother, I need to talk with you about my future." Augustine kept pace with her as they strolled around the columned peristylium. The room was open to the sky. At its center was a pool which collected rainwater used to water the herb garden.

"Have you found who you will apprentice under?"

"I have no need for further education, for I wish to become an educator myself."

Monnica stopped walking. "What do you mean? Do you no longer wish to be a lawyer? That was your father's dream for you."

"I shared his dream for a long time. But I have changed and so have my desires. I want start a grammaticus here in Thagaste. Romanianus has already approved of my plan and has agreed to send his son. That is, if I have your blessing."

The *domina* looked down at her grandson sleeping peacefully in her arms. "Teaching is an honorable vocation, a method of serving others. And the town needs a grammaticus. It was difficult for us sending you away to Madaura. Every day your father and I worried about you, just a boy so far away."

"Now I can spare other families such hardships and save them money. Do I have your blessing?"

"Of course. I am very proud you are choosing a path of service over ambition. Will you attend church with us tomorrow?"

"I will be busy visiting acquaintances, looking for more students." He refrained from telling her about his new faith.

Galla prepared an elaborate four course meal, putting as much effort into it as if cooking for a fancy dining party. She served the food herself, placing only vegetables in front of Augustine.

Navigius noticed and frowned. "Is there something wrong with the meat?"

"No, I just have indigestion and have been avoiding meat for a while." Augustine hoped the lie would deflect their curiosity for a while. Eventually he would share his new beliefs, but now was not the time.

Monnica picked up a chicken leg basted in a spicy sauce and took a bite. Her face filled with delight. "My son is right. This is the best tasting fowl I have eaten."

Galla smiled in relief, feeling she had found her place within the household.

Over the following month Augustine visited prominent townspeople, inviting their sons to become his students. Having Romanianus's favor opened doors for him, quickly leading to support from over a dozen families. He rented a room near the market to use as a class once summer break was over. Didus was often by his side as they explored the town, watching plays or attending races. They spent long hours together discussing books and philosophy. By the time Perpetua's wedding arrived, Didus had secretly converted to Manichean.

Unlike her mother so many years ago, sixteen-year-old Perpetua was radiate and jolly on her wedding day. She had met her groom Isauricus several times over the last few months and felt tenderness for him, certain he would be a kind, loving husband, though he was twice her age. She was to be his second wife, as his first had died several years ago during childbirth.

The wedding party lasted for hours, with musicians playing late into the night. Augustine and Didus avoided the wine and groups of guests debating politics. They were attracted to the philosophical conversations. A half-drunk youth bragged about his knowledge of Virgil. Augustine baited the young man, asking him sly questions, trapping the youth by his own words. The man became angry when he realized he could not counter Augustine's points.

As he marched away, Didus and Augustine winked at each other and laughed, feeling superior to the intellects around them. The youth returned with several friends who attempted to outwit Augustine. The exchange attracted the attention of others curious about the new grammarian's oratorical skills. Augustine skillfully weaved through the augments of his opponents, allowing their own faulty logic to be their undoing. They became more frustrated, changing topics several times. The first youth was determined to win at least one point.

With polished words Augustine said, "What is the nature of God? The Stoic believed that the element of fire constitute the visible universe, endowing life and wisdom, creating the universe itself. Fire, in fact, was God to them. They and other lesser philosophers could only understand God as being a material thing, existing from substance which they were familiar with. The Platonists came closest to the truth, seeing God as spirit, immutable. Nothing which changes can be a supreme God."

The youth countered, "God can be material, as he walked among us, eating with us, and dying on the cross."

Augustine moved in for the kill. "Then is God like Zeus, taking on the form of man to woo women? Did Mary birth a demigod, another Jason or Hercules?"

"Jesus was God and the son of God at the same time."

"You repeat what you hear in church without understanding its meaning. How can an object exist while being its own begotten? Can anyone birth themself? Explain how Jesus can be God and his son at the same time."

The youth faltered, glancing at his friends for help but they were also speechless. "He…just is."

"Just is. That is your best defense? I think you need to sign up for my classes."

Spectators laughed. The youth and his friends left, muttering angrily.

Romanianus patted Augustine on the back. "You make for fascinating entertainment. So what is the answer to your question?"

"The only logical answer is that Jesus was not God." Several people nearby gasped in shock and began whispering. Augustine ignored them.

The councilman studied Augustine keenly. "You speak not the words of a Christian."

"I do not embrace my mother's faith but have found truth elsewhere."

"In my lengthy travels, I have met many who claim to know truth. Who do you believe holds it?"

"The great teacher Mani."

A few onlookers called out in anger, "Heretic! Demon worshipper!"

Augustine looked them in the eye. "You who embrace Christianity dare call me a heretic? Have you forgotten that not too long ago it was your religion which was branded as evil? Nero used your kind for torches to light up his races, enjoying watching Christians writhing in flames as his horses thundered across the sand. Just because something is forbidden does not make it evil. Do not be so quick to judge what you do not understand."

"More wine," called Romanianus, beckoning a slave over. "A grammarian's job is to make others think. You have been quite successful in that tonight. Drink everyone. Dance and enjoy yourself."

Some drank deeply and grabbed a partner, forgetting the discussion, but others whispered urgently, passing on the word that sweet Monnica had a sacrilegious son.

Romanianus whispered to Augustine. "Drop by my villa next week. I wish to probe your beliefs more. But be wary of sharing your thoughts publicly."

"Did fear of death stop Christians from speaking about their faith? I will not be silent either. Yet I will heed you by remaining cautious."

Rumors spread fast across the small community, yet it was several days before anyone dared mention them to Monnica. While delivering clothes to a widow, Monnica was asked how she dealt with a renegade son. At first she thought the question referred to Augustine having a concubine, but when she learned the rumors about her son, she became devastated. She hurried home, finding him reading in the garden, Galla sitting on the ground rolling a leather ball to Adeodatus.

Face pale, Monnica asked, "Is it true?"

"What is?" Augustine sat the scroll down, knowing what she referred to.

"Are you a...a...Manichean?"

"Yes, Mother, I am."

"How could you? I taught you differently." She glanced at Galla. "Did she change you?"

"Do not blame Galla. She is as Catholic as you. This was my choice. I saw through the deception of all other religions including yours. Mani holds the truth."

"But he knows not God."

"His writings are completely about God."

Distraught, Monnica sought some way to save her son, "He knows not the true God. You must turn away. Go to evening prayers with me."

"I will not step into a church again. It is a waste of my time."

72

"Please come. Talk with the priest. Let him explain God's word to you."

"I have heard sermons most of my life. I tried reading your sacred word. It is poorly written, full of illogical nonsense. I will have nothing more to do with it."

Monnica began weeping. Augustine rose to comfort her, but she pulled back. "Until you come to Christ, Navigius is the only son I have."

"What are you saying? I am still the son you birthed."

"You are not my son!" Monnica turned away then slowly slid to the ground, her body trembling as agonizing tears burst forth.

Augustine touched her shoulder. "Mother, you weep as if I am dead."

She did not look up. "You are dead to God and so are dead to me. Leave."

"Mother?"

"Leave! Out of my house, now!" She remained on the ground, rocking her body in agony.

Galla picked up Adeodatus, her timid eyes moving between Augustine and his kneeling mother. Augustine was dumbfounded. He knew Monnica would be upset, but not this much. He stared for a long moment. Slowly shock turned into anger. How dare she cast out her own son! Augustine marched away, Galla silently following him to their bedroom where he packed. As they left the villa, Monnica still remained on the ground, desperate prayers pouring forth.

The couple down the road in the gathering dusk, Galla clutching her son tightly. Augustine was too livid to speak, Galla too frighten. The sky darkened with thick clouds on the horizon. They stopped at a crossroad.

Gingerly Galla said, "Adeodatus will need a place to sleep soon. Where we will go? An inn?"

Augustine laughed bitterly. "Where will we get the money for an inn? My mother was the only income I had, and my job has not started yet. We are homeless and broke. Do you still love me, Galla?"

"Yes, of course. You will find a way. You always do." She smiled reassuring then tended to her hungry son.

The young father sighed, watching her breastfeed Adeodatus. "Didius's parents hate me since they learned their son has converted. Perhaps Romanianus will be merciful to us."

They walked to the wealthy patrician's estate. A slave guided them inside to the atrium. A short time later Romanianus arrived, dressed in a tunic instead of the toga he usually wore when meeting guests. Broad-shouldered, and muscular, Romanianus looked commanding no matter what he wore.

"I did not expect your visit so late." The man glanced at Galla holding her son close and the bags that rested by Augustine's feet. "Has something happened?"

"My mother learned that I am a follower of Mani and has kicked my family out."

"I warned you to be careful about your private faith. You may find it difficult to fill your classroom."

"We are Romans. Our society has absorbed countless religions. Many Christians send their sons to schools to be educated by pagans. Why should it matter if I am Manichean? My mother just overreacted. Tomorrow she may feel different."

Romanianus nodded, "Parents are like that sometimes. I will have an apartment prepared for you tonight."

"We do not wish to inconvenience you."

"I have many rooms to spare." Romanianus ordered slaves to bring food and wine. As the couple ate, their host noticed Augustine did not touch wine or meat. "Is the food unsatisfactory?"

"There is nothing wrong with it. I am following Mani's teachings."

Romanianus questioned further, and Augustine gladly began explaining the forbidden writings, grateful the patrician was not closed-minded like his mother. They talked for hours. When Galla fell asleep on a couch beside them, Romanianus had slaves gently carry her and Adeodatus to bed. It was not until the watchman called three in the morning that the men finally ended their conversation. The next morning after Romanianus had finished dealing with his clients, he continued the discussion with Augustine. They sat in his large library, debating the meaning of ancient scrolls, their discussion finally ended when Romanianus's son reminded his father it was time for their daily horseback ride together.

As Augustine watch father and son head towards the stables, he wondered what type of relationship he would have with his own son. He tried not to think about Patricius much. His father had been a volatile mixture, stern to those who angered him but showing joviality to those he wanted something from. He had been more concerned about the opinions of others than the happiness of his own family. Augustine had never felt close to him. He hoped to avoid such strife with Adeodatus.

A slave entered the library. "Didius wishes to see you."

"Send him in immediately."

Looking very concerned, Didius sat at the table across from Augustine. "I went to your house, but your mother said she had sent you away." He glanced at the open scrolls laying in front of him. "I see you are making yourself at home. Why did you not come to my house last night?"

"I doubted your parents would permit me entry. I may be the most hated man in all of Thagaste."

"You overstate your fears. Many care not what religion you are. It is just the traditional-minded Catholics like our parents who are upset."

"How did my mother look when you spoke with her?" Augustine felt a stab of guilt, seeing her again kneeling, face full of grief because of him. He pushed the image away. It was her decision not to accept his beliefs.

"Upset. I could tell she had been crying. She apologized that her erred son had led me into falsehood. When I tried to reassure her that now I see truth for the first time, she burst into fresh tears. I knew not how to comfort her, so I left seeking you. Romanianus is very generous to take you in."

"He is like-minded like us, a seeker of truth. He may soon become one of our brothers. We have been discussing the writings of Pericles." Augustine picked up a scroll and began reading to his friend, forcing the image of his weeping mother from his mind.

The summer break flew passed. Several Catholic families withdrew their sons from Augustine's school, but the spots were quickly filled by others. The lure of educating a son without the expense of boarding him in a big city attracted many parents. The first day of class, Augustine stood in front of the youths. His school only consisted of a single room, but it was large enough for his two dozen students. They sat on wooden stools, their silent eyes noting he carried no cane. All of them had completed primary and knew firsthand the harsh penalty for failure.

"Each of you are here because high expectations have been placed upon you by your families. The question is, do you expect the same for yourself? I can teach you the skills to be a wordsmith, but the path to success lies in you. Are you willing to eat, sleep, and dream the great speeches of our ancestors? To heed their wisdom from beyond their graves? Can you pull out a quote with perfect timing to counter your opponent? Can you think logically under pressure or cave in to emotions, allowing your opponent to control you?"

He then gave their first assignment, calling each to the front to present their defense of their view. The day flew past. Augustine enjoyed the experience even more than he expected. The boys were quiet and respectful, many nervous as they began speaking but gaining confidence as Augustine praised their efforts, keeping criticism gentle.

Back at Romanianus's villa, Augustine cheerfully took a long walk in the cultivated gardens with Galla. The path wove between statues of gods and exotic flowers from across the empire. He went into great detail about the lesson, how each boy responded, who had the keenest mind, the most promising talents. Galla spoke little.

When he finally finished, she gently said, "I have little to do here. They have no need for a cook and Romanianus's wife stopped me when she saw me cleaning, saying that was what the slaves are for. I tried to befriend the slaves, but they see me as too high in status. I have no place."

"You have our son to attend to."

"Which I do. But I wish to do more. I cannot be like you, finding pleasure in reading a book all day. Perhaps if you would go back to your mother and ask, she will take you back."

"She rejected me, remember. I will not apology for being what I am, nor will I beg like a dog for forgiveness."

"A mother and son should not be divided. She adores Adeodatus." Galla thought about her own parents, whom she missed acutely. Though her father had been upset about her choice to take Augustine as a lover, he had never turned her away. Whenever she visited, he always gave her choice cuts of meat without her asking.

"Speak no more about her. If she cannot accept me as I am, then her claim of a mother's love is very shallow indeed."

Augustine turned away from Galla and spent the rest of the evening alone in the library trying to find comfort in reading the words of men long dead. On marble pedestals were busts of Cicero, Pericles, and others famous orators. Where any of them abandoned by their own mothers? Monnica claimed to serve a loving God, yet she was so quick to disown a wayward son. So much for Christian love.

In the afternoons after teaching, Augustine began spending most his spare time with Didius. Rarely did a day go by when they were not visiting friends or debating opponents together. Among some circles, they were often invited guests at dinner parties, but other groups despised them. Augustine's elite education and witty tongue drew admirers, leading several other youths to convert to Manichean. When it became public knowledge that even the great Romanianus had become one, Augustine was considered one of the most influential men in town, despite his young age of twenty.

Summer break drew near. Augustine looked forward to the extra time it would provide for him to read the ancient writers. One day as he sat in the library reading out loud to himself, a slave entered and announced that Monnica asked for an audience.

"Tell her I am busy."

"She said she will not leave till you speak with her."

Augustine sighed and put down his scroll. He knew too well she would keep her word. He followed the slave to the large atrium with marble columns and tiled floor. Monnica's hair had a touch of gray, but her face was at peace. Son and mother sat across from each other for a long moment.

Finally Monnica said, "I have come to ask for you to eat at my table again."

"You said I was dead to you."

"You are dead until you allow the true God to awaken you. Nevertheless, I wish for you to come back home. I miss my grandson. I miss you."

"Why the change of heart?" Augustine frowned, not quick to forgive the banishment.

"I tried to change you, even begged a renowned priest in another town to come speak with you, to refute your false doctrine. But he would not come, saying you were not yet ready to learn, still too conceited with the novel excitement of the heresy. Though he lives several towns away, he had heard stories about how your many trivial questions have disturbed the untutored minds of townspeople here. As I continued to press him, he told me that when he was a small boy, his mother had handed him over to the Manicheans to study their books. Eventually he had come to his own conclusion that their religion was best avoided. When I dropped to my knees begging and crying for him to come, he became irritated and said, 'Go home. As you live, it cannot be that the son of these tears should perish.' To me, it seemed as if the words sounded from heaven itself."

Augustine sighed. "For this reason you wish me back? If I come, I will still be open about my beliefs."

Monnica shifted uncomfortably. "I know. But it will not always be so."

"I will not change."

"During my darkest hour when I was crushed with grief, I had a dream that I stood on a huge keystone. A cheerful handsome young man appeared. He asked why I cried daily. I told him about your predicament. He said I should have no more anxiety then told me to look. Suddenly you stood beside me on the keystone. The young man said, 'Where you are, there he will be also.' Thus the dream ended."

"It was but a dream, Mother."

"It was a vision. You will one day be a Christian."

"Then perhaps you misunderstand its meaning. Maybe it signifies you should not despair becoming what I am."

Without hesitation, she replied, "The word spoken to me was not, 'Where he is, you will be also', but 'Where you are, there will he be also.' I no longer despair because now I know for certain that you will know God."

Augustine looked into her sober, trusting eyes. He had caused her much grief and was tired of the fight. Besides, Galla preferred the small, homely villa to the grand mansion they now stayed. "I will come back if you stop trying to change me."

She smiled. "I will leave that for God."

Chapter Ten

Bright sunshine kissed olive groves and ripening wheat fields. Augustine walked down a country lane with a dispirited youth lagging behind him. Without glancing at the boy, Augustine turned off the path, marched up to a small villa, and knocked on the door. The woman opening the door turned pale at the sight of Augustine. During the three years he had taught at Thagaste, he had earned a reputation of fairness along with being a firm discipliner.

"What has he done now?"

Augustine kept a stern face, remembering his own childhood of mischievousness which led to meetings between his concerned parents and strict teachers. "Another fight. When he loses with words he resorts to fists. If this happens again, I will be forced to expel him."

The mother placed hands on hips and glared at her son. "After all we sacrificed to provide an education for you. Do you wish to throw everything away?"

The youth kept eyes downward, staring at the ground. "Licinius said my speech was stupid."

"It was," said Augustine. "Your logic was faulty and poorly thought out. The use of violence will not make a bad speech better but only shows you are a tyrant. A master orator has no need for swords or fists. How can you remedy the situation?"

The boy remained silent, kicking a stone with his foot.

"Well, answer him!" barked the mother.

"I am to study harder, memorize more."

"And will you?"

"Yes, Mother." He looked up for the first time. "I will make you proud."

Leaving the repentant boy with his mom, Augustine headed back to town. The cases presented in the forum today would be over by now, but there would still be groups meandering about outside, discussing the day's events. As he reached the plaza beside the forum, he glanced for Didius but did not see him.

Augustine drifted among the groups of men, hearing which cases had been won or lost, which lawyers were credited with giving the best speeches.

Still not finding Didius, he decided the other must have already returned home. He walked through Thagaste until arriving at his friend's home, a modest villa a few streets over from the market. A slave let him in. As he walked across the atrium, Didius's stern mother stopped him.

"My son is sick today and will receive no visitors." She glared at Augustine like he was a loathsome insect. An uneasy truce existed between Didius's parents and Augustine. They had tried various methods to dissolve the friendship between the two young men, even resorting to threatening to banish Didius if he continued to hang out with Augustine. Didius called their bluff, saying he would move in to Romanianus's far larger home, spending even more time with Augustine. They had backed down, but still feared Augustine's influence over their son.

"He will receive me." Without further word, Augustine strolled past her and enter Didius's small bedroom.

The young man was pale, sweaty, but smiled when he saw his friend. "I have been quite bored today. Mother would not permit me to leave this morning when she saw I could not keep my breakfast down. Read to me."

Augustine picked up the latest book they had been discussing and read until Didius fell asleep. On his way out, he ignored the dark glares of Didius's parents. Instead of heading directly home, he enjoyed a long walk through the fields of his mother's land which he would one day inherit. Having just finished the hay harvest, male tenants and Navigius were washing.

The brawny fifteen-year-old fell in step with his taller brother. He could have studied under Augustine, but books did not interest him. "This season's harvest has gone well. The rain has worked in our favor this year."

"Father would be proud of all you have accomplished."

"No, he would be disappointed to see a son getting his hands dirty. He believed a patrician's role was to only supervise. That was why our farm never produced well. I get far more accomplished when I put my hands to the plow than bark at our tenants to plow."

"You have Mother's heart and Father's strength."

"But not your tongue, wordsmith. Good thing, since the olive trees would die of boredom if I stood around lecturing them with lengthy speeches."

Augustine laughed then said, "How did Mother's meeting go today? Fausta is indeed fair."

Navigius grinned. "Her parents agreed to the marriage proposal. We wed in four months when she turns of age."

"As she is their only child, you stand to inherit their ten acres."

"If I was after land, I would have wooed a far richer maiden. I love Fausta. Neither she nor I am ambitious like you. We will be happy with a small farm and lots of children. Will you attend our wedding or do your Manichean vows keep you from that?"

"I will make an exception for you."

As they reached home, four-year-old Adeodatus dashed to his father and raised his hands high. Augustine picked up his prattling son, paying little attention to what the boy said as weariness from the day's work settled upon him. He still had to prepare for tomorrow's lessons.

"I saw a bug with five legs. I counted twice. Mommy said one must have broken. I tried to find the leg to fix the bug but it was nowhere to be found. Can you fix him, Daddy?"

"Your uncle is better with animals than I. Ask him."

The child turned his sorrowful eyes to Navigius. The uncle smiled, despite being tired. "Come on. Let's go on a bug hunt. Then you can help me check for eggs."

"I know where the big red hen hides her nest. I will show you." The boy grabbed his uncle's hand and led him towards some bushes in the garden.

Relieved that the boy's attention was fixed elsewhere, Augustine followed his nose to the kitchen where Galla was finishing up cooking dinner.

"Smells delicious." He kissed her on the cheek.

"That is the fish, which of course you will not be eating. Leeks and figs for you."

"No radishes?"

"Only if you pick some. I did not have time."

"I will make due."

As Statilia and Turia began sitting the table, Monnica walked in carrying a bouquet of freshly picked flowers. "Ah, there you are. Perpetua has invited us for a visit when your summer break begins."

"I can escort you, but we can stay no longer than a week. I have much studying to do."

When supper was over, Augustine sought out a quiet spot to prepare his lessons for tomorrow. After Galla had put their son to bed, he snuggled with her, feeling he would never tire of her smooth skin, silken hair, and sumptuous lips. The next morning Augustine rose with the sun and ate a light breakfast of fruit and nuts. Then he walked to Thagaste, barely arriving ahead of several of his students. The day progressed well. No fights this time. After school, Didius was still not at the forum, so Augustine went to his friend's home. Didius was worst, fighting a high fever, unable to keep food down. Augustine kept his visit short, promising to return tomorrow.

Didius slipped into a coma, not awaking for many days. Concerned, Augustine daily sat by his friend's side, using a wet rag to wipe sweat off Didius's feverish face. The youth's parents began to despair as they watched their son fading away from them. They made arrangements with the priest to have their dying son baptized. A week later Didius awoke to the anxious faces of his parents and Augustine peering at him. He smiled weakly, trying to reassure them. His mother hand-fed him soup, fretting he had lost too much weight. When Didius was told he had been baptized during his deep sleep, he took his father's hand and squeezed it, a tear running down his cheek.

When the parents finally left the room, Augustine joked, "Catholics. A little fever and they cry, 'Call the priest.' Waiting until you are weak then dunking you in water, like that element can purify your soul. They would not listen to me when I told them they were wasting their time. Predators of souls they are."

"Do not speak so," Didius's voice was harsh and scratchy. "They baptized me because they care. If you wish to remain my friend, you are to never speak ill of my parents again."

Augustine was surprised by his friend's anger. "I apologize for the offence. You need rest. I will visit again tomorrow."

Didius recovered slowly over the next week. Augustine spent every afternoon with him, but he noticed a difference in his friend. Didius avoided discussions about Mani. One day as Augustine walked into his friend's bedroom, he spotted Didius tucking a scroll under the blanket.

"What are you reading?"

"Just a letter."

"From who?"

"Someone named Paul."

"Paul the apostle? Surely you have not taken an interest in that Catholic nonsense. Mani teaches that the letters have been altered, corrupted."

"Can the Manicheans show us an untarnished version?"

"No, but what does it matter?"

"You would not understand. When I stood at death's door, everything that I held as important looked like decaying rubbish. I was left with nothing to hold on to. Never do I desire that experience again."

There was an awkward silence between the two. "Today was the last day of school. Tomorrow I will take my mother to visit Perpetua."

"It is good that you are kind to your mother. Enjoy the trip."

Perpetua lived half a day's walk north. She cheerfully greeted her mother and brothers. Her husband threw a dinner party in their honor. Married life suited the young woman who was well-trained for overseeing a thriving household of stepchildren and slaves. She entertained her family with the lyre while Augustine recited, as in the days of their childhood. She glided her family on long walks through the fields, proud of her husband's flourishing farm. Too soon the week passed.

The day after arriving back home, Augustine went to visit Didius. When he walked into the villa, he found the atrium filled with mourners, both men and women weeping loudly. Most were genuinely grieving but a few were professionals paid to cry at wakes.

Hesitantly, he asked the nearest person, "Who has died?"

"The young man Didius, struck down in the pride of his youth," the woman answered in a dramatic voice. Probably she had never even met Didius before.

"But he was fine when I left."

"His fever came back three nights ago. Already weakened, he could not overcome it. Such a pity. He left no heirs."

The room seem to spin as Augustine looked this way and that, unable to accept the truth. Surely his friend would be in the next room, full of vitality and laughter, ready to attend the next race or debate a new opponent. Then Augustine saw Didius's parents. One look at their grief-filled eyes and he knew he would never see his friend again.

Augustine approached them. "I share the pain of your lost."

Through her tears, the mother said, "At least God answered our prayers. We begged for your influence to be removed from our son's life so he would come back to the truth." She sobbed, her shoulders slumping, "We just did not know it would be this way. He is in heaven where you can never corrupt him again."

Augustine took a step back, for once at a loss for words. "I am…sorry…you think that way." He left, feeling the accusing stares of the mourners. His mind numb, he wandered out of town, blundering down country lanes until dark. When he arrived home, Galla took one look at his face and immediately knew something terrible had happened.

"What is wrong?"

"Didius died."

"Dead? I thought he had recovered." She wrapped her arms around him as he buried his face into her soft hair. When they finally pulled apart, she said, "I have leftovers from supper for you."

"I am not hungry."

Augustine went to bed, awaking in the morning to misery. Throughout the day he kept expecting Didius to walk in. He tried finding comfort in books, but whenever he read something interesting, out of habit he would think about telling it to Didius. Then the grief would hit anew as he remembered he would never again share a poem or a story with his friend. Augustine cried for days, then weeks. The weeping could be triggered by anything: a beautiful cloud, music in the distance, a rider dashing past on a gallant stallion. Everything reminded him of his friend, and he began to hate all because he could not share it with the other half of his soul. In his dark musings, he felt that Didius and he were one soul living in two bodies.

Galla tried to comfort him, fixing his favorite meals, joining him on long walks. It was to no avail. Not even the pleasure of sex stirred him anymore. Illiterate Galla, beautiful to look upon, could touch his body but not his soul. He pushed her away, as he did the rest of his family. Years before, his father's death had barely phrased him. Now for the first time Augustine felt the deep grief of loss. He began to hate death itself, yet feared it. With his friend gone, he felt life itself must end along with all of humanity. He found no comfort in his Manichean beliefs that a soul was reincarnated repeatedly until it reached perfect purity. Didius was separated from him. Only when he wept did it bring some release to his torment. But even the weeping had to end, leaving him with only emptiness and despair. The lost life of the one who died became the death of the one still living.

As the end of summer break drew nearer, Augustine knew he could not face a classroom of students in his depressed state. He needed to get away to start over. One night Galla walked into their bedroom and found him packing.

"Are you going on a trip?"

"We are going back to Carthage."

Galla smiled, pleased she would be seeing her family again. "When? How long will we stay?"

"We leave tomorrow before daylight. And we are never coming back."

"Never? Will not your family be upset? What about your brother's wedding? You promised to be there."

"Navigius will forgive me."

"Rent in Carthage is expensive. How can we afford a place to stay?"

"Romanianus gave me enough money for the trip. Perhaps we can share an apartment with one of your relatives. I will take on new students, and you will be near your family. You would like that, will you not?"

"Yes." She looked into his dark eyes, glad he was finally doing something besides mopping about. "I will tell Adeodatus he needs to say goodbye to his grandmother."

"No. She is not to know until we are gone."

"You are not telling your mother we are leaving?"

"She will try to stop us, begging and pleading. I have not the stomach to see her weeping again. I have already written a letter explaining why I must go. She will find it tomorrow."

"Are you sure this is right?"

"Of course."

Chapter Eleven

The tired couple climbed the finals steps to the fourth floor apartment as the sun began to fade outside. Adeodatus sleepily leaned across his father's shoulder. Several times on the long trip, he had burst into tears, asking for his beloved grandmother.

Galla hesitated outside her sister's apartment before knocking. Would she still be welcome after three years absence?

A scraggy stranger opened the door. "Who are you?"

"Is Sulpicia here?"

The scrawny man stepped away, and they entered the small living quarters where half a dozen people chatted. Several kids dashed by in play. An elderly woman finished washed dishes in a corner then a young man dressed in a ragged tunic tossed the dirty water out the window. Sulpicia, stomach swelled with a coming child, cheerfully arose from a stool and rushed over to hug her sister.

"When did you get back to Carthage?"

"We just arrived today. We have no place to stay."

"There are a couple of empty rooms here, if you wish to rent one."

Augustine said, "That will be suitable to us."

Sulpicia led them down the narrow hall to a tiny room only six feet by eight. Nothing was left in the room by the last occupant except a dirty bedroll which probably contained lice, bedbugs—or both. Augustine laid his sleeping son on a blanket which Galla pulled out of their bag. The thin wooden partitions which separated their area from the other bedrooms were smeared with layers of grime. For the same amount of money they would pay for this tiny space, they could have rented an entire house in Thagaste.

"I will clean tomorrow," said Galla, eyeing the bedroll suspiciously.

Sleep was elusive as Augustine worried, tossing back and forth on the hard floor. After the trip, his funds were low. With the new school year starting just a few weeks away, he would need finances. Rhetoric professors made more money, but the start-up cost was higher. He would need to secure a lecture room in the public forum. Parents had to be cajoled to turning over their sons to him. In

Thagaste where he had been the only grammaticus instructor, students were easy to come by, but in Carthage there were dozens of reputable teachers. Rhetoric instructors were only paid by parents at the end of the school year, which meant Augustine would not have a source of income for many months. How would he afford rent and food? He must quickly find local patrons who would support him.

Next morning while Galla scrubbed the floor, Augustine headed off to visit a rich Manichean who he had met at the secret religious assemblies several years before. At the villa, he waited with other clients until a slave called him forth. Using his charm and wit, he flattered the man while telling of his own predicament. Before he left, his new patron had offered his nephew as a student and recommended several other families to contact. Patience and persistent, Augustine had a dozen students by the time school started, most from Manichean contacts. Additional finances had been donated for a classroom. Apartment rent, unfortunately, was another matter.

He had just finished dismissing his students after the first week of class when he noticed a black-skinned man watching him from the doorway. "Nebridius, it has been a long time." Augustine smiled in greeting.

"I heard rumors you were teaching here at the forum. What brings you back to Carthage?"

"The need to start anew. Tell me the news in your life. How is that beautiful bride you were engaged to?"

Pain flicked across Nebridius's face. "We had a wonderful but short marriage. She died two months ago in childbirth."

"And the child?"

"He died too."

"I am deeply saddened to hear that. Grief also has been my constant companion for the last few months. I lost a close friend who I have known since childhood." Busy preparing his classroom and obtaining students had helped pull Augustine away from the deepest part of his depression, but in quiet moments melancholy still haunted him. He kept occupied as much as possible to avoid that.

The two walked through the magnificent courtyards of the huge forum, sharing stories about their loss. Talking with someone who also suffered from raw grief lightened Augustine's depression. Soon they were debating like old times. While munching on hot bread and cheese purchased from a vendor, they discussed if Julius Caesar's murder was necessary or only prolonged the inevitable fall of the republic. As they relaxed in the heated waters of the Antonius Baths, they argued over if Homer's *Iliad* or Virgil's *Aeneid* was superior. While weaving through the crowded, narrow streets to Augustine's apartment, they disputed Epicurus's claim that all matter was created from indestructible atoms flying through a void.

Nebridius said, "The Greeks believed material existed which we cannot see. In *About the Nature of the Universe*, Lucretius gives several examples. Trodden flagstone wears down over the years. Sometime dry clothing becomes damp. Other times wet clothing becomes dry. Water is present yet we do not see it. Lucretius supported two principles. One, nothing is ever created by divine power out of nothing. Two, nature dissolves all things turning them back into their constituent atoms. By this theory, we can conclude that gods have nothing to do with creation or destruction. It is the atoms reforming."

"You have no need to convince me that invisible particles do exist, but they are corrupt as all matter is. They can only be purified by being breathed out by the exalted Elders."

"Still holding onto Mani, I see. He writes of war between spirit and material, between light and dark. What proof do you have of this ongoing battle?"

"The very sky cries out, shedding its tears of rain. The sun and moon are blotted out in eclipses." Augustine paused outside his apartment. "I would invite you up but our lodging is unsuitable for visitors."

"Or you are trying to find a way to avoid pressing your point, knowing it is pointless. Nevertheless, I will bid farewell, after inviting you to my father's villa next holiday. Bring your family."

As Augustine climbed up the narrow stairs of the insula, he reflected on his conversations with Nebridius. He had gone the whole evening without once thinking of Didius. He still missed his friend but had found rejuvenation. When he reached his shabby apartment, he told Galla about the invitation. She was delighted and immediately began planning what she would wear.

A few weeks later a litter sent by Nebridius arrived to carry them to his large county estate. Nebridius's family greeted them warmly. This was one of the few places Galla felt comfortable when away from her own family. Here no one looked down upon her for being born a slave. Soon she was sauntering in a garden with Nebridius's mother and sisters while Adeodatus dashed about in play with other children. Augustine joined the young men playing a game at the ball court. Later as they relaxed on a terrace, Nebridius's father bragged about a new wing being constructed to the villa.

"It will give us a second banquet room well-heated during the winter. My wife is proud of the sunroom where she will grow vegetables all year." Dacien excitedly pointed towards the half-built areas, his chubby arms a testimony to his wealth when the average Roman barely had enough to eat each day.

"You have been very prosperous," said Augustine, admiring the view.

"At tonight's dinner party you will meet several of my business associates and one of my many enemies. I delight in showing off my estate to him, watching him being eaten by envy."

"Father has the vice of vanity," said Nebridius with a teasing smile.

"Vanity? Our opponents derogate us for being freedmen, gossiping that it is wrong for us to have more money than many patricians. If they were not so foolish squandering their profit on gambling, mistresses, risky investments, and appeasements to the gods then they would have finer estates. I will not be ashamed of being wiser and wealthier than they."

"It is a pity," said Augustine, "that wealthy freedmen cannot buy full Roman citizenship, as some did in the days of old."

The father called over a child who sat cheerfully on his lap. "This is our youngest, born after our manumission. She is the first in our family to be a Roman citizen. I may not be able to run for office or hold a high military rank, but one day my grandchildren will. When she turns of age, I will marry her to one of the richest and most powerful families in Carthage. Let my enemies stew in their jealousy then." After kissing the child on the forehead, he sent her off to play.

Later Augustine and Nebridius explored the large collection of books in the well-stocked family library, debating their favorite authors. As they flipped through bins of scrolls, Nebridius said, "You speak enthusiastically of teaching these great works to your students. I find myself envious of you having a purpose in life beyond simply searching for wisdom."

"As a teacher of liberal arts, I can combine my own pursuit for wisdom with sharing it with others. I delight when a youth's eyes light with understanding. You also could be a teacher. I would vouch for your qualifications."

"I doubt my own ability to teach. As you know, I had never officially attended a school. Still, it would be nice to assist part-time. It would not interfere much with my own private study time."

"I welcome you to my class anytime."

"Perhaps we could share an apartment like before."

"It would be my delight, except, alas, my funds are too lacking to afford one worthy of your quality."

Nebridius grinned wickedly. "Your concubine can make up for that." He left the library and headed to the promenade where several women sauntered about in conversation.

The women had finished dressing for the upcoming party. Galla's long blond hair had been curled into several stylish braids encircling her head. The deep red of her lips stood out against her powered face and rouge cheeks, her eyelashes blacken with ash. The dress she had borrowed revealed bare shoulders. A thin gold belt under her chest highlighted her curvy body.

Augustine gawked, "You look like a goddess."

She blushed. "Ulania is very generous helping me."

Nebridius's mother smiled, "Every woman deserves to feel beautiful."

With a mischievous look, Nebridius said, "Augustine and I have been discussing sharing an apartment, but his funds are meager. I am considering paying his share if you will cook your succulent dishes for me."

Galla beamed. "I would be delighted."

As other guests arrived, Augustine kept near Galla, relishing the envious looks several men directed at him. They ate the five course meal while reclining on couches. This time Galla lay beside him, carefully tasting the rich flavors, commenting on how she believed each dish was made. Once back home, she would create her own less expensive versions of her favorites. The courses of sow udders and sea urchins had little appeal to Augustine. Instead, he was enthralled by Galla's closeness, her perfume overwhelming his senses as he stroked her smooth skin. While the night was still early, they left the party to enjoy the privacy offered in a luxurious bedroom.

Several days later they arrived back at their tiny, dingy apartment. Galla broke the news to her sadden sister that they would be moving out. Nebridius came the next day and guided them to a suite he rented near the forum which he shared with only two other boarders. Galla was excited by the large rooms and comfy beds.

She purred to Augustine, "I was right in choosing you, my love. You have provided well for your family."

Facing his students the next morning, Augustine was cheerful. Almost all of them had completed their assigned reading of Aurelius Symmachus's writings about the impact of religious tolerance.

"Is it right for Christians to force their beliefs on traditional Romans, closing down their temples, depriving the priests of state revenue and privileges?"

As the debate became heated between two students, Augustine noticed a dark-haired youth standing quietly in the doorway listening. He recognized the teenager as Alypius, a native of Thagaste who had been his student last year until the boy's father became upset with Augustine and had withdrawn his son. When the class ended, Augustine greeted his former student.

"I did not realize you were in Carthage. I recently visited with your uncle Romanianus."

"I saw him just a few days ago too." Alypius had the bronze skin of a Berber and keen eyes of his uncle.

"Who is your teacher now?"

"Pulcher. He taught my uncle long ago, and Romanianus still thinks highly of him. But I find Pulcher boring. Not as animated as you. How did you put up with him for two years?"

"I found he had much wisdom to share. Anytime you wish, you may visit my class."

The youth glanced at the empty stools. "My father has forbidden me to have contact with you. He is still upset about a comment you made against Catholics."

"Christianity may be the state religion now, but I will not refrain my criticism of its faults. As a rhetoric teacher, it is my duty to train students to examine all sides of an issue. I present controversial topics to develop students' orator skills. Someday in the public arena you will face opponents who will speak disagreeable about subjects you feel deeply about. If you flee because you dislike what you hear, how will you prove your point?"

The teen shuffled his feet. "I must go."

Augustine watched the youth disappear down the corridor. Pulcher had noticed Augustine talking to Alypius and decided to give friendly advice to his own former student.

"Do not waste your time befriending him," said the elderly teacher. "The boy will not make it. Spends more time at the circus than in my class."

"He was one of my brightest students at Thagaste. Well-mannered and cultured. His father is on the town council." He sighed, worried about the boy. As Alypius was from his hometown and related to his patron, he felt both kinship and responsibility for his former student.

"Here he is just another county lad sucked into the folly of distractions. I have seen too many like him." Pulcher sadly shook his gray head. "They waste their money and talent, eventually disappearing. Does not stop me from demanding payment at the end of the year though. I teach, even if my students choose not to show up."

Augustine glanced back down the now empty hallway dividing the curtained classrooms, determined to find some way to help the youth.

Chapter Twelve

Chariots pulled by horses thundered around an oval track, kicking up sand in their wake. The charioteers held reigns in one hand and long whips in the other. As the leader rounded a corner, his wheels brushed against his opponent's horse. The animal stumbled, causing its harnessed partner to slow. A third chariot bumped into the horse. The second driver lost control as his wheels hit the *spina* running down the middle of the track. The wooden chariot broke apart against marble decorations, sending the driver flying through the air. He landed in front of oncoming racers who did not slow down as hoofs and wheels crushed the man's body. Thousands of spectacles screamed in delight, relishing the violence.

Alypius leaned forward, enthralled, heart pounding in excitement. He yelled as his favorite crossed the finish line first. Too bad he had not placed a bet on this race. He had already lost five sestertii this morning, his allowance for the whole week. The sun had reached its highest point, and Alypius sweated in the heat. Sighing reluctantly, he rose and made his way through the crowded stone benches to an exit. Outside in the shade of the high circus walls, he used his last bronze coin to buy wine then gulped it down. His stomach growled but he had no money left for food. He should have saved that last sestertii to eat with for the rest of the week. Tomorrow morning he would visit Senator Manlius Theodorus, an old friend of his father, and hint of his need for funding.

The teenager ambled to the forum. For his next letter, he needed at least a little information to report about his education to his father. He peeked into Pulcher's classroom, but the droning voice of the old man repelled Alypius. He desired excitement, not a dull lecture about history. He drifted down the hallway to Augustine's class and sat on a stool in the back of the room. The teacher was animated, one hand waving in the air as another held a scroll. Despite his father's opinion, Alypius had always liked Augustine. What did it matter if the man was not Catholic? Neither were any of his grammaticus teachers in Madaura who worshiped traditional Roman gods.

Deep into expounding upon *The Golden Ass*, Augustine barely acknowledged Alypius presence. "Lucius's folly is his desire to practice magic. He is drawn to it out of curiosity and excitement. When he tries to preform magic himself, he is turned into an ass. It is like the circus fans of today who are drawn to the excitement of the races, willingly throwing away their money, squandering their lives, their talents. Over time, they transform themselves into foolish, broken asses."

Students snickered at the joke. Alypius face reddened, feeling the heat of several staring at him. He was certain Augustine had made the comment about him. For a moment he was angry then weariness overtook him. His stomach rumbled from hunger. Skipped meals, failing class, begging for money. The nagging terror of the day he must finally admit it all to his father. No more. He would not become one of those nameless beggars who had ruined their opportunity for fame.

After the class ended, Alypius sat in the bright sunshine under a colonnade and wrote a letter to his father, confessing his weakness for the circus and the positive influence of Augustine. Using polished persuasive skills he had learned in class, he pleaded for permission to switch teachers. It may be months before he received a response for the letter had to be given to a trustworthy acquaintance traveling to Thagaste. During the meantime, he stopped attending the circus and focused on his classes. Still he disliked Pulcher's methods, and often sneaked out to attend Augustine's more dynamic lessons. Finally he received a reply back. The next morning he proudly marched into Augustine's class to show off the letter giving him permission to attend.

Alypius threw himself into his work, determined to regain his father's trust. His parents had already decided he was to be a lawyer, and he became determined to earn glory for his family. Often he visited the home of Senator Theodorus, a friend of his uncle Romanianus. He enjoyed being surrounded by luxury instead of his tiny, dingy abode. He built contacts with other respectable young men of high birth.

One night while walking through the streets after attending a dinner party, Alypius accidently let it slip during the conversation with drunken friends that he was a virgin. They insisted that he remedy the situation immediately and guided him to the nearest brothel. He knew his Catholic parents would disapprove, but friends' opinions were more important to him. Soon he was alone in a small, dirty chamber with a middle-age woman who began to undress. He panicked, uncertain what to do. The woman moved closer and pulled up his tunic. When he emerged several minutes later, his friends took one looks at his pale, anxious face and burst into laughter. They jibed him all the way home. Alypius vowed to himself to never be put in such a situation again.

The next day, he had difficulty concentrating on his lessons. During the midday break, he tried to develop a declamation for an exercise Augustine had assigned. Alypius paced back and forth in front of the basilica for court cases, wax tablet and stylus in hand as he jolted down ideas, paying little attention to what was happening around him.

Another rhetoric student from a different class walked pass, trailed by a six-year-old slave carrying a bag. In a shadowy niche where several buildings meet, Gavros knelt on the ground and took a hatchet out of the bag. He began hacking at a lead grating which covered a silversmith's workroom. Below, the smith heard the banging and whispered out a plan for co-workers to capture the thief. Gavros heard the whispering and realized he had been discovered. He dropped his tool and dashed away, followed closely by his young slave.

Alypius noticed the fellow student rushing pass. Curious about the reason, he backtracked their flight and came across the damaged grate and hatchet. He picked up the tool, bemused, wondering about its abandonment. Suddenly several men grabbed him.

"Thief! We finally caught you."

"Thief? I just picked it up. It was just lying there. I am a student here. My teacher is Augustine."

The men dragged him out into the open, catching the attention of visitors coming to the forum. The muscular silver workers bragged loudly about their catch, drawing a larger crowd.

"We finally caught the bugger who has been terrorizing our shops."

The crowd became energetic, shouting, "To the magistrate!" "Scourge him!" "Lion feed!"

Terrified, Alypius yelled that he was innocent, but only insults and threats resulted. The men dragged the youth down the street, the enraged crowd following closely. Alypius cried in frustration, pleading for someone to believe him. As more bystanders pushed in to see who the thief was, the chief architect who oversaw Carthage's public buildings recognized Alypius.

"Unhand the lad," barked the architect wearing a toga declaring his high status. "His uncle is a close friend of Theodorus. I have seen him at the senator's home many times."

The brawny silversmith refused to let go of Alypius's arm. "It does not matter who his relatives are. We caught him red-handed and are turning him over for punishment."

"Do you want the senator's wrath against you? Let me talk with the lad." The patrician stared down the silversmith until he let go of Alypius. Taking the youth's hand, he led Alypius a short ways from the crowd. "Now tell me what happened."

Alypius poured out his story in a rush, relived someone was listening to him.

"Do you know the name of the student you saw?"

"Gavros. He is not in my class."

"Do you know where he lives?"

"No, sir."

The stern architect man turned back to the crowd. "Who knows where Gavros the rhetoric student lives?" Several people called out directions. "Thank you. Now I ask all you who have gathered for justice to come with me. We will find the truth of this matter."

The crowd, still rowdy but a bit more subdued, followed the architect and Alypius through the narrow streets to the house where Gavros stayed. A six-year-old played in the street with other children.

"That is the slave of Gavros," said Alypius. He pointed to the hatchet that one of the silversmith workers held and asked the boy. "Whose is this?"

"Ours," the child promptly responded, too young to understand his was compromising his master.

The architect questioned the child further, revealing the misadventures of Gavros. The crowd was confounded at the sudden change of culprits. Soon they were demanding for Gavros to be dragged out of the house. As the home was raided, Alypius slipped away after parting words of gratitude to the architect. Still upset, he headed back to the forum and found his trodden school bag, his stylus broken from being stepped on by the crowd. Shakily, he made his way to class.

When he entered, Augustine said, "Trying to skip your declamation? Your turn now."

Alypius looked at his peers staring at him. "I…uh…have no defense…except you should not judge on appearance. Just because superficial evidence points towards one person does not mean he is really guilty. You should always question carefully, seeking truth."

"A point of merit, yet you still have not answered properly. What is your defense for this specific case?"

The youth ducked his head and said no more.

Augustine noticed the youth's tear-stained eyes. "Take a seat." After class, Augustine beckoned Alypius over. "What happened which has upset you?"

Alypius poured out his story, leaving nothing out, his heart quickening with the realization that his future career and even his life almost ending today.

"From this experience you have gained wisdom to aid you in becoming a great lawyer, if you heed the lesson."

The youth nodded. "I will never forget. Truth saved me. From today onwards, it will be my life's focus."

Chapter Thirteen

Jugglers entertained the crowd, tossing balls high into the air towards each other. The crowd cheered as more balls were added. Then someone whispered that a famous gladiator would be fighting soon. The crowd melted away, eager to attend the new attraction. Augustine strolled past the abandon jugglers, barely giving them a glance as they picked up the few coins that had been tossed on the ground for them.

Surely he was far enough away that he would not be recognized in this part of the city. He slowed down and entered a tiny bookshop. He glanced about, soon finding what he sought—a scroll about astrology. After purchasing it, he hid the book in his tunic. Mani forbad astrology. Augustine had tried to stay away from it, yet the lure of futures foretold pulled at him. He own attempts at predicting friends' horoscopes were right half the time, if only he could improve the success rate. Still, it gnawed at him that he was breaking another rule of Mani. Try as he might, it was impossible to avoid every temptation. He sought absolution for his failures by routinely joining other Hearers with visits to the countryside where they harvested fruit to be sent to the Elect.

Leaving the shop, he headed home. Just a few streets away, Alypius greeted him. "Hello, old teacher."

"Old? I am only five years your senior. How does your jurisconsult training precede?"

"Well. I may be assigned to my first advisory panel next year. Still, I miss your class. What stimulating debates we had." Alypius had grown taller over the last few years, reflecting his uncle Romanianus's olive skin and handsome face.

"Ah, you were one of my brightest students." Augustine paused, considering an idea. "There is a room which recently opened at my abode. Would you be interesting in becoming a boarder?"

The twenty-year-old smiled. "I would enjoy that very much."

"I must speak with Nebridius first, putting in a good word for you. Stop by in a few days after the annual poetry contest."

"I am certain this year you will win the wreath."

"I did so once, when I was younger than you."

Seeing a soothsayer's booth, Alypius called out, "Seer, will my friend win the heart of the gods and the praise of the people at Apollo's tournament?"

The bent, wrinkled woman held out a hand and Alypius dropped a coin on it. She pulled out a bag containing bones. After shaking them, she poured the bones onto the dirty wood counter and studied them. "The odds are favorable, but there is another who also pleases the gods. For a sestertii I can offer a sacrifice to appease the gods, ensuring your victory."

Alypius reached into his moneybag, but Augustine said, "No, I will not have an animal's life taken on my account."

"Do as you wish." The soothsayer placed the bones back into the leather pouch. "And the gods will do as they wish."

As the men walked away, Alypius asked, "Is there a special reason why you wish to spare a fowl's life?"

"Mani teaches that we are to do no harm in all areas of our life including taking the life of animals. I will win on my talent, not by magical enchantments." Augustine ignored the astrology scroll rubbing against his chest under the tunic.

The next day Augustine stepped onto a stage surrounded by thousands of listeners. He was the twenty-fifth poet to recite, yet many still waited their turn to charm the crowd. From a lifetime of training, Augustine recited a poem he had written about the beauty of light bathing the countryside, using symbolism of Roman pride for the humble beginnings of their great empire. Using perfect pitch and dramatic pauses, he fused emotion into the words. When he finished, the audience responded robustly. Later, it was Vindicianus, a renowned proconsul and former doctor to Emperor Valentinian I, who placed the wreath of victory upon his head. Augustine soaked in praises from the crowd, feeling as if the whole world exalted him.

As he walked home with his beaming son and Galla, Augustine continued to enjoy the congratulation from strangers who spotted his wreath. Augustine treated his family to a delicious meal at a restaurant. Seeing the victory laurel, the owner asked for Augustine to give his recital again. Happily Augustine complied, earning a round of applause from the dinners and a free meal from the owner. Six-year-old Adeodatus clapped the loudest, laughing in delight at his father's speech. Galla smiled, hiding fears that had haunted her for weeks.

Every day she expected Augustine to notice her belly slowly growing larger. Perhaps he was too involved in his teaching and studying to pay her much attention except in the dark of night. She had not seen him this happy in a long time. Better now than later to tell him.

She waited until bedtime. Galla nestled against his firm body and whispered in his ear, "God has blessed you richly. You are to be a father again."

Startled, Augustine pulled away. "Are you certain?"

"Yes, I am pregnant."

Long silence followed. "I will take you to an abortionist tomorrow." There were various concoctions which could induce miscarriages, but they did not always work. Best to make sure it was done right the first time.

"But you may have another son."

"I have told you that I cannot bring more evil matter into this world. It is forbidden."

"So is having sex with me, but still you do it."

Augustine flinched. "Someday I hope to be freed from even that longing, to become completely liberated from desires of the flesh. Nebridius can teach my class tomorrow."

Galla's voice became desperate. "It is one child. Surely you have picked more than enough pears for the Elect to make up for the weight of a tiny infant."

"I told you years ago this was the way it would be."

"And have I not done all that you have asked of me? Taking the foul conceptions, careful of our dates for intercourse. Still God has given us this child."

"It is not a gift but a curse from Darkness."

Galla begin to sob. "I want this child. I have longed for a daughter for years."

Augustine's voice became harsh. "Still your tears. I will heed no pleading."

He turned away from her, trying to ignore her stifled weeping in the darkness. Part of him softened, and he wished to comfort her. But this must be done. He had broken so many of the Manichean rules like it was. He hid what he could, like the astrology books he brought or wine he occasionally drank when alone. While it was known to the Elect that he kept a concubine, having a child was a grave offense that would not be overlooked.

The next morning Augustine arose with the sun. During breakfast, Adeodatus sensed uneasiness between his parents and noticed sadness in his mother's eyes. When he tried to question her about it, his father quickly sent him out the door to school. Augustine gave Nebridius his lesson plans then left with Galla. As they walked through early morning traffic, she moved slowly, her eyes pleading. Augustine kept a grim face, ignoring her pleading. As they neared the small apartment of a midwife, Galla hung back. He firmly grabbed her arm, propelling her forward.

As they walked into the small room, a thin middle-age woman studied the tense couple. "What service can I render you today?"

"The removal of a problem before it grows larger."

The woman, bent from the onset of scoliosis, moved to Galla. "Has there been a quickening in your womb yet?"

Galla only stared, speechless.

Augustine cut in, "It is too young for movement." He opened his money pouch and handed over several coins.

The midwife beckoned a strong slave to prepare tools while she poured a foul smelling concoction into a cup. "Drink. It will help with the pain."

After waiting several minutes, she ordered Galla to lie on a table. Augustine held his lover's hand tightly as she lay trembling. The slave stood nearby, his strong arms folded, his face blank. The midwife inserted a long needle into Galla's womb, killing the fetus. Then using a hooked curette, she began pulling out pieces of the unborn. Galla screamed and fought against the slave who held her down. Augustine continued to hold Galla's hand, promising it would be over soon. He watched the stern mid-wife's experienced hands move quickly, dropping bits of human flesh into a wooden bowl. A tiny hand attached to a severed arm landed on top of the bloody heap of flesh. Augustine looked away, disturbed, keeping his eyes averted until it was over.

The midwife stood up as much as her diseased spine would allow and said, "It is over now. You have done well, child."

Galla's only answer was to turn on her side and weep.

The midwife gave Augustine instructions. "There will be bleeding, perhaps a discharge of bits of flesh, but I removed most of it. Mix this powder with wine and give it to her twice a day."

Augustine coerced Galla up and led her back to their apartment. She lay in bed, curled up in the fetus position. He attempted to cook lunch, but she refused to eat. When Adeodatus returned home, he ran to his mother to tell her about his day. Seeing her ill, he sat on the floor beside her bed, trying to comfort her. She stroked his blond hair, tears running down her cheeks. He reached out and held her hand, not understanding why her heart was saddened.

The next morning, Augustine headed to work, leaving Galla in bed, depressed. She skipped breakfast. Augustine worried about her throughout the morning. During his lunch break, he hurried back home. She had still not risen from bed. He brought her water and food. She nibbled the bread, speaking little. Augustine rushed back to his classroom, arriving late. Some of his students milled about in the hallway, others played a dice game on the floor.

"Why are you not reading your assignment?" he barked.

A boy gestured towards the room. "Because we cannot sit down. The Wreakers have been here."

Augustine peered in. The stools were all smeared with dung. Already a foul stench hung in the room. This was not the first time pranksters had struck his room. Cussing, he directed students to carry the stools outside for washing. As the room was cleared out, he spotted greasy words on the cloth wall. "Apollo sends his blessing." He clenched his hands in anger. The prank may have been committed by a random group of students or encouraged by a rival teacher enraged at losing the poetry contest to him.

When Augustine reached home, tired and grumpy, Alypius was there to greet him. Augustine forced a smile, pretending cheeriness as he introduced his former student to Nebridius. After an evening of chatting, the three headed out to a restaurant to eat, for Galla still had not risen from bed to cook.

Days went by before Galla began tending to housework again. Augustine and Nebridius spoke gingerly when around her, Adeodatus quick to volunteer for chores. When Alypius moved in, he was told nothing about Galla's condition. His jokes brought laughter again to the apartment. The men sat around for hours discussing literature. Alypius took an interest in the teachings of Mani, asking numerous questions. Galla began cooking again, seemingly back to her normal self, yet sometimes melancholy set in for days.

Because of Augustine's poetry victory, the proconsul Vindicianus invited the young teacher to a dinner party. As guests reclined on soft couches using their hands to eat the lush dishes, the topic of astrology came up. When Vindicianus perceived that Augustine had an addiction to horoscopes, he became concerned.

In a fatherly voice, the old man said, "In my youth I studied astrology quite studiously. Even considered taking it up professionally. I thought that if I was capable of understanding Hippocrates, I could understand these books. Over time, I realized the folly of their claims. Not wanting to make a living deceiving people, I turned to medicine instead."

"I have not found them to be erroneous." Augustine casually separated the cooked vegetables from the pork on his patter.

"You have the profession of rhetoric teacher by which you earn your living in society. You are pursuing this delusory subject in your free time, not out of any necessity to raise additional income. You should be inclined to believe my view of the matter, considering that I worked hard to acquire a thorough knowledge of astrology to exclusively earn my living."

Not wanting to offend the powerful man, Augustine carefully said, "Can you answer me, then? Why do many of their forecasts turn out to be correct?"

Vindicianus placed the sow udder he was about to eat back on his plate, the topic interesting him more than the food. "When someone listens to a poem being read about one subject, sometimes the listener perceives it to relate to an entirely different topic. It is a wonder that the human soul, by some higher instinct, unknowingly senses what goes on deep inside one's self and finds patterns which fit personal circumstance."

"You should meet my companion Nebridius who also finds divinations nonsensical. He has tried to convince me for years, but I will not change my opinion unless absolute proof is presented to me that can demonstrate astrology as false."

They continued the discussion for some time. Augustine swatting away Vindicianus's points, but tiny tentacles of doubt began to encircle his mind.

A few evenings later Augustine sat in his apartment, eating a plain bowl of beans. Galla could turn the humblest of vegetables into a delicious feast, but lately everything she served him was plain and unseasoned. He looked across the table to Alypius, also eating beans. The recent convert to Manichean was usually enthusiastic about his beliefs but tonight he stared wistfully at young Adeodatus and Nebridius eating roasted beef strips, melted fat dipping down their fingers.

"How come our food is never that good?"

"You are supposed to be giving up the pleasures of the flesh. That includes taste," said Galla, pouring wine into a cup for Nebridius.

Alypius licked his lips, mesmerized by the red liquid. "Which year would that be?"

Nebridius held the cup up and deeply breathed the alluring fragrance. "The best year of my life."

"Could you spare a week or perhaps a day of that enjoyable year?" Alypius held out his cup.

Galla batted the cup away with her hand. "None of that. You, sir, are on a strict diet. No fruit of the vine for you unless freshly plucked." She glanced at Augustine out of the corner of her eye.

Her lover sipped his water loudly. "The most important drink in the world, revitalizes life itself."

"Glad you enjoy water so much, since it is the only liquid which can pass your lips."

Adeodatus giggled and took another big chomp of his beef strip. "Yum, spicy. The best, Mother."

Alypius took several more bites of lukewarm beans then sat the bowl down in disgust. "I cannot take it anymore. A man should eat proper." He reached out and grabbed a beef strip off Adeodatus's plate.

"Hey," complained the boy, secretly giving his mom a wink.

Mouth full of spicy meat, Alypius closed his eyes in delight.

Augustine sighed. "There will be penance for you to pay."

"I will happily pick a bushel of apples every day to justify eating from Galla's table."

"We do not eat apples as they are the fruit which led Adam and Eve into sin."

"Too bad," said Galla. "For dessert I have roasted apple in honey sauce."

Adeodatus cheered, and Nebridius boasted she should be cooking for the emperor. Alypius held out a plate, "I have already sinned. Might as well make the best of it."

Augustine breathed deeply, trying to keep his temper in check. He knew Galla was still upset about the abortion, but for her to undermine the training of his new recruit was going too far. He turned to Alypius. "You have vowed to follow the teachings of Mani. When will you begin keeping your word?"

Between slurps of wine, Alypius said, "When you begin sleeping alone, I will begin eating like a pauper."

Frowning, Augustine went back to silently eating his beans.

Chapter Fourteen

Students bent over their wax tablets, quietly concentrated on writing words into the smooth surfaces with their wooden styluses. Nebridius walked among them, occasionally giving a comment or suggestion. At the front of the classroom, Augustine listened to a student reciting a famous speech by Cicero. Suddenly six youths rushed into the room, screaming wildly. They knocked over a table holding supplies and kicked stools out from quiet pupils. Then they ran from the room and melted away into other classes before Augustine could reach his door to yell at them. Frustrated, Augustine turned around to see his class in disarray. Students picked themselves off the floor, one holding a broken stylus. Two helped Nebridius pick up the overturned table and gather its scattered contents. Nearly half an hour passed before the upset students settled down enough to focus again on their work.

"This is the third time this month," complained Augustine after class to Nebridius and Pulcher. "Something must be done."

The veteran teacher said, "Students have always behaved this way in Carthage, including when you were my pupil."

"I never joined the Wreckers in misbehaving. They should be persecuted under the law and whipped in public."

"Alas, they are minors, and many are children of prominent citizens. They feel themselves immune. Also, be aware that some of your students may be guilty of pranks too, seeking revenge against those who invade their class. The cycle is unending."

"I never tolerated misbehavior from my students in Thagaste. If there was a problem, I went directly to the parents who dealt with it immediately."

Pulcher sighed. "Perhaps the atmosphere of a different city would meet your approval. I have heard that students in Rome are better behaved. I have considered moving there a few times myself, but my family is here."

Nebridius gathered the scrolls used in the day's lessons. "Our comrade Alypius recently sailed to Rome to begin his career as a jurisconsult."

The old teacher smiled. "Ah, he is a shiny example of why I continue to teach. A great future awaits him. Perhaps one day he will become a proconsul."

Augustine resisted pointing out that Pulcher had once predicted failure for young Alypius when the youth had been addicted to the circus. "Have you had the opportunity to read my book *On the Beautiful and the Fitting*?"

"Aye, the writing is well styled. Your topic of beauty is universal. Interesting comment that we love an object because of its beauty."

"Through Alypius I sent a copy to Rome to be delivered to the renowned orator Hierius who I have heard much about. I would be delighted if he finds my book insightful."

"Perhaps he will. I have used several quotes from Hierius in my own lessons."

Augustine and Nebridius slowly meandered home through the crowded streets, pausing at bookshops on the way. A scroll about predicating eclipses caught Augustine's eye. As he perused it, the contents began to disturb him. He turned to Nebridius who was haggling with the seller over the price of a book.

"Have you heard of Thales from Miletus?"

"Of course. He was a Greek philosopher, one of the famous Seven Sages. He rejected mythological explanations and looked to science to explain nature. I have read about him in depth. Fascinating work with geometry. Using triangles he calculated the height of the pyramids in Egypt." Nebridius turned back to the vendor. "One sestertii for it."

"Nay," said the seller. "I will take nothing less than five sestertii."

Augustine looked back at the scroll in his hand. "The author claims Thales predicted an upcoming eclipse years before it happened. A war lasting six years was spontaneously halted when the sun blackened, causing the enemies to make peace immediately. How could he possibly predict an eclipse? They are the random results of the war between Light and Darkness."

"Buy the book," said the merchant. "Then you will have plenty of time to ponder the mysterious of the universe. All for just five sestertii."

After haggling their books down to three sestertii each, the friends returned home and spent the evening reading. Long after he should have been asleep Augustine continued to study by lamplight. Thales and his disciples were credited with producing charts which foretold eclipses for both the sun and moon. They were accurate down to the exact day and hour. Augustine was baffled. According to Mani, predicating events in nature should be impossible.

The next morning, tired and groggily, Augustine headed to the forum to teach. While in front of his students, he was self-assured, seemingly knowing all life's answers. Yet uncertainty plagued him. During the lunch break, he wandered among the many plazas and courtyards of the bustling forum. Crowds gathered around popular orators. On the steps in front of a tall building, Augustine paused to listen to a lecture from a man named Elpidius who was attacking Manichean. A few days earlier Augustine may have stepped up to counter the man's arguments, but today he only listened as seeds of doubt deepened their roots in his mind.

Augustine began reading every book he could find about the scientific observations of the world and comparing their teachings with Mani. Mathematics accurately predicted the rotation of seasons and the visibility of stars. Mani's writings seemed foolish when compared with rational accounts for solstices, equinoxes, and eclipses. At meetings, Augustine questioned the Manichean teachers, asking for a logical explanation which would explain away his confusion.

But the elders were stomped, only telling him, "Wait until Faustus comes. He is a great bishop, an elegant speaker who will answer all your questions."

So Augustine waited and waited, doubt eating at his soul while he publicly pretended all was well.

Months later Monnica arrived in Carthage, escorted by Navigius who would only stay for a few short weeks before heading back home to be with his expectant wife. Happy to see his grandmother, Adeodatus greeted Monnica with a big hug.

"Let me look at you," said Monnica, studying the tall, blond boy. "So handsome, like your father. How old are you now?"

"Twelve. I have not forgotten the stories you used to tell me about God's servants."

The grandmother smiled, her gray hair more pronounced. "It lightens my heart to hear that."

Galla added, "He is top in his grammaticus class."

"I would expect nothing less from my grandson. I knew when he first began talking that he had inherited his father's keen mind."

Feeling the comment had been a sly insult against herself, Galla hid a grimace. "He does not share his father's faith but yours and mine."

"Has Augustine taught him about…Mani?" There was dread in Monnica's voice.

"Some, yes, but Augustine has never prevented me from taking him to services. Augustine believes that Adeodatus should learn the fundamentals of all major religions to help with his future career. Adeodatus has already decided that

Christianity reveals the true path to God." With pride, she added, "He remembers whatever he hears and can recite many scriptures."

"You have done well raising Adeodatus. Where is my son?"

"Still at work. He will be home in a few hours."

They sat for a while talking. Then Galla began preparing dinner. Monnica ambled about the apartment, inspecting it. She frowned at dust in corners. Disliking the arrangement of some of the furniture, she had Navigius and Adeodatus move the items about.

"The table should be nearer the window for better lighting. Where is your broom kept?"

In the midst of roasting a chicken, Galla kept her irritation to herself. She was only a concubine, Monnica the *domina*. When Nebridius and Augustine arrived home, they found an extremely clean, newly arranged abode. Augustine greeted his mother formally while Nebridius wondered where his writing utensils and half-completed letters had been moved to.

Conversation during dinner mainly focused on events at Thagaste—which relative was doing what, who were the latest clients of Romanianus, where the newest villa was being built. Navigius said little, letting his mother control the topics, but his face lit with excitement when he spoke of his wife and coming child. While Galla stood in a corner washing dishes, Monnica carefully changed the topic to religion, probing her son's beliefs. Augustine treaded carefully, mentioning he attended Manichean meetings but spoke nothing of his doubt. He did not need his mother clawing away at the cracks of his uncertainty.

The apartment seemed far smaller with Monnica and Navigius staying there, though there had been other boarders over the years. Monnica got along well with most of the household, including Nebridius once he found all his missing items. Galla resented another woman telling her which meals should be cooked, how to organize, and what to clean. Augustine felt as if he walked on eggshells around his mother, always guarding what he said. He became even more cautious when Galla told him that sometimes in the mornings Monnica could be heard praying and weeping in her bedroom, saying Augustine's name over and over.

In public Monnica was outgoing and industrious, quick to volunteer for church activities. Soon she was part of a circle of women visiting the sick, bringing food and clothes to the poor. She also visited various shrines scattered around Carthage which were dedicated to martyrs. Following local custom, she offered wine at each location, taking only a small sip before saying prayers. During holidays when school was out, Adeodatus often escorted his grandmother on her many errands. As they navigated the bustling streets, they discussed things he could not talk with his parents about. His mother was uneducated and his father too wrapped up with his Manichean teachings and busy life. Monnica would listen patiently to her grandson's questions. If she did not know an answer relating to religion, she boldly walked right up to a priest and asked for an elucidation.

Augustine avoided home as much as possible, attending parties of prominent men late into the night, sometimes breaking his vows to abstain from wine and meat. At home he continued to put on a show of being a strict Manichean. At last, word came that Bishop Faustus had arrived in Carthage. Eager to meet him, Augustine attended several public lectures. Faustus spoke boldly in the open, unafraid despite his religion being illegal. Large crowds gathered to hear his elegant words. Surrounded by spectators, Augustine was frustrated, his private doubts unanswered. His could not ask controversial questions at the public lectures, and Faustus kept to topics Augustine had heard countless times before. The only difference was that Faustus worded his answers far better than others. Augustine began visiting influential Manicheans, hinting he wanted to personally meet Faustus.

Finally he was invited to a dinner party the other was also attending. When the timing was right, Augustine put forth his question. "You know the teachings of Mani better than any other. I hope you can illuminate an issue which has disturbed my thoughts."

The middle-age bishop was cordial. "I will share what God has illuminated to me, though some matters he keeps to himself."

"I have studied the mathematical calculations in books which accurately predicate many events of the heavens. The books by Mani describe the signs of the heavens quite differently. Which one is right, or are both versions somehow correct?"

Faustus pursed his lips. "I am unaware of these calculations you speak of. Can you elaborate on them more?"

As Augustine began explaining, his hopes sunk. Faustus was an honest and friendly man, well-educated in classic literature, but he had little knowledge of liberal arts. If the Manichean bishop could not answer his questions, who could? Still, Augustine formed a friendship with Faustus, visiting him often. Faustus was eager to learn about new topics, so Augustine brought books to discuss with the bishop. Augustine kept nagging doubts pushed to the back of his mind, but they refused to be vanquished.

As the school year began to draw towards its end, Augustine's frustrations grew. Student pranks became more vicious. Letters from Alypius and other friends in Rome sung praises of the preeminent city, claiming Augustine could earn better wages and high honors there. Perhaps in Rome he could finally silence the uncertainty which plagued him. He began discussing with Nebridius the idea of moving. Nebridius approved, as he longed to visit the renowned city with its famous scholars and orators.

Using Manichean contacts, Augustine gained a teaching position in Rome. Once he was certain about the job, he told his family. Adeodatus was eager for adventure, but Galla preferred to live near her family in Carthage. Still, she would go wherever her lover went. Monnica advised against the move, fearing her son would truly lose his path in the ancient city dedicated to pagan gods.

But Augustine would not heed her, instead arranging for a merchant to take his mother back to Thagaste after they sailed. Their belongings were packed and sent ahead to a ship in the harbor. Monnica followed, begging Augustine to change his mind. When they reached the sea, she reached out and grabbed his arm, tears running down her cheeks.

"Son, you break my heart. Do not leave me or your kinsmen. Return with me to Thagaste. Did you not enjoy teaching there? Your soul has had time to heal from Didius's death."

"Mother, my appointment has already been made. I cannot turn back."

"Then I will go with you."

"What of Navigius and Perpetua? You have other grandchildren beside Adeodatus to tend to."

"My entire household is saved but you. I cannot….will not leave you."

Augustine sighed, looking about in frustration. Thinking quickly, he lied, "We will not sail until another friend of mine arrives and the wind it right. The Shrine of Cyprian is nearby. Let us go and pray there for a safe voyage." Their ship was not scheduled to actually leave until earlier morning during high tide.

"You would enter a church again?" Hope sparked in Monnica's eyes.

"Yes, for you."

The whole party walked into the stone shrine which had stood for over a hundred years on the spot Cyprian had been beheaded in front of thousands for his faith. Galla and Adeodatus comfortably kneeled beside the *domina* at the wooden altar at the front to pray. Augustine and Nebridius kept to the back of the sanctuary, feeling uneasy. Other petitioners came and went, some staying all night for prayer and worship. Monnica wept beside other visitors, pleading to God that her son would finally understand truth. Her words caused Augustine to wince. After the sun set, Nebridius knelt for a few minutes in prayer then walked to the side of the room.

Augustine stared at him. "You too, Nebridius?"

"It is a long voyage. I thought it could not hurt to ask for safety. Who am I to say that no god exists? Out of the thousands, perhaps at least one is real. The Christian God is more pleasant than most."

"They worship the same deity as us Manicheans, but they go about trying to reach God the wrong way."

Nebridius studied the sincere worshipers singing a psalm. "Your Manichean God is hard to appease. You are forever trying to reach out to grasp him. The Christian God cared enough to reach down to touch mankind."

"Strange talk from you."

"Maybe it is just anxiety for the coming trip. How long do we wait?"

"An hour or two until her attention fades."

Late into the night when Monnica was deep in prayer with a group of women, Augustine secretly beckoned his family and Nebridius to leave. They walked down the dark, unlit street to the circular harbor, its massive stone walls protecting hundreds of merchant ships. Military vessels were docked in a second connected harbor which encircled an island fortress. No other city in the world had such an imposing design which had allowed the original Carthaginians to dominate the Mediterranean for centuries until the Third Punic War with Rome. After boarding their ship, Augustine could not relax until the tide had risen and the wind filled their sails.

Galla stood by her lover at the stern of the ship, watching the shore slowly disappear, wind tossing about loose stands of blonde hair. "You are breaking your mother's heart yet again."

"Rome is no place for her, and Thagaste is no place for me. She will be comforted when she returns home and sees her new granddaughter."

"She grieves not for your absence from her, but your absence from God."

Augustine looked away, troubled. "Then she will grieve for a long time."

Part III

"The person who knows truth, knows it, and he who knows it, knows eternity."

~Saint Augustine, *Confessions, 7.16*

Chapter Fifteen

Triferus looked up from the scroll, tired from deciphering its words. He had been reading on and off for days, struggling with its Latin words. He could have asked Possidius or another priest for help, but anger still raged within him. They trusted in God while the world crumbled around them. He hated the priests for their blind faith. Hated Boniface for inviting the enemy here. Hated the Vandals for destroying his world. Hated himself for living while his family was dead. Most of all he hated God for allowing it all to happen. Better to hate than be debilitated by grief.

Reading allowed him to focus on something besides the wretched conditions around him. He found himself disliking the Augustine in the book. How could this arrogant man who abandoned his mother be the renowned bishop of Hippo Regius? They were nothing alike. Triferus had heard the elder Augustine preach, a wise man who spoke with authority, loved by his congregation. What had changed him?

Triferus limped back to the library to return the scroll. *Confessions*, like most books, was compiled in a series of scrolls, often circulated among friends before the last chapter was even written. Triferus had learned that Augustine often held public readings for the latest chapters of his books, allowing anyone to critique his work. The suggestions were then used in the shaping of the final version of the text which went into general circulation. Copies of published books were held in the monastery's library where trusted individuals could borrow copies to read or reproduce. Certain monks spent long hours every day copying the text of cherished books. Wealthy people who wanted a duplicate would either pay the monks for their version, hire someone to copy the text for them, or have an educated slave reproduce it. Creating books was a long, laborious process, keeping their cost high. Book sellers who made a living off books often had an entire room of workers who transcribed the words while one individual read the text aloud. It was the cheapest, fastest method to create multiple copies of the same book.

After placing the chapter he had read in its bin, Triferus glanced at several monks moving among the shelves. Possidius was scanning sermons of Augustine, attempting to organize them in related categories. The sermons had been transcribed by stenographers who had been present at the services. Triferus turned to leave, but the bishop spoke to him.

"Does *Confessions* suite your taste?"

"Not really. He breaks the narrative too often to quote scripture."

"God's word is a lamp unto our feet and food unto our souls."

"I would prefer real food for my stomach."

"When food falters, the Word does not." Possidius smiled. "Like you, I do wish for a real meal with meat, fresh fruit, and cheese."

"And honeyed rolls for dessert." Triferus relaxed slightly. Possidius may be a priest, but he still felt the same pangs as everyone else.

An aid to Heraclius, the co-bishop of the city, entered the library and hurriedly glanced around. Possidius noticed. "Is there something we can do for you?"

"Boniface has asked for a priest to give last rites for several soldiers. So many of our brothers are busy today. Could you spare the time?"

"Certainly." Possidius glanced at Triferus. "Would you like to aid me?"

"I…uh…" Triferus never wanted to see death again, yet he could not refuse the gentle priest who had saved his life. "Yes, I will come."

They walked through the city overcrowded with refugees. Most people they passed were gloomy and despondent. Terror of the Vandals poisoned the citizens, choking away happiness and hope. As food became scarcer and prices sharply rose, even the rich could no longer enjoy proper meals. Everyone suffered. It was rare to meet someone who had not lost family, friend, or home. While the churches were packed every service, so were the taverns, brothels, and entertainment businesses. When the liquor and lamp oil ran dry, people still came, huddled in darken rooms, seeking comfort in shared misery.

Possidius kept the pace slow for Triferus who had to pause occasionally to rest his crippled leg. They reached a crest of a hill, giving Triferus a view of the lower city and the massive city wall which stood between them and eighty thousand barbarians waiting to slaughter the townspeople. Sometimes weeks went by in relative tranquility as the enemy fortified their camp, providing the Romans opportunity to reinforce weak areas in the wall. Today was not a day of peace.

The sky was full of high flying arrows launched from Vandals' catapults. Many harmlessly hit the terracotta roofs of houses, but others bit into the soft flesh of livestock or people dashing through the streets near the wall. Most people stayed hidden in their houses, but fiery arrows mixed into the barrage sometimes caught hay or dry wood on fire. Civilians and soldiers rushed about, fighting fires. Triferus watched in horror as a military stable burned, grooms trying to lead frighten war horses out. A man caught fire, his tormented screams reaching Triferus's ears. Someone tossed a bucket of water on the man withering on the ground.

Triferus looked away, his body trembling. Possidius placed a comforting hand on his shoulder. "The hospital is near. You do not have to go further, if you wish."

The teenager swallowed. "I…I said I would come. I always keep my word."

They entered a warehouse which once stored imports from cargo ships. Now it held the dead and dying. Near one wall lay over a dozen bodies awaiting disposal. The main area of the floor consisted of the injured and sick, many victims of the latest plague devouring starving people living in overcrowded apartments. Physicians and volunteers moved through the dim light, aiding as they could. Several nuns and monks bound wounds and fed those too weak to feed themselves.

Spotting the bishop robe of Possidius, a young monk barely older than Triferus greeted the newcomers. "Father, several are asking for last rites. We thought it best if a consecrated priest did it."

"In times like this, it does not matter one's station. Please lead the way."

They stopped before a soldier crazed by high fever, his right arm now only a bandaged stomp. The young monk said, "An arrow was removed, but then the flesh began to rot. A doctor removed the arm, but now his whole body burns. He will not tarry long in this world."

Possidius knelt by the man whose eyes fluttered open. "Can you understand me?"

The soldier reached out with his good arm and grasped the priest's hand. "You came. Tell me, can God forgive me? I have broken his trust."

"Yes, my son, God forgives sincere hearts."

"I…broke my marriage vows. It has been two years since I have seen my wife." He gnashed his teeth together in pain. "God punishes me. I was alone, so alone. I began visiting the brothels."

"You were never alone. God is with you, even now."

"Tell him I am sorry. My wife. My kids. I should have been a better father."

Possidius held the man's hand which clenched as another spasm hit. "God does forgive you. Let us pray together, and you tell him yourself."

The soldier and priest closed their eyes, their lips moving in prayer. Feeling pity for the injured man, Triferus also offered a silent prayer for him.

Possidius then turned to Triferus. "The oil and wine."

Triferus passed over a small vial of oil which the bishop opened. He placed a small drop on the soldier's forehead. Then he placed a tiny piece of bread on the man's tongue. For the last step, he gave the man a sip of watery wine. The viaticum completed, the soldier could now face eternity with his soul cleansed.

The man relaxed, despite the pain. "Thank you, Father."

"Rest in peace, my son." Possidius turned to the young monk still watching. "Who else needs me?"

As Possidius walked down the row of sick people, Triferus awkwardly knelt down beside the sick man. "You sacrifice yourself for the protection of your family. What greater love is there?"

The soldier smiled. "None. Perhaps God will be merciful to my soul, and I will not tarry too long in purgatory."

Triferus rose to catch up with the bishop, but he had only traveled a few steps before a feverish woman caught his brown robe. "Pray with me, Father." She lay on a bedroll, pale skin tight against bones, lips cracked from dehydration. The smell of decay clung to her. "Please."

He almost told her he was no priest, but as he looked into her desperate, pleading eyes, he remembered his own mother. Awkwardly he knelt down beside her and took her hand. What did one say when praying for a stranger? Especially one near death? He mumbled through a prayer, using jargon he had often heard. The woman relaxed, her eyes closing peacefully.

Again, Triferus tried to catch up with Possidius, but he was sidetracked by a doctor who waved him over to a soldier whose deep wound had just been sewed up.

"He asks for a priest."

"I am not…" Triferus glanced at the bishop halfway across the warehouse administering last rites to someone else. The teenager sighed and asked the sick man, "How can I help you?"

The soldier lay on a dirty mat. His face marred by old battle scars. "This time I will be visiting Saint Peter. I have a letter which must reach my father. We departed on…unhappy terms. My pride has kept me from apologizing in person." The man reached into his bloody cloak and pulled out a sealed scroll. "Here are a few coins to cover the cost."

Triferus swallowed, realizing the momentous task this stranger was entrusting him with. "By God's providence, I will see it delivered when the siege is over."

It was a long time before Triferus caught up with Possidius. The need of the dying was so great. Triferus was not qualified to administer the viaticum, but he could pray with those who requested it, fetch water, hold a cloth over a feverish face, or just listen to the lonely talk about their lives. Over and over Triferus thought of his own family, that no priest had been there to pray with them in their last moments, how he now lived only because a neighbor took time to help a dying boy. So Triferus continued to kneel painfully beside the sick, not flinching among the hideous odors of death, vomit, and decay.

Triferus did not know when it happened, yet it did. Sometime in the midst of helping others, Triferus forgot to hate. A gently peace filled his soul as he looked beyond his own loss to what he could do to ease the burdens of others.

Late evening Triferus and Possidius left the make-shift hospital and wearily walked up the steep hill. At the top, they paused to look out over Hippo Regius. A furious battle was now taking place along one section of wall. Vandals were scaling ladders, attempting to gain control of several guard towers. The Romans fought valiantly, their swords flashing in the fading sunlight. Archers from the towers rained arrows down upon the invaders. Among the chaos marched a tall Roman, barking out orders. Even from this distance Triferus was certain it was General Boniface.

As he watched the barbarian wave repelled, he realized the burning hatred he felt for the commander was gone. Only relief that the city walls still held.

"There will be more injured who need help," observed Triferus.

"Yes, there will be," said Possidius, his face lined with exhaustion.

"Tomorrow, can we come back?"

"Yes, son."

Back at the monastery, Triferus could not sleep, despite his tiredness, the day's events replaying through his mind. He wandered about the quiet hallway to the library, finally picked up the next scroll of *Confessions*. Then he sat by an oil lamp in a kitchen corner and continued to read while several monks finished scrubbing pots.

Chapter Sixteen

The ancient city of Rome was built upon the ruins and blood of other nations. Established over fifteen hundred years before, it had grown to a population of two million. Its empire controlled most of the known world. Powerful nations had crumbled before its mighty armies. Entire populations were slaughtered or turned into slaves to serve the needs of the Romans. Architectural wonders of temples, monuments, statues, and arenas dotted the city landscape. But Rome was also a city in decline. Fifty-three years earlier Emperor Constantine had moved the imperial capital to the city of Constantinople to be closer to Roman troops protecting the frontier. After his death, the nation split into two realms with the city of Milan claiming the title of capital for the Western Empire.

Upon arriving at Rome, Augustine saw little of the city. His family had been invited to stay for a short time at a villa of a prominent Manichean. They had not finished unpacking before sickness struck Augustine. He lay in bed shivering and sweating, fever ravishing his body. Fanciful dreams blended with nightmarish images. Didius and he strolling through ripened wheat fields at Thagaste. Fire suddenly leaping up the stalks. Didius enflamed. Augustine reaching out to save his fiend, but when their hands touched, the fire which trapped his friend crawled across his own skin, waking him with screams of pain.

Always by Augustine's bed sat Galla, tending him by placing a damp cloth on his forehead or spoon-feeding him soup. Nebridius visited often along with Alypius when he could pull himself away from his busy schedule of a jurisconsult. Their Manichean host stopped by daily to see how his guest was doing. When the fever finally faded, Augustine's clarity returned, but his weaken body forced him to lie in bed for days. Trapped with nothing to distract him, Augustine was plagued by doubts about Mani. If he had died during the sickness, would he really have ascended to God? No, his impurity was too great, dooming him to be reborn into a lowly life. How many lifetimes of eating fruit and refraining from fleshly entertainment would it take to be embraced by the Light? Depression clung to him, crushing his spirit. Augustine warned his host against placing too much trust in Mani, but the man brushed Augustine's worries away, seeing his guest still inflicted from the sickness.

Nebridius and Alypius tried to cheer up Augustine by reading to him for hours, but when they left, the depression returned. By pooling their money, Nebridius and Alypius found an affordable house to share. When Augustine's strength returned, he moved his family there. The house was too simple to be called a villa, but it was large enough that each man had his own bedroom and Augustine could hold classes in the main central room. Using his powerful Manichean contacts, he soon had over thirty students, some the sons of senators. He pushed them and most thrived, winning public debates against peers and earning Augustine higher esteem in the public eye. Overall, his students were well behaved, but he was warned by friends that some Roman parents, to avoid paying the yearly tuitions fees, would withdraw students just before the end of the school year.

Each morning Galla would fix a light breakfast. Then Adeodatus headed off to grammaticus and Alypius to the forum to hear cases. Soon students arrived at the house. Augustine oversaw the main lessons while Nebridius pulled small groups aside for further exercises. During the lunch break, the students headed either home or to vendors for food. Adeodatus often popped in for a quick meal with his parents, other times he ate out with friends. Students returned for afternoon classes. Sometimes Augustine took the whole group to the forum to hear speeches of famous orators or have his pupils debate students of other rhetoric teachers. During the evenings, guests regularly came for dinner and stayed for hours discussing various topics. Adeodatus often sit in a corner, listening quietly to the adults, his keen mind absorbing everything. In the background, Galla quietly went about her work, cooking and cleaning, bringing the men snacks and filling their goblets.

"Have you heard word from Hierius yet?" asked Augustine one quiet evening after dinner.

Alypius looked up from the scroll he had been reading. "Not yet. His slave who I gave your book to said Hierius was highly sought after and may take many months to read what is sent him."

Augustine sighed. "It has already been months."

"I am sure he will find your words inspiring. What was it you wrote? 'Beauty is what charms and attracts us to the things we love.'"

"Yes, without the grace and loveliness inherited in them, they would not move us."

"Father," said Adeodatus, looking up from his homework of writing a declamation on his wax tablet. "Does that mean you only love what is beautiful and despise that which is ugly?"

"Do we not value the athletic and spurn the disfigured?"

"If I have been born deformed, would you have spurned me, perhaps exposing me on the rocks?"

The question caught Augustine off guard. He opened his mouth to respond but said nothing. Looking into his son's deep blue eyes, he could not speak the truth.

Galla, who had been sweeping the floor, intervened. "It is not your place to interrupt adult conversation. Back to your homework."

Adeodatus obeyed, returning to his writing, but his probing eyes silently darted back to his father. Augustine ignored his son by resuming his conversation with Alypius and Nebridius—but choosing a new topic. Galla went back to her cleaning, noticing the calluses on her hands from years of scrubbing floors. She was still beautiful. Augustine often told her so during passionate nights where she fed his insatiable appetite. What about in another ten or twenty years? Would he still love her when she became wrinkled and gray? Disturbed, she scrubbed the floor harder until no blemishes remained.

Life in Rome was lonely for her. Lacking Augustine's charisma, she found it difficult making new friends. Daily she chatted at the well with other women waiting their turn for water, but the conversations were superficial. Trying to appear important, Galla would brag about the latest party her lover had attended or which famous people he had spoken with. While her words made an impression on the others, the result was the other women distancing themselves further from her. She was too high-class for them who were only slaves or servants sent to fetch water. Neither was she able to befriend wives of the wealthy for Augustine did not invited Galla to the dinner parties he attended.

Her life revolved around chores and shopping for the household. She was proud of her son's accomplishments at school, but she understood little about what he studied. He was always polite to her, obeying in anything she asked of him. Daily they attended evening prayers at a nearby church. From the age of a toddler, he was full of questions, asking about the meanings of sermons. At first, she could answer his simple questions, but within a few years he outgrew her limited knowledge. When Monnica lived with them, Adeodatus spent many hours discussing deep topics with his grandmother. Keeping to a habit Monnica had taught him, after services ended, he would hang back until most worshipers had departed then ask the priest to explain a point bothering him. Galla loved her son but she still longed for a daughter who she could bond with. Who else could she pass on the recipes from her own grandmother? Who else would understand her long days of labor and isolation? Still, she felt pride as she served guests. There was her handsome lover, dressed formally, chatting with powerful men. She may have been born a slave, but her lover taught senator's sons. How many freedwomen could boast of that?

Life was pleasant for Nebridius. With no need for money, he spent each day as he wished. Mornings he helped Augustine with teaching. Afternoons he either read books or listened to speeches at the forum. Sometimes he attended court cases Alypius was working on. In conversations, he challenged anyone whose answers were too superficial, demanding they probe deeper into the problem. Always he sought truth, studying the renowned Greek philosophers. Sometimes he still missed his young wife who had died during their third year of marriage. At night he still had nightmares of her screaming in labor. The hideous sounds seemed to go on for hours. And the blood. So much. Then silence. No crying baby, only the weeping of his shattered dreams. After watching her die, Nebridius had sworn to himself he would never marry again. He could never endanger another woman's life like that. So he spent his days chasing wisdom, but she was a finicky lover who was hard to pin down.

Following his parents' wishes, Alypius pursed a career in law, but his true interest lay in adventure. As a youth he dreamed of traveling to every province and writing about his tales of discovery. But his parents had stripped him of that dream and pushed him into law. The incident of almost being arrested for being a thief weighed heavily on him, leading him to develop a deep sense for truth and justice. As a jurisconsult, he was expected to have an in-depth understanding of the law and to offer legal advice to both commoners and officials. At most trials, a panel of jurisconsults observed the proceeding then offered their opinions to the judge before the verdict was rendered. Many jurisconsults had a more thorough knowledge of the law than even the judges trying a case. The influence of jurisconsults was so strong that even governors often consulted them before making important decisions.

With thirteen hundred years of ever-changing laws, the Roman Empire at times had become its own worst enemy. It controlled provinces on three continents and rarely did a year go by when the nation was not involved in a war in at least one territory, with simultaneous battles sometimes taking place hundreds or thousands of miles apart. New laws were slow in reaching the outer provinces. Months and even years passed before outlaying cities and towns became aware of new rules. During the meantime, yet another law may have already changed the meaning of a previous one. Added to the confusion was that many ancient laws were still in effect but forgotten over several generations. It was the jurisconsults' duty to know both the newer and older laws, and to declare which was currently in effect.

Alypius was now fulfilling his third appointment on a panel. Each day he sat at the front of the room with other jurisconsults listening to petitions for the Court of Italian Treasury, which oversaw funding for the entire providence. Some cases were of commoners complaining that tax collectors were taking more than their fair share. Others were greedy patricians demanding reinterpretations of laws so they may gain more money. Alypius was disturbed when some of his peers gave advice to judges which were outright lies. Overtime he realized that his peers and even some judges were accepting bribes.

During lunch break one day, a powerful senator approached Alypius. "You have a keen mind, son."

Alypius quickly swallowed the bread he had been munching on. "I have studied hard."

"I have heard you carry great respect among your peers. If you would sway the others my way, I will reward you well."

Alypius felt outrage burn inside of him, but he replied formally. "If the law had supported your position, I would gladly have done so with no bribe needed. As the law clearly states your request is illegal, I cannot do so."

The senator frowned, danger lurking in his eyes. "You do realize that I have the power to crush your career or see it prosper."

"And you do realize that without honest jurisconsults like me, the laws you pass in the Senate are useless. If you do not like the laws, then change it. I will do my duty to enforce them."

The senator's calmness melted away. "With a naïve view like that, you will never prosper in politics."

"I will leave that to you. I simply seek Truth, wherever she may be found."

"You may find her in Hades soon."

"Then she and I will have a nice chat in the Elysian Fields, a place I believe you will never be permitted entrance."

Fuming, the senator marched away. His trailing slaves glancing back at the bold youth who dared to stand up against their master. Alypius hurried back inside and found the judge overseeing the case. He told the elderly man about the bribe.

"You were foolish to anger him."

"We stand for justice. If we give in to the whims of every rich man, what does that say about Rome? Does money and greed rule our nation? If so, we are doomed to a short future. Cicero said...."

"Quote not Cicero to me. I know his words by heart." The judge sighed, weary of the many painful compromises he had wrestled with over the years. "I have wanted to refuse the senator's petition, but I cannot stand against his wraith. You have only yourself to think about while I have sons whose careers can easily be destroyed by a few words by such men as he."

"You cannot let injustice win. If so, I will resign my post and tell any who ask exactly why I did so."

"You are rash but courageous. Those such as you become the heroes of our stories, much admired. I will do as you ask, denying the senator, but I will tell him it is because of your opinion that I do so."

Alypius nodded. "Thank you. Justice is all I ask for."

"Do not be so quick to thank me. Remember, most of the heroes in our stories face tragic endings."

That evening at home Alypius described in detail the events. Augustine and Nebridius laughed with him as he mimicked the furious face of the senator when his learned he had lost the case.

"Where you not afraid," asked Augustine, "to stand up against such a powerful man?"

"Why should I be afraid when truth is on my side? I would prefer to die a thousand honorable deaths than live one corrupt life."

Nebridius shook his head in awe. "And I thought your sense of justice was too presumptuous when you refuse to use the government discount to get your books transcribed cheaper."

Alypius walked in boldness for days, enjoying the admiration directed towards him by peers. His self-rightness grew, leaving him vulnerable. One evening he strolled with several fellow law students along the narrow streets, debating where to eat. They passed through shadows cast by the immense circularly structure of the coliseum. The roar of the excited crowd could be heard from within.

One of Alypius companions glanced at the entrance with envy. "The best competitions are always saved for late evening. I wonder who is fighting today."

"Might be a historical reenactment. Navy battles are my favorite," said another jurisconsult.

Alypius was aghast. "Surely you do not attend such barbaric displays. Gladiator fights should be permanently banned."

"Have you even seen a fight?"

"Of course not. I have never been tempted by such lewd entertainment."

"You judge quickly. If you have never watched a fight, how do you know it is lewd? You cannot judge something unless you have first experienced it." With a wink at his companions, the young man grabbed Alypius arm and pulled him towards the entrance.

Alypius resisted. "If you drag my body into that place and force me to sit down, do not imagine you can turn my mind and eye to such a spectacle. I shall be as one not there, and so I shall overcome you and the games."

The others laughed. Gently but firmly they prodded Alypius through the entrance and up into the stands. Alypius sat on a stone bench, keeping his eyes shut. Around him the rowdy crowd of spectators yelled at the gladiators fighting below in the vast circle of sand. Alypius tried to keep his curiosity at bay by focusing on the smells around him. The most powerful odor was the rank, sweaty bodies of the packed crowd pressed closely together. Whiffs of tantalizing food caused his empty stomach to growl. Fifty thousand voices blended together, becoming almost one entity as they cheered a gallant maneuver or jeered clumsiness. The fight below intensified, and the crowd's voices reached such a fevered pitch that the very stone Alypius sat on vibrated.

Suddenly from the spectators came both shirks of joy and groans. Curious, Alypius peeked. A gladiator lay on the sand, his head half severed from his body, his body twitching, blood spurting onto the combatant who had just slaughtered him. Alypius was both horrified and fascinating. He had never seen anyone killed before. The gruesomeness and savagery repelled him, yet he could not tear his eyes away from the dozen other skirmishes taking place simultaneously. His focus shifted from one pair to another. A swordsman against a pike. A net against a dagger. Two had dropped weapons and where hitting each other with bloody fists.

Without realizing what he was doing, Alypius groaned when a net tripped a valiant gladiator who had just sliced his own opponent's neck. As the Goth struggled to quickly regain his footing, yet another gladiator pounced on him. Excited screams reverberated across the coliseum. The Goth was a favorite with many wins. Alypius leaned forward, yelling with the others for the Goth to succeed, wincing when a blade raked across the gladiator's side. Ignoring the pain, the Goth jumped to his left and stabbed his sword into the abdomen of his enemy. The crowd roared in pleasure, Alypius's voice blending in with fifty thousand others.

That night when Alypius came home, he could not stop talking about the games, his eyes wide with excitement. "You must come with me tomorrow."

Augustine shook his head. "I have classes all day then a dinner invitation from a famous poet. Besides, why would I want to watch such butchery?"

"Because it is more thrilling than even the races at the circus. The closest we will ever get to a real battle front. Surely Nebridius you will come? You have much spare time."

The other frowned. "One of my cousins died as a gladiator. His costly death given at the expense of cheap thrills from spectators who quickly forget he ever existed. I will never set foot in such a place."

"Well, I am going back tomorrow after work. The games only last three weeks. Then we have to wait months until another is hosted. Augustine, you must find at least one free day to come."

"Wisdom is not found in such superficial entertainment." Augustine picking up a scroll and began reading out loud, ignoring further pleas.

Chapter Seventeen

Augustine had been warned. Still he felt bittiness and betrayal when four of his students dropped out of class a few weeks before the school year ended and their parents refused to pay the annual tuition. The absence of expected funds would not destitute him, but their conduct enraged him. For nearly ten months he had trained the students, giving them the tools to becoming successful politicians. One had even won a public debate. How did the parents thank him for his countless hours of labor? By withdrawing their sons and refusing to pay. What type of example were they setting for their sons' future careers? Augustine could always sue for payment, but it was a long and tedious process.

His grumpiness did not subside when he arrived at the Manichean meeting where a renowned Elect would be speaking. Augustine sat quietly on a mat during the lecture, barely paying attention to the words. Nothing new was ever said. No sudden insight would be kindled, answering all of Augustine's doubts. He now only attended the meetings for strengthening contact with influential men. After the speech, attendees split into small groups to chat. Augustine mentioned to several men his frustration with his students' refusal to pay.

An elderly patrician said, "Such an offensive could be forgiven if the parents' estate had suddenly fallen on hard times, but for rich citizens to treat a fine rhetorical teacher such as yourself like that, it is unforgivable. My grandson has only praise to speak about your classes. I have seen him blossom with self-confidence, which his last teacher failed to achieve. I have heard about an opening in Milan for a professor of rhetoric paid by public funds. Only senators' sons are accepted as students. If such a job interests you, I could speak a word to Symmachus, Milan's prefect who has been charged with filling the position."

Augustine's heart leaped. It was the highest level an educator could achieve besides being a private tutor for an emperor's son. Unlike most teaching positions where tuition was paid by parents, this highly coveted position came with a fixed high salary, along with the bonus of shaping the minds of the next generation which would govern the nation. "I would be highly honored to be included as a candidate for the position."

"Then I will visit Symmachus tomorrow and drop your name to him. Like all candidates applying, you will be required to give a speech to show off your orator skills which I have heard so much about."

"I look forward to fulfilling your confidence in me."

Back home, Augustine gushed about the job opportunity. "It will place me in the center of politics. The going-ons of the empire happening around me every day. What influence I can achieve!"

Alypius caught his friend's enthusiasm. "My seat is almost finished. Milan is the perfect spot for my next appointment. Think how high we can climb, perhaps even become proconsuls one day."

"What about Wisdom?" asked Nebridius, looking up from his reading. "In your pursuit of power, will you forget her, your true love?"

"Of course not," said Augustine. "I will teach the wisdom of the greatest writers the world has ever known to students who will become the most powerful men of our nation. No greater job could any teacher desire. Will you join me, friend?"

"If you go to Milan, I will too."

As the men dreamed of exciting futures, Galla filled their cups and washed their dishes. Milan was even further away from beloved Carthage where her family and friends lived. She harbored no doubt that her lover would win the position. Whatever he sat his mind to, he always succeeded. Perhaps in the imperial city, she would not be lonely, and there would be exciting events to brag about in her letters home. Communication was slow, with only two messages received from her family in the last year. Adeodatus wrote the letters for his mother then she would place them with other correspondence Augustine was sending by a trustworthy acquaintance traveling to Carthage. When the letters finally reached her parents, they would have to hunt for someone to read the correspondence to them. Then they had to pay or seek a volunteer to transcribe their response. How she would love if some method existed where she could talk instantly to her family without the long tediousness of writing and waiting. To hear her mother's voice, even for a moment, would ease her isolation.

A few weeks later Symmachus invited Augustine for an interview. Dressed in a toga he had recently brought to fit the image of an esteemed professor, Augustine stood in front of the perfect and several of his powerful friends. Honeyed words Augustine had practiced every day since he had heard about the job easily flowed from his skilled lips. Symmachus smiled and nodded several times during the speech. Afterwards, Symmachus invited Augustine to his private office.

"Your name came to me highly praised. I thought they must be exaggerating your talents, but you have proven me wrong today." Symmachus leaned back in his chair, studying the candidate. He snapped his finger and a youth standing in the corner moved forward. "Bring wine for us. No…just me. I forget that you Manicheans are forbidden the drink of the gods."

"Water will do just fine." Augustine did not mention that he had begun occasionally drinking wine at parties.

"Your religion intrigues me. I am certain you are aware of the growing persecution against our traditional Roman religion. Christians, rather they be Catholic like my cousin Ambrose or Arian like our Emperor, are all the same. Forcing our hands at every turn. Senators chose me to deliver an epistle to Valentinian II, petitioning him to restore funding to our beloved temples, pleading for tolerance. During my speech, I saw his young face soften and knew he favored my request. While he was still pondering a final decision, my horrid cousin wrote to him, claiming our 'gods of nations are demons.' Using his position as bishop of Milan, my cousin claimed he would debar Valentinian from worshiping in church if funding was restored to 'pagan temples.' By Hades, Ambrose has overstepped himself!" In anger, Symmachus brought his fist down, sloshing wine over the edge of his goblet. A slave hurried forward to wipe the spill. "How dare he tell an emperor where he may or may not worship!"

Augustine sipped water, trying to keep his comments neutral. "The boy is only thirteen but carries the weight of an empire."

Symmachus sighed. "Valentinian's tender age is used as a weapon by others to force their will upon him. His mother Empress Justina holds much sway. A woman bossing an emperor. What a disgrace our proud nation has sunk to. Whatever she asks, her son will do. Things were bad enough when Gratian controlled the strings of power."

"As the emperor matures, let us hope he becomes more like his father." Augustine knew it was essential that he understand the political environment of Rome if he was to win the appointment. Gratian was Valentinian II's older half-brother. Their father, before he died, had appointed Gratian the title of Augustus, but the generals chose the four-year-old as emperor instead because they believed they could control him. The brothers had split control of the empire until Gratian had been assassinated by a general the year before.

"Ah, Valentinian I was a noble ruler, leading his troops into countless battles, winning glory for Rome. Though he was a Christian, he tolerated other religions. Alas, both his sons have turned against us. There are some of my colleagues who believe the empire is doomed to fall after Gratian removed the Altar of Victory from the Senate House in Rome. Could there be a more blasphemous ruler? He confiscated temples and turned their revenue over to the state. I had hoped with his death would come tolerance but Valentinian II yields to the influence of my cousin Ambrose."

"One of my assignments this year was for my students to defend the freedom to worship the traditional gods."

Symmachus nodded, pleased. "I knew as a Manichean you would understand, as your religion is also persecuted. Professor of rhetoric is a position which carries weighty influence. Each year, the professor delivers a panegyric to the Emperor and consuls, publicizing the programs of the court. Carefully constructed phrases could sway a young ruler to new ideas."

"I have made my career in molding young minds."

Symmachus smiled. "You will hear my answer for the appointment soon."

Augustine headed home with confidence that the position would be his. A few days later when the public announcement was made of his posting, his friends celebrated with him. Preparations were quickly made for the move. A rich acquaintance who had several homes offered Augustine use of a villa in Milan.

The city lay three hundred and fifty miles north in a basin just below the Alps Mountain. Half a millennium ago, Romans had captured the city from a Celtic tribe then turned it into a prosperous trade center strategically connecting major roads heading deeper into Europe. More beautiful than overcrowded Rome, the city spiraled outward from a center surrounding the elaborate palace and forum. Hundreds of villas dotted the lush countryside. Many rich patricians had homes both in Milan and Rome. Few pagan temples remained, some having been converted into churches. Beyond the city, stockades guarded nearby passes into the frontier were hostile tribes roamed.

The view from the villa Augustine and his friends would live was gorgeous with tall mountains rising in the distance. The owner, who spent most of the year in Rome, always left behind several house slaves to tend to the villa. Galla found herself in charge of them, a strange feeling for her as she had never commanded anyone but her son. Now with a few words, she could order the floors scrubbed, walls washed, water fetched, and garden weeded. She saved cooking duty for herself, shopping for the best deals at the market, then laboring for hours to prepare sumptuous meals. Augustine had begun eating meat again, and she was delighted to serve him and his important guests.

Within a few days of settling into their new abode, Augustine made polite visits to various dignitaries befitting his level. His saved his visit to Ambrose for last, expecting to be received coldly but was surprised by the bishop's warmth and kindness to someone appointed by an enemy. They chatted cordially for several hours about literature. Augustine found Ambrose to be well-read and keen-minded.

Alypius contacted various magistrates and soon had another appointment as a jurisconsult. As Augustine's assistant had already been appointed by Symmachus, Nebridius looked elsewhere for a job, soon accepting a position as aid to Verecundus, a seasoned rhetoric teacher who held classes in his own villa. Augustine again encouraged Nebridius to become a fulltime instructor, but his friend wished for freedom to study wisdom without the heavy responsibilities that teachers carried.

Augustine's classroom was located within the palace complex near the public offices. Out of his own salary, he was expected to pay for a veil keeper. The more curtains a visitor had to pass through, the higher the rank of the dignitary. Each veil was guarded by a slave or servant who would turn back any forbidden visitors. Only one veil was passed through to reach Augustine's tidy class. His students were sons of the richest families in the city, and each bore heavy expectations from parents. Each day Augustine drilled them on memorizing historical speeches, baited them in debates, and pushed them beyond their comfort levels. He openly criticized and praised them in front of their peers, preparing them for the day when they would enter the public arena where a poorly worded phrase could be used by an enemy to destroy their careers or even their lives. Over the centuries, many officials had been ordered to death by offending an emperor.

Political power was constantly swinging back and forth, with those on the edges switching sides to whoever seemed the most powerful. Valentinian II's authority was considered weak by many, but he was strongly supported by Theodosius, the emperor of the east kingdom, despite disagreements on religion. Four years previously Theodosius had declared Catholic Christianity as the only legitimate Imperial religion, ending all state support of traditional gods. Valentinian II and his mother took the Arian creed and supported its version of Christianity, despite most bishops at the latest official council were Catholic and viewed Arianism as heretical. Anger and even bloodshed broke out, especially in North Africa where Arian extremists became very violent.

Augustine and Alypius joined the ranks of countless ambitious men at Milan attempting to win flavor and renown. In the evenings after work, they visited homes of the powerful, dinning with the wealthy. Guarding their words carefully, they developed a strong network of influential friends. Nebridius refrained from most parties, as he preferred spending quiet hours with his books, but if a famous philosopher or scholar was a guest, he would make an exception.

During the school year, Augustine rarely had a moment alone but was surrounded by students, peers, and friends. He kept doubts about religion at bay by staying busy, but no longer did he called himself a Manichean in public. When the summer holiday arrived, he roamed the bookstalls, looking for something different. One vendor, puffed up on pride, claimed to have the writings of the greatest philosophers the world had ever known. Augustine brought several of the Platonists texts and devoured them, finding insight which broke the final hold of Mani upon his mind.

Many quiet mornings he discussed the writings with Nebridius, debating their complex meanings. Frustrated one day, he tossed down the scroll he had been reading aloud. "I have been searching for thirteen years and I still have not found the wisdom Cicero so highly praised."

Nebridius looked up from a letter he had been writing to his parents. "Which section has upset you now?"

Augustine read Plato's words, "'The supreme power can use evil for a noble end, and is capable of transforming formless things to give them a new form.'" Augustine frowned. "How can God use evil for good? Where does evil even come from? Manicheans see good and evil as co-existing. Plato claims a supreme god of purified intelligence created the universe with the first cause. He is so powerful and perfect that even evil bends to his will. How is this possible?"

"Perhaps you need to simplify your question. First, decide how to define something as evil."

"My students would say evil is the opposite of good."

"And you would not accept that answer from them."

"No, it is too simple a response." Augustine sighed, deep in thought. "The Christians might claim evil is the twisting of good. Of taking what is beautiful and using it for selfishness. The Plotinus say evil is the turning away, of separateness, from that which is bigger and more vital than oneself."

"For that answer I give you a passing grade, but not top marks."

Both men laughed. Glancing out the window, Augustine saw the sun dipping down towards the horizon. "Are you sure you will not accompany me tonight?"

"To hear endless flatters flatter endlessly? I think not. I have better uses for my time."

Augustine arose and dressed for the dinner party. Galla wrapped the long toga around his body, arranging the drapes to give a noble appearance. She smiled at the results.

"You are as handsome as ever, my love."

Augustine kissed her lips. "I look forward to you undressing me when I return." They had lived together for fourteen years, yet his craving for her shapely body had not diminished.

Galla smiled alluringly. "When can I accompany you to a party? I wish to learn new recipes for you to taste."

"Like I have said before, these parties would bore you."

The freedwoman hid a grimace, knowing the truth was that he considered her unworthy to show off to acquaintances with their cultured wives. "How will I cook fashionable meals for guests when you host dinners?"

"I will try to bring back leftovers."

He headed out the door, already pondering which jokes he would use at the party. Adeodatus, coming back from an outing with his friends, greeted his father. Augustine gave a brief nod then continued down the street. At the forum, he met up with Alypius, and they walked together to the villa of Firminus, an orator known for his wit and wine. As the evening progressed, slaves kept cups full as guests ate the lavish courses with their hands.

"A friend of mine said you foretold his future by studying his constellation when he visited Carthage a few years ago." Firminus took no notice of warm grease dripped down his hand.

"I used to give readings but have not done so in several years."

"Will you read my future? I am intrigue to know what you believe the stars have to say about me."

Augustine took a sip of wine to buy time. "I can do so, but I warn you that my lack of accuracy has almost persuaded me that it is a vain practice." And Nebridius's many debates against astrology, but Augustine kept that to himself.

"My father was extremely curious about it to the point of obsession. He had a friend equally enthusiastic. They use to record such trivialities as the position of the stars at the moment a dumb animal gave birth then observed the fate of the beast to see if it followed their predictions. About the time my father learned of my coming birth, his friend had a slave who also was due to deliver. As the expected due dates were the same for both infants, the men corroborated, recorded the exact time of our births then sending a messenger to the other's estate to pass on the information. The messengers meet in the middle, confirming that the slave and I were born down to the exact minute. Can you predict what the stars foretold about me?"

"The obvious answer is that you would grow up to become a wealthy man of high honors."

"And the slave?" Firminus slurped on jellyfish whose stingers had been removed.

"As you both shared the same star alignment, he also should have been wealthy and famous, but my own prediction is he is still a slave who owns not even the clothes he wears."

"Observant you are." Firminus held up his goblet, and a slave hurried over to fill it. He nodded to the slave who was the one from is story. "When I grew up, I bought the slave that interested my father. Can you explain why the slave and I have different fates but the same constellation? Is this not against the rules of astrology?"

"Because I can predict your future by your circumstances, not by the stars. My faith that the heavens control the fate of men grows ever dimmer."

"A pity. I have had hopes that perhaps the slave would one day be blessed by wealth, though not as rich as me, of course."

"That is something you have the power to control, not the stars."

On the way home Augustine pondered the conversation, saying little to Alypius. They walked along the quiet, dark streets. Their only light came from a few lamps in windows of homes where the occupants had not yet went to sleep. He no longer believed Mani held truth. Astrology was a fabrication. The pagan gods of his father were mythical. What else was he left to believe in? Was there more to life than the reality he saw every day? He paused to look at the night stars which twinkled brightly in their sea of blackness. An awareness of beauty, of something mysterious and wonderful lay just out of his reach. He tried to hold onto the feeling, to understand it, but it slowly faded away. In the morning, he knew the sun would rise and vanquish both the stars and alluring colors of dawn. The humdrum of life would continue.

Chapter Eighteen

The center of the world revolved around Augustine as he stood in the middle of a vast marble chamber with hundreds of dignitaries listening to him. Today the official panegyric was to be delivered on the emperor's birthday. The most powerful people in the nation were listening to his words, his opinions. Fourteen-year-old Valentinian II, dressed in a splendid toga, sat on his throne, observing the events around him. People lived or died by the boy's command. Empress Justina hovered near her son's side, her keen eyes missing little, her face authoritative. Consuls, senators, and several military officers sat on stone benches encircling Augustine.

Even with endless practice in front of friends, Augustine was still nervous. Over the years, he had delivered countless speeches, won orator contests, taught the secrets of rhetoric to students. Still, this was a terrifying experience. Each phrase had been deliberately structured, it's many meanings carefully examined by his roommates. The speech was full of flattery and fluff, bragging about how wonderful Valentinian's rule was. Serious issues were avoided except in brief, neutral comments. Owing Symmachus for the appointment, Augustine did include a veiled appeal for religious tolerance, but even that line was left open for interpretation by the listeners. If someone was offended, Augustine could later claim the line had a different meaning.

The syllables rolled off his skilled tongue, his voice strong. Here every word, every phrase was his building blocks in crafting his future, his career. But even as he spoke, his soul quivered in disgust, shamed that his speech was full of lies. Even as the listeners laughed at his jokes against the emperor's enemies and clapped with enthusiasm at the end, Augustine felt empty inside. Seeing the serious face of the youthful emperor who carried the weight of a fragmented kingdom reminded Augustine of his own youthful dreams of beauty and wisdom. At the age of thirty-one, he had become just another ambitious flatter, the antithesis of who he desired to be.

Applause surrounded him, the echoes in the marble chamber rolling over him and through him. He had achieved so much. Yet greater honor beckoned.

Why then did this victory feel hollow? Why did the praise of men which had motivated him since childhood no long bring satisfaction?

Finishing his speech, Augustine took his place on the benches as others spoke. The feast which followed was prepared by a professional chief creating tasty dishes inspired from cultures across the empire. Galla would have loved it, but Augustine had not invited her. This was no place for the illiterate. Patricians greeted Augustine, praising his speech and inviting him to future dinner parties. Augustine charmingly accepted each time, speaking by rote when inwardly he felt bleak. The feast over, Augustine went back to the lavish villa serving as his home and buried himself in reading, seeking elusive wisdom that continued to beckon but he could not grasp.

A depression slowly crept into Augustine's soul, a poison that could not be cured with the renowned books of the Platonists. They only heightened his sense of perplexity. His friends detected his gloomy state but could not understand its cause. Nebridius had long ago accepted that wisdom was a lifetime pursuit that never ended. Alypius was too caught up with the lures of the imperial city to fret over unanswered philosophical questions. Galla worried about her lover and attempted to cheer him up with succulent meals and passionate nights.

Summer break drew to an end, bringing with it visitors from Thagaste. A few months before Romanianus had written, bragging about how proud he was of Augustine's achievements and asking if several local youths could come to the imperial city to be educated. Augustine had agreed, making the needed arrangements and finding a suitable apartment for them.

One hot afternoon, a slave announced visitors. Augustine left his study cluttered with scrolls and strolled into the roofless atrium. Sunlight beamed down on the Thagaste natives standing in the center of the tiled floor. A few sat on benches in the shade beside potted plants. Slaves brought refreshments on trays, ignoring two youths splashing each other with water from a marble fountain.

Romanianus held out a strong hand and clasp Augustine's arm in greeting. "Well done, friend. I knew from the first moment you spoke as a youth visiting my villa with your father that you would rise high. You have many admirers back home."

"I hope the voyage was not difficult." Augustine glanced at the other faces of the visitors, recognizing two of his young cousins along with his mother and brother. Immediately he felt a tightening of his stomach. Why did she have to come?

"Actually, it was alarming. We were caught in a storm so vicious that even the seasoned crew feared our ship would capsize. To be truthful, every man on the ship quivered in terror, even I who has made the voyage many times." Romanianus glanced at Monnica. "It was your mother who comforted us in our darkest hours, calm in the midst of great danger."

Monnica gave a polite smile. "God had already promised our safe arrival in a dream I had before leaving Thagaste. What had I to fear? He has never broken a promise."

"Your mother is a fascinating character. We have spent many hours in deep conversations about God. I can see where you get your intelligence from."

Augustine kept his grimace to himself. Leave it to his mother to turn a trek into an evangelistic mission. If she stayed here long, she might soon have all his students baptized. "I am grateful for your safe passage. This must be your younger son Licentius. He barely reached my waist when we last met. I remember he was bright with curiosity."

Romanianus beamed. "You will still find him eager for learning, a sponge who soaks up your knowledge. I should know, for he never tires of asking me questions. And this is Trygetius, a close friend of his whose father is on the city council."

"Greetings to you both. And to my cousins Lastidianus and Rusticus. In your first letter home, send my greetings to your mother. I am pleased to be teaching fellow Africans. But I will warn you, in my class I will show no favoritism. It matters not if you are the son of a senator or my relative. I push my students hard, and in return I expect you to dazzle me with your elegant speeches. If you come to just enjoy the sights of Milan, then I suggest you return home with Romanianus and save your fathers some money."

The four teenagers immediately replied they were ready for any challenge. To prove it, Licentius stepped forward and quoted a passage from the *Aeneid*.

> Friends, where are you bound? I beg you now
> By all the brave things you have done,
> The wars fought through, your leader, great Evander,
> With my own hopes of emulating him,
> Put no faith in retreat. The way ahead
> Has to be cleared by cold steel through the enemy.
> There where the mass of them is heaviest
> Your proud land calls you forward, and calls me.

The youth looked boldly at Augustine. "We are ready, sir. The deep sea lies behind us. There is no retreat."

Augustine smiled. "You have fortitude, soldier. Good, as you will need it. I have an apartment already chosen near the forum. I expect you to all be on time to every class." Augustine next turned his attention to his mother and brother. "How long is your stay?"

Navigius said, "I will sail back with Romanianus. I do not want to be away from my family for long. My daughters are growing like wildflowers."

"Bright girls they are. I will miss them, but my place is here." Monnica gave Augustine an audacious look. Her hair had faded almost completely to grey, her face revealing more wrinkles since Augustine had last seen her on the night he had abandoned her at the seaside shrine.

He sighed, knowing this time he could not simply vanish. "You will find Galla in the kitchen cooking."

"And my grandson?"

"He is out someplace with friends. Now to show my newest students their home."

Augustine led the four youths through the streets to their apartment. Romanianus approved of its quality and location. The teenagers' excitement of being away from home reminded Augustine of his own youth when he first arrived in Carthage, dreaming of romance and adventure. He had discovered both but too soon was grounded with the responsibilities of taking care of a family he had not been ready for. Hopefully they avoided such a fate.

When he returned to the villa, Monnica was already quickly settling in, having the slaves rearrange furniture in her new bedroom. "Mother, are you aware I do not own this place? We are only guests here."

"Yes, I have already been informed. But I need my bed turned so I may have better lighting when the sun rises. When the owners return, I will have it moved back if it displeases them." Monnica took her son's hands and peered deep into his eyes, into his soul. "Are you well?"

Augustine pulled away, troubled. "My health is fine."

"Galla says you are no longer a Manichean. Will you go to church with me tomorrow?" There was no gloating in her voice, just calm expectedness.

"I am busy. Besides I have already gone a few times to critique Ambrose's oratorical skill."

"Your verdict?"

"That he is not as soothing and entertaining as Faustus, but he is more learned. A pity he turned from politics to religion. He could have risen far."

"Perhaps he sees the path he chose as rising higher than what the world has to offer."

"I hear the calling that supper is ready to be served."

As Augustine and his mother crossed the mosaic floor of the atrium, Adeodatus walked through the front door. Seeing Monnica, the teenager's face lit up.

"Grandmother, you came!" The youth rushed over and hugged her.

"How could I not come to visit you? You are my favorite grandson."

"I am your only grandson," laughed Adeodatus.

"Let me look at you. Nearly as tall as I am. So handsome. How old are you now?"

"Thirteen. How I missed you. Will you need an escort around the city to the shrines of the martyrs? I know where each is located."

"I would appreciate that."

Augustine cut in, "They do not offer wine and bread here. Ambrose forbade it."

Monnica frowned. "The martyrs are still honored in Milan, are they not?"

"Yes, people worship at the shrines, but they carry no offerings." He studied his mother, watching for a reaction of anger at being deny something she strongly believed in.

Monnica only shrugged. "If the bishop has forbidden it, I am sure he has a good reason. Adeodatus, I would appreciate a tour of the city tomorrow."

They ate on an elegant table displaying patterns created from small, colored tiles. Nebridius and Alypius greeted Monnica and her younger son, both casting curious glances at Augustine, asking silently if she was staying. His nod confirmed their suspicious. Galla directed slaves to serve the food, herself too busy preparing the next course to sit down and eat with the others. Monnica observed the occasional interactions between Augustine and Galla, a slight frown creasing her face.

With the new school year starting in just over a week, Adeodatus spent every spare moment he had with his grandmother, even introducing her to his friends who she greeted warmly. They toured the imperial city, visiting every shrine, discussing the fate of each martyr. Just outside the city wall, they watched builders placing stone for the foundation of a new church to be called Basilica Martyrum. Just like in his childhood, Adeodatus was eager to talk with Monnica for she understood him in ways his parents could not. They attended church services in Milan, where Monnica introduced herself and Adeodatus to the bishop. Ambrose gave her names of like-minded women to contact who had a ministry of helping poverty-stricken widows.

The four Thagaste students were eager to explore the city before classes started. As Licentius was Alypius's cousin, the jurisconsult gave them a tour of the large forum complex, and they watched several court trials he was helping with. They relished plays at the theaters and chariot races at the huge circus. Coming from a small town, the teenagers were thrilled. The gladiator battles where not in session, but Alypius praised them highly, describing his favorite battles. Romanianus attended several of their outings, enjoying the attractions with his son. When school began, he reminded the youths that high expectations rested on them and they must not bring dishonor to their parents. Then he and Navigius departed, beginning the long trip home to Thagaste.

Augustine poured his energy into teaching, pleased to see that the African students held their own against the native Milanese. He avoided home and his mother as much as possible, spending most evenings out with friends, dining with the powerful. Occasionally he did attend church services with his family, so as to have material to comment on at parties. In certain political circles, Ambrose's name came up often. Augustine had long ago lost interest in sermons, as most priests lacked a rhetoric education. Augustine's schooling had trained him to judge a speaker based on elegance and diction. Many priests only had a basic education, their sermons simple and unrefined. They spoke from the heart, but were unable to impress Augustine.

Ambrose was different than any priest Augustine had met before. Highly educated, Ambrose had risen up the ranks of politics, becoming a popular governor of the province of Liguria. When the late bishop of Milan died, a heated debate broke out between Catholics and Arians over who should receive the new appointment. Fearing a riot, Ambrose went to the church, giving a speech to calm everyone. Somebody called out, "Bishop, Ambrose!" The chant was quickly taken up by others who saw Ambrose as a balanced candidate, though he was a professed Catholic. Ambrose refused the office, reminding them he had neither been baptized nor was a theologian. They pressed him, declaring him bishop without his consent. Ambrose fled to a friend's house and hid, refusing to leave despite demands in the streets. Emperor Gratian heard about the matter and wrote to the friend, praising the choice of Ambrose. The friend felt it was his duty to turn Ambrose over, and within a week the former governor was baptized and ordained, becoming the duly consecrated bishop of Milan. Another individual might had become bitter about being ripped from power and thrust into a completely different vocation. Ambrose spent weeks in prayer, leading him to accept the position as God's will. He poured his passion into the ministry. The skills he had developed as a politician served him well as bishop, and he remained highly popular, his influence felt by the elite of the empire, including his enemies like Symmachus.

At first Augustine came to church services only to critique Ambrose's oratorical skills, but soon he was drawn into the content. The bishop smoothly wove quotes of Virgil and the Platonists into sermons while explaining how their understanding of God fell short of the holy scripture. The Manicheans had heavily criticized the lives of the Patriarchs. Ambrose presented them as a stately procession symbolizing souls purified by wisdom. He expounded on the figurative meaning of verses, examining their multifaceted implications. Augustine found himself rethinking his understanding of Catholic beliefs. He had perceived the whole universe as material and God a spirit made up of particles that came from the material. Ambrose, like the Platonists, saw God as otherworldly. Augustine went back and reread the letters of Paul, discovering new meanings that had been invisible to him before.

Left with nothing else to believe in, Augustine became a catechumen. Many were dedicated believers who spent months attending daily services, memorizing scriptures, seeking deep understanding. Once a year at Easter the new converts were baptized, publicly declaring they would live a holy life. Then there were catechumen like him. Christianity was currently the popular religion of the elite who held power, and many ambitious men claimed the religion in order to mingle among the ranks of the influential. Doing so allowed them to be accepted by baptized Christians without the expectation of keeping to all the strict rules. Some, including Constantine, the first emperor to make Christianity the state religion, remained a catechumen until death approached. Then they were baptized, living sanctified lives their few remaining days.

Augustine took the easy path, declaring himself a catechumen without the commitment, waiting until another appealing road came along.

Chapter Nineteen

Guests applauded dancers clad in scanty outfits, wiggling their bodies to the thumping of drums. Colorful mosaics on the walls displayed adventures of gods and heroes. Iiertoer coupling with a bull, leading to the birth of the Minotaur. The centaur Eurytion trying to rape a bride, sparking the battle of Lapithae. The orgies of Bacchus, couples entwined with grape vines. Zeus pursuing yet another beautiful woman.

Augustine reclined on a couch beside Firminus who hosted the party. The guests ate lavish dishes with their hands. Nearby on another couch Firminius's wife flirted with a handsome guest half her age. Her husband took no notice.

"You, a catechumen? I laughed when I heard." Firminus emptied his wine goblet. "Do you really believe such a move will lift you into the inner circle of power? Marriage is the only way to insure a permanent position."

"I have a concubine who satisfies me."

"I have a lover who satisfies me too." Firminus fondly patted the hand of the young slave filling his cup. The boy had not quite reached adolescence. "Why should that prevent you from marriage?"

Augustine glanced towards Firminus's wife deep in conversation with her neighbor, her hand sliding down his arm. "Your wife is acceptable of this?"

"Of course. Even when our nation was a republic such arrangements were common. Ambition men rising in politics must wait years before their ranks are high enough to earn marriage into a reputable family. A man has needs in the meantime. Once married, a man is expected to put away his lovers, but some of us find the attraction too strong." Firminus smiled at the boy. "I did my duty and fathered two heirs. But why should I restrain myself? The gods have limitless lovers. Are not we humans supposed to imitate them?"

"Still, I cannot send away my concubine. She birthed my son."

"So? There are many slaves who carry the bloodline of their masters. And why do you need to send her away? Keep both." The slave boy placed grapes one by one into his master's mouth. "Or if it eases your new Catholic conscience, reward her well for her services when you kick her out. That is what I do when my lovers reach adulthood, if they have pleased me." He winked at the youth who smiled shyly. "I give them emancipation and startup money. Some have become successful businessmen, thanks to my patronage. Of course, if a lover dissatisfies me, I crush them completely. But rarely have I needed to deal with that problem."

Firminius's words became hooks in Augustine's soul as he pondered his future. Many men took this path, including his own father. Why should he not also have a proper wife from a prosperous family? Without wealth how else was he to gain a government position? Surely he was not fated to spend his whole life teaching future politicians while he never become one himself. He was talented and deserved a political post. What power and influence he could achieve!

The next afternoon when only Nebridius and Alypius were in the study with him, Augustine discussed getting married. The more he talked, the deeper became Nebridius's frown. Alypius at first was repelled but stayed open-minded.

"What about Galla?" Nebridius leaned forward on his couch, his scroll lay forgotten beside him.

"What about her? She will benefit by living in a house that is really mine instead of borrowed."

"Have you asked her feelings in this matter?"

"Perhaps when you were married, you asked your wife's permission before acting, but I am a Roman citizen. My lovers do what I say."

Nebridius flinched at the reminder that as a former slave, he would never have the rights of full citizenship. He stood up, hands clenched in fists for a moment then allowed himself to relax "You are setting yourself up for misery, *friend.*"

"I apology for my hasty words."

"I think my time will be better spent at the forum today." Nebridius walked out of the room.

Augustine turned to Alypius. "Do you also think I am wrong?"

"Of course. Have I not said many times that I find your robust cravings for sex disgusting? Why do you seek yet another lover? Is one not enough?"

"Sex is the most extreme pleasure a man can have. You cannot base your whole opinion on one fleeting incident you had in your youth. Your celibacy is unnatural."

"You did not claim celibacy as unnatural when you were aiming to become an Elect among the Manicheans."

Augustine frowned, not wishing for the reminder. "Yes, I will admit it was the one vow I could never keep. Imagine the authority you could gain with the right wife. Perhaps becoming a proconsul. And you could experience the true pleasure women were designed for."

Alypius tapped his fingers, considering. "Perhaps I have been hasty in my judgment of marriage. I have not been given a new appointment for over a year, only giving private advice to individuals. A rich wife could gain me the attention I need."

Augustine smiled, relieved to have one understanding comrade. "You will not regret it. Now to deal with my mother."

He waited until she came back from evening prayers. She smiled when he invited her for a stroll in the large, cultivated garden. They ambled along the brick path bordered by fragrant flowers and stone benches. Among the fruit trees they discussed Ambrose's latest sermon. Then Augustine casually brought up his desire for marriage.

Monnica's steps faltered. "Marriage?"

"Have you not wanted this for me my whole life? I leave it to your judgment to find the perfect wife for me. She must be rich, from an influential family. Young, not set in her ways."

"Have you told Galla and your son yet?"

"I will tell them soon."

Monnica studied her son. "A marriage pleasing God is the right decision, but it will be difficult for Adeodatus to lose his mother."

"Why should he grieve? Galla will still be living here."

Monnica gasped in shock. "You cannot commit such a sinful offense."

"Why not? Father did so."

"And I bore the agony and shame of his sins. You are not your father. I had hoped I raised you to be better than him. You cannot treat Galla like this. It is unfair to both her and your future wife. Marry but send Galla away."

"This is my life, my decision. If you wish to not choose my wife, then I will find one myself."

Monnica closed her eyes, lips moving in silent prayer. When she finished, she looked at her son with steel determination. "I will help you in obtaining a wife." As her son walked away, she whispered quietly, "Perhaps this is the path which will finally bring you to God."

Augustine waited to tell Galla until late that night, after their bodies were intertwined. As he stroked her blonde hair, he casually said, "I have discovered a path to furthering my career."

She snuggled closer, her arms wrapped around his lean torso. "What is that?"

"I must marry into a rich family."

"Marry?" Galla stiffen then pulled back. "Marry? What about me? Your son?"

"You will both continue to live with me. It will be a political marriage and you will be my bed companion most of the time, though I must still preform my husbandry duties."

"You cannot do this. It is a great sin." Galla's voice was on the edge of panic.

"And us living together is not?"

"You know the law forbids a marriage between freed slaves and patricians. As long as we are loyal to each other, our relationship is….partly acceptable."

"I have already asked my mother to begin looking for my bride. It takes money, much of it, to climb high in politics. I cannot be a teacher my whole life."

"What is wrong with being a teacher?"

"You would not understand a man's desire to become something more, someone great who is admired throughout the ages."

"Nor do you understand a woman's need to be truly loved." Galla climbed out of bed.

"There is no need to become upset. I marry not for love. It is your beauty that fulfills my longing. Besides, you will benefit from my marriage too. With my wealth you will have new dresses and jewelry."

"Am I just a harlot to you? One bought with fancy clothes?" She pulled on a dress and fled from the room, breaking into sobs when she was out of his sight.

Augustine lay in the darkness. Why was Galla being so difficult? Countless Roman families had such arrangements. Why did she have to take her Catholic beliefs so serious? He sighed and rolled over, drifting slowly back into sleep. Surely tomorrow reason will set in and Galla will understand he did this to bring greater honor to the family.

But Galla refused to share Augustine's view. She remained isolated, leaving the slaves to prepare bland meals. Her weeping could be heard from behind a closed door of an extra bedroom. Monnica tried to comfort her, but Galla responded venomously, blaming the mother for the son's rejection. Galla only allowed Adeodatus into her room. The youth tried to cheer up his mother, but his words of comfort were hollow, himself feeling the ache of betrayal. Why would his father treat his mother this way?

For a week Augustine ignored Galla's moping. Finally tiring of it, he entered her room despite her protests for him to leave.

"Enough of this crying. If you wish to keep my love, stop weeping, clean yourself up, and focus on your duties again."

She looked at him with teary eyes. "How have I dissatisfied you? Am I no longer beautiful?"

"You are a radiant star, your hair a halo of sunshine."

"Words of flattery come so easily for you. Is there any sincerity left within you?"

"I am sincere in that I miss you." He stepped closer. "My bed is a desolate crypt without you."

"You will have a wife soon enough to comfort you."

"It is you I long for." Augustine wrapped his arms around her slender waist, pulling her close. She tried to pull away but he kissed her. She resisted only for a moment then melted against him. Augustine held her close, relieved that the crisis had passed. Tonight he would enjoy their passionate making-up.

Galla attempted a different approach. She poured herself into cooking the most elaborate meals she had yet made, every dinner having at least four courses. Despite the long hours she spent in the kitchen, she dressed in her finest clothes, her hair braided into the latest styles. Determination and despair motivated her. If she could just be beautiful and useful enough, he would forget about taking a wife.

When home, Adeodatus's keen eyes constantly observed his parents. His mother's obsession for the perfect meal and the cleanest rooms. His father claiming the meals were delicious then withdrawing to read with his friends or headed out for another party. Only with his grandmother was Adeodatus able to speak openly of his fears. She tried to comfort him but promised no happy future, gently reminding him that his parents' relationship was outside God's blessing.

Several tense months later, Monnica approached her son with the news she had found a potential bride. Augustine put down the letter he had been writing to Romanianus. "Who is the family?"

Monnica was about to speak when Galla walked into the study with a tray of refreshments. When she hesitated, Augustine prompted her, "Speak openly. It is no secret that I will marry." Galla's hands trembled as she sat the tray down, but he pretended to take no notice.

"Lovernianus. He and his wife seek a distinguished husband for their second daughter."

Augustine allowed a brief smile to flirt across his lips. "An influential family with connections to the senate. Well-spoken of at church. You have done well, Mother."

"They do have one condition. They will not wed their daughter to anyone who has a concubine. You must agree to live two years without yours."

"Two years?"

"That is when the daughter turns of age for marriage."

A cup fell from Galla's limp hand and crashed to the floor, its contents soiling the edge of Augustine's toga. He jumped up. The angry oath he was about to unleash froze on his lips when he saw her pale face and trembling lips. For a moment he could find no words to speak. Finally he said to his mother, "Could you not find a better arrangement? One that accepts concubines?"

"Not among Christians. Such a thing is forbidden."

"Then look to pagan families."

"I will not." Monnica's face was firm, her resolve ready for any battle. "I will not willingly allow any of my children to marry anyone who is not a Christian."

"I can bypass you and find my own wife."

"Yes, you could. But we both know that nearly all the most powerful political families are Christian. You will not find a better offer than this one."

Augustine looked between his calm mother and quivering lover. "I will need time to consider this offer." He turned and walked out of the study.

A sob escaped from Galla as she sunk to the tiled floor among the broken shards and spilled wine. "How could you do this to me? He will choose her."

Monnica knelt beside Galla. "It is time for you to let go of my son."

"Get away from me," spat out Galla. "You have always despised me, seeing me unworthy of your son. Well, you finally got your way. Go brag to your saintly friends. The whore is finally being sent away."

Monnica flinched. "You misunderstand my intentions. I have never hated you, but was disappointed you were living in sin with my son. You knew from the beginning that imperial law forbid a holy union between the two of you, yet you still chose to move in with him. You did not have his excuse to being blind to the truth. You knew God's commandments and chose to disobey. Now you must live with the consequences."

Galla burst into tears. "I love him. How can that be wrong?"

The older woman's face softened. "Oh, Galla, if you just had been patient and waited. Did you not think that if you had asked, God would have sent you a Christian husband? He may not have been a rich patrician, but he would have chosen you over a career."

A sob escaped Galla. "A daughter. I always wanted one, but Augustine forbad me to have more children." Galla looked up, strains of hair clinging to her wet cheeks. "What am I to do? Who else would want me now? I am too old. And I have a son."

"You are not old. But why do you need a man at all? Seek God instead. Take it from someone who has been through the trials you are about to endure. God will never leave you nor abandon you. He will comfort you in your darkest hours."

"I cannot survive without Augustine."

"You have made my son the god of your life. Now it is time to make the Son of God the sole ruler of your life."

"I have not your strength, nor education, nor money. I am nobody."

"Not to God. Surrender your life totally to him, and you will find new purpose. And it is not to be someone else's concubine."

When Augustine finally returned, he found Galla red-eyed and pale, but resigned to her fate—making it easier for him to announce his intentions. "Pack your things. I will pay for your passage back to Africa where I am certain your family will take you back in."

"And our son?" Galla's voice quavered.

"I will provide for him here where he can receive the finest education and best opportunities."

Acting quickly, Augustine secured passage with a friend who would be traveling to Rome in a few days. From there Galla would travel to a port and take a ship back to Carthage. The parting was painful for all. Adeodatus hugged his mother, trying not to cry, but a single tear ran down his cheek. Monnica pressed an extra bag of coins into Galla's hand, promising to pray daily for her. Alypius and Nebridius gave Galla letters to be delivered to their families.

"My parents will welcome you anytime," said Nebridius. "Stay with them for a while."

"Perhaps I will after seeing my own family." Galla forced a smile, her deep grief barely kept in check. "I appreciate the kindness they showed me."

Augustine escorted Galla to his friend's house. They spoke little, but his heart felt torn from him. What choice remained to him? He needed a proper wife. Galla could never be that. When he turned to leave her, he found his feet rooted, pain in his chest crushing him. She had supported him when he was nothing more than a youth with big dreams and little money. She had stood by his side when he was homeless, tended him when depression overwhelmed him.

Seeing him waver, Galla said, "Go, my love. A bright future beckons you."

"You have been loyal even when I took you for granted. If there was just some way I could have you and a wife too." He touched her cheek.

She pulled back. "Nay, do not tempt me. I have already made my peace with God and will know no man again."

He held her hand until she pulled it from him. Without another word she turned and walked into the house. The door shut, leaving him alone on the narrow street. Nearby buildings blocked the morning sun, casting Augustine into shadow.

Chapter Twenty

The child stood placid in front of the adults discussing her future. Hair curled, dress white, face blank, she looked like a doll. From the moment of her birth, she had been groomed for becoming a bride of a politician. Her education and training centered on running a household. Only ten, she knew weaving, harp playing, financing, and reciting classic Greek literature. Her potential husband and mother-in-law asked her several questions which she answered in polite, sophisticated words as she had been trained to do. Then her parents dismissed her to continuing studying with her governess.

Augustine gave his approval, and the haggling over the dowry began. Her parents liked Augustine's charisma and charm, believing he had a bright political future ahead of him. They respected his mother, and though they knew Augustine was only on the verge of Christianity, they trusted he would grow more religious over time. Promises where offered on both sides, the dowry agreed upon, and the wedding date set two years in the future, once the girl turned twelve, the legal age for marriage. The child's opinion of the matter was never sought.

Monnica was pleased that her son was finally engaged, and she eagerly looked forward to more grandchildren. She was certain that by him marrying into a Christian family, he would draw closer to God. Augustine, though, was tormented. He missed Galla more intensely than he could ever have imagined. Walking along crowded streets, he unconsciously sought her face, his heart quickening when he caught glimpses of blonde hair. Then disappoint when it was always someone else. Meals cooked by the household slaves were bland. He avoided eating at home, dining on the succulent dishes at dinner parties, trying to forget how much Galla would love tasting them. Nights were the worst. He lay in the empty bed, missing her touch, her comforting body.

The depression that had plagued him for months deepened its hold, sucking all happiness from him. He taught classes by rote, putting little enthusiasm into his lessons. He read every Platonists book he could find, believing someplace in the ancient text he would finally discover true insight. Sexual desire grew till it began to overwhelm him. Two years without a woman was asking too much.

Despite his craving, he refused to visit a brothel, viewing them as lewd entertainment. One day at the market he noticed a peddler flirting with customers. Her body was well endowed, so he flirted back. He came by her booth every day for a week. She always greeted him alluringly, so he asked her to move in with him. No love was involved, only lust. He was just one of a long list of lovers for her. When one tired of her, she just moved on to the next.

Monnica was furious when her son came home with the peddler. "You promised two years without a concubine."

"Clara is not a concubine. She knows I am engaged and this is only a temporary arrangement."

"What happens when Lovernianus finds out? He might call off the wedding."

"Then do not tell him, Mother. You do want me properly married after all."

She tried to reason with him, but he brushed her concerns away. She withdrew to the nearest church to fast and pray.

The prick of Augustine's conscience was strongest whenever he looked at his son. Adeodatus had his mother's blue eyes and blonde hair. Father and son rarely saw each other, as both avoided home as much as possible. When they did happen to meet, Adeodatus stared silently, but accusingly at his father. Augustine felt the youth's anger but chose to ignore it. He told himself that one day his son would be thankful to have a well-connected father.

One morning Augustine's lessons fell apart when two students began hitting each other with their wax tablets. Discipline was hard to restore, so his dismissed the class early. When he returned home, he was surprised to find his son dragging a heavy woven bag through the atrium.

"Why are you not at school?"

The fourteen year old kept a firm grip on the large bag. "I had something to do. Why are you home earlier?"

"I am the one asking questions here, not you. I am paying for your education and you are wasting it by not attending classes. How dare you throw away the opportunities I have provided for you."

Anger flared in Adeodatus's eyes. "You see me but are blind to who I really am, Father."

"I am not blind."

"You cannot see truth when it stands right in front of you."

Augustine searched his son's face and saw pain in the youth's eyes. "I know you hate me right now, but what I do is for you also. As you begin your career, you can use my contacts to advance yourself."

"Do you even know which career I have chosen?"

"Politics, of course."

"Nay, Father. I will become a teacher like you."

Augustine opened his mouth, surprised. "A teacher? The pay is too low. The profession is decent only as a stepping stone. You must aim higher."

"You once believed teaching was an honorable occupation."

"No longer. If you want to be a teacher, then why did you skip school today? What is in that bag you are carrying?"

"You still judge without truly seeing. I did go to school. My instructor is promoting a clothing drive for the needy at church. I came by to pick up cloth Grandmother donated."

"Donations?" Feeling chagrin, Augustine changed topics. This was the longest conversation he had with his son months. "I know you are upset about me sending your mother away, but it was for the best."

"I have accepted that, Father. Away from your tarnishing, my mother can finally be baptized and take her proper place as one of God's sanctified."

The forthrightness of his son jolted Augustine. "I see you have been strongly influenced by your grandmother."

"And by the priests. I do pay attention to sermons."

"Yet you are still angry with me. Are you concerned that when I have more children, you will be left out of the inheritance? I will make certain to include you in my will."

Adeodatus frowned in disgust. "Is money all you think I am after? You do not know my heart at all, Father. How many times after school have I practiced speeches with my friends, dreaming of one day earning your praises like the ones you shower on your prizewinning students? When I do practice in front of you, all I receive is criticism."

"I am trying to help you improve your delivery."

"I know. For years, all I wanted from you was for you to be proud of me. But no longer. My fury is too great to care what you think about me. I hate that you have brought in a woman barely better than a harlot to replace my mother. I am trying to forgive you, as you are yet blind. But it a difficult struggle for me."

"You keep referring to me as blind, yet I see far more than most men. Barely older than you, I was able to comprehend books others struggled with. Even my rhetoric teacher could not understand Aristotle's *Ten Categories* without attending lectures. But with one reading I was able to comprehend it without any need of an expositor."

"Truth is not complicated, Father. Even a child can understand it." Adeodatus picked up the heavy bag and stepped out of the villa, alone.

Augustine watched his son leave, realizing Adeodatus had grown into a young man, intelligent and capable, but to Augustine he was a stranger. "I have become my own father," Augustine whispered, loathing himself. Like Patricius, he was ambitious, seeking admiration from the public, but emotionally distant from his own family. "I was going to be a wiser man than he. Why have my dreams faltered? How have I turned into the very image of what I despised the most?"

He stared at water running endlessly in a marble fountain. No matter how high a droplet splashed after it burst forth from the lead pipe, it was doomed to fall into the marble basin, merging with the mass of churning water. Was his life as pointless as a droplet that fleetingly glistened like a jewel in sunlight only to fade away into oblivion?

In February an argument over church property stirred up heighten tensions between Catholics and Arians. Empress Justina, supported by several clergy and military officers, demanded that two basilicas be turned over for Arian worship. Ambrose refused, giving a powerful speech at the council, persuading most of Valentinian II's ministers to support his side. The next day Justina sent the prefect of the city to persuade Ambrose to give up the recently constructed Basilica Martyrum. Viewing Arians as a heretical sect, Ambrose refused to give in to their demands.

Threats were issued by Justina. Ambrose spoke to his church leaders and congregation, informing them of Justina's degrees. Crowds of angry citizens marched through the streets. Justina placed her court courtiers under curfew, fearful they might join in the usurper. A court official placed a large imperial flag on the basilica, declaring it government property. Hundreds of Catholics flocked to the church, united in their stand against the Empress. Concerned that the church would be taking by force, Ambrose asked for volunteers to keep vigil in the building both day and night.

Monnica was one of the first to step forward. She helped organize volunteers, encouraging those who felt their cause was hopeless, bringing meals to those who were taking part in the vigil. Many nights she knelt for hours on the stone floor of Basilica Martyrum, praying for Justina' heart to change and that of her son.

Several intense weeks later, Augustine walked into his villa after only teaching for an hour. There was too much tension in the streets and he thought it safer for his students to be in their homes. His mother was busy packing a lunch while Adeodatus filled old wineskins with water.

Augustine frowned as he watched his son work. "Where are you heading today? It is too dangerous to be in the streets."

Monnica did not pause in her preparations. "We are going to Basilica Martyrum."

"Have the harpies stolen your sanity? Empress Justina has pulled troops from the frontier. They arrived yesterday."

"I am aware of that. Adeodatus, pass me that loaf."

"You are going to have a picnic in the midst of a massacre?"

Monnica looked directly at Augustine. "The basilica is dedicated to the martyrs who lost their lives for taking a stand for God. We are asked to do no less. Goodbye, son."

She grabbed one basket and Adeodatus the other. Augustine stared for a moment, speechless. Then he sputtered, "I forbid you to go."

Monnica turned her sharp gaze on him. "Forbid? Need I remind you that I am *domina* and you cannot do so?"

"But I can command my son. Adeodatus, go to your room and study."

The youth looked between his grandmother and Augustine. "I obey you in most things, Father, but in this matter I must answer to a higher power."

The teenager walked out of the villa with Monnica, leaving Augustine fuming— yet puzzled. The logical course of action was to stay home, safe from the chaos. Why risk lives over a building? It was just stone and wood. What if Emperor Valentinian realized that Augustine's family was taking a stand against his policies? Would that endanger Augustine's career? The teacher clenched his fists, angry that his mother was so selfish, worrying more about a building than how her actions impacted her family.

When Adeodatus and Monnica arrived at Basilica Martyrum, it was already packed with hundreds of people from all classes, their feet scuffing the shiny marble floor. Richly dressed patricians stood beside peasants in rags. Children dashed about, enjoying a holiday from classes and chores. The building still smelled of newness with the recently cut lumber beams supporting the terracotta roof. The window frames held glass panes, a rarity as glass was expensive to make. Most buildings only had window openings which were protected by wooden shutters during rain or cold weather.

Ambrose walked to the dais and everyone quieted. "God will bless you for standing with him today. The psalms we sing are dignified but cheerless. I would like to introduce you to the more vibrate musical style of the East whose hymns have touched me on my visits there. Today we worship victoriously."

With his strong voice, he sung a psalm they were familiar with but the melody was more upbeat. As he repeated it a second time, the congregation joined in, hundreds of jubilant voices blending together. For hours they sung, learning the new hymns. When word circulated that the troops had arrived, they chanted even louder, their voices carrying far.

Adeodatus moved to a window and looked out at the burly soldiers encircled the building. The troop was Gothic, pulled from the hostile frontier. Few, if any of them, would be Christians. They would harbor few qualms about attacking a church. Centuries ago, Roman officials had discovered the best way to defeat a powerful enemy was to make that enemy one of your own. Grant them citizenship, give them titles and land, and their soldiers would stand with you against other invaders.

Beyond the Goths was a cluster of Roman soldiers guarding Justina, her son, and powerful supporters who had come to watch the showdown. Through the heavy glass pane, Adeodatus studied the emperor who was his own age. Even from this distance, he could tell Valentinian II bore himself proudly, walking with the authority of those far older than himself. An official left the cluster and walked through the stern Goth soldiers. Then he entered the church. The singers quieted down and stared at the intruder.

The man said in a loud voice, "This church is the property of the empire. You are to leave immediately. When it opens for Arian worship, you may join with us if you wish." Several listeners booed. "If you continue to defy Emperor Valentinian, you will be arrested."

Eyes turned expectantly to Ambrose who calmly stood on the apex. "If you demand my person, I am ready to submit. Carry me to prison or to death. I will not resist, but I will never betray the church of Christ. I will not call upon the people to aid me. I will die at the foot of the altar rather than desert it. The tumult of the people I will not encourage, but God alone can appease it."

People in the crowd called out their support for Ambrose, promising to remain with him, no matter the cost. The official turned promptly and walked out of the church. The congregation began singing again, louder than ever. Through the glass, Adeodatus watched the official deliver the message to the royal family. Justina gestured angrily to the Gothic troops, ordering them to arrest Ambrose. Her son gave a nod in agreement. The solders tightened their circle around the church then a dozen of them entered through the front doors. Adeodatus's pulse quickened and he slipped through the crowd to be by his grandmother.

The brawny Gothic soldiers entered the large doors, their sharpened swords belted at their hips, ready for use. Catholics immediately blocked the way. Men and women, young and old, rich and poor, stood shoulder to shoulder refusing to budge. Monica was at the front of the group, Adeodatus beside her, his heart

154

pounding in fear. He looked at his grandmother, taking courage from her resolute.

The Gothic leader pulled his sword, glancing back across the street at the young emperor surrounded by nervous Arian clergy who wanted the building—but not a bloodbath. The royal youth looked from the soldier waiting for permission to use force to his angry mother and the nearby Arians muttering that the church should not be defiled by blood. Uncertainty showed on his tender face. Then a Roman general whispered into the emperor's ear, suggesting that force be withheld.

The emperor frowned but waved the Gothic soldiers back. Yet his eyes betrayed his relief to use any excuse not to issue the command which would take lives.

For hours the two sides were at a standstill. Jubilant singing poured from the church while the Gothic troops listened with blank faces. The Roman soldiers, on the other hand, had Christian relatives or were themselves converts. Attacking a church disturbed them. As the sun began to set, Valentinian finally ordered all soldiers away.

Frustrated at the division among his own followers, the young emperor complained, "If Ambrose gave you word, you would hand me over in chains to him."

Justina desired to come back tomorrow with even more soldiers, but Valentinian overrode his mother, weary with the whole issue. The Catholic had won. Monnica and Adeodatus returned home, cheerfully singing a new hymn. When they arrived, Augustine was relieved to see them alive, but complained that their defiance of the Emperor might cost him a future job promotion. He tried returning to the book he had been reading, wanting to forget their elated faces. They had faced death and survived, excitement and joy food for their souls. He survived on the words of dead philosophers and dreams of future power, but for what purpose? Did he believe strongly in anything that he was willing to die for it?

During June the streets were again filled with Catholics, this time in celebration. The bodies of two martyrs Gervasius and Protasius had been unearthed. The jubilant crowds followed the procession, carrying the holy bodies to Basilica Martyrum where they were buried with honor. The event meant little to Augustine, whose depression still clung to him, weakening his body, his throat beginning to hurt when he spoke for long periods. Sharing his bed with Clara did little to lessen his longing for Galla. Clara cooked no better than the household slaves and the pleasure she provided at night was shallow and brief. Nothing satisfied Augustine.

He wanted to question Ambrose about the books which disturbed him, but the bishop was a busy man. When Augustine greeted him at church among the crowd, Ambrose praised Monnica's devotion to various ministries. Augustine tried visiting during the evenings, but the bishop was often busy dealing with church matters or out helping others. Occasionally he saw Ambrose resting in the library. The bishop read silently, an unusual method for most scholars. Augustine came in and sat with other visitors, but no one dared disturb the weary bishop.

Late July, Augustine paid a visit to Simplicianus, a highly respected priest who had baptized Ambrose many years before. The elderly Roman greeted Augustine kindly and invited the teacher into his house. His friendliness and keen insight helped Augustine to relax. Soon Augustine felt comfortable enough to speak of his own spiritual wanderings.

Augustine sipped the water he had been offered. "I have been recently reading books by Plato which have been translated into Latin by Victorinus. I have heard that Victorinus was a rhetor in Rome who died a Christian."

Simplicianus nodded as memories of the past became alive again. "You have done well choosing to study the Platonists over other philosophers who are full of fallacies and deceptions. Years ago when I lived in Rome, Victorinus was a close friend of mine. He was extremely learned, an expert in all liberal disciplines, tutor to numerous noble senators. To honor his distinguished qualities, he was given a statue in the Forum of Trajan. Until old age, he was a firm worshipper of idols, including the foreign cults from Egypt. He defended these with such a robust voice that he terrified opponents. He studied holy scriptures of many religions, paying special care to Christian books. One day in private he told me, 'Did you know that I am already a Christian?' I replied, 'I shall not believe you or count you among us unless I see you in the Church of Christ.' He only laughed and said, 'Do walls make Christians?' We had this conversation many times. Victorinus was afraid to offend his devil-worshipping friends, fearing them turning against him. But through his reading of holy scripture, he began to long for courage, finally telling me one day he was ready to be counted a Christian.

"What joy I felt accompanying him to the church. As is our custom in Rome, new converts say our creed in front of the baptized on an elevated platform. The presbyters offered him the opportunity to say it in private, as they do to protect those embarrassed or afraid. Over the years Victorinus had used his own words in front of frenzied crowds of pagans. Now he would not be afraid to speak words praising God. I still remember that day as he climbed the steps in front of the congregation. Immediately he was recognized. Who there did not know his great works? The people spoke his name in delight, turning it into a chant, 'Victorinus! Victorinus!' Then as he began to speak, they all fell silent, eager to hear his vow. When he finished, they happily embraced him in joy." The old man's eyes lit with excitement at the memory.

"It is a well told story." Augustine said, feeling a hungry in his soul he could not understand.

Simplicianus smiled. "It is one of those golden moments when all of life blooms in beauty. A moment that stays with you forever, which you pull hope from during dark times."

"Was Victorinus shunned by his friends?"

"By some, yes. Others accepted the change, a few becoming Christians themselves because of his stand. Several years later when Emperor Julian passed that law forbidding Christians to teach literature and rhetoric, Victorinus welcomed it, preferring abandoning the school of loquacious chattering rather than God's word."

"He was fortunate to have the freedom to dedicate all his time to studying. The dream of every philosopher."

As Augustine walked home, he felt both envious and tormented, longing for the happiness that both Simplicianus and Victorinus had found. But the rules of Christianity were too harsh. Some he agreed with and others he could live with. But celibacy unless married? If he could not give up sex for Mani, how could he for God?

Chapter Twenty-one

The morning sun climbed higher into the bright sky. Alypius read from a scroll as Augustine listened. Breathing problems had been plaguing Augustine lately, causing him difficulty when lecturing students. He could not speak long before his chest burned in pain and breathing became laborious. Today was a holiday. Augustine and Alypius were relaxing, sluggish from staying out too late at a party the night before. Nebridius was away visiting friends, and Carla still slept. Adeodatus had already left to explore the city with several youths. Monnica sat in a corner, skillfully mending worn cloth which would be made into a new garment. A slave entered, announcing a visitor.

Augustine preferred turning the visitor away for his voice was unsteady, but Alypius set down the scroll he had been reading and said, "Send him in."

Ponticianus, an inspector for the imperial bureaucracy, walked into the room. Like Augustine and Alypius, he was a Berber from North Africa with olive skin and dark hair. Though born in a small town, he had risen high in the imperial court. "Greetings this fine morning. I came to borrow that book you mentioned the other day."

"Ah," said Alypius. "I have already loaned it to another. Perhaps it will be here on your next visit."

"A pity. I was looking forward to our discussion about it." Ponticianus glanced around the room cluttered with scrolls. He reached over and picked up the nearest which lay on a gaming table. Glancing at it, his eyes opened in delight. "You are reading Saint Paul! I was guessing this book would be one of your dull school texts. I too find Paul fascinating. Have you read Ephesians where he uses the imagery of wearing the armor of God?"

"No," said Augustine, his attention perking, forgetting the burning pain in his throat. "But his writings are part of a study I have been undertaking."

"I was baptized only a year ago myself, so my knowledge is also growing. The many hours I spend in prayer at church have strengthened me. I have been especially encouraged by the story of Antony the Great."

Augustine glanced at Alypius in puzzlement. "I know of no conqueror by that name."

Ponticianus laughed. "Antony did not conquer nations but himself. Surely you have heard of this famous desert hermit from Egypt? He is well-known. His life story was written down by Anthanasius of Alexandria."

Alypius leaned forward. "Tell us about him."

"Antony lived not long before our time. He was from a wealthy family but illiterate. His parents died when he was eighteen, leaving him in care of his young sister. During his early thirties, he took Jesus's words to heart, 'If you want to be perfect, go, sell what you have and give to the poor, and you will have treasures in heaven. Come and follow me.' Antony did exactly that. He sold his estate, donated the money, and placed his sister with a group of consecrated Christian virgins. Then he traveled to the desert to become a hermit, living an ascetic life devoted to worshiping God. Though he lived in isolation, his fame grew and many began seeking him out for advice. Even Emperor Constantine wrote to him, asking for prayer. Over the years many have been inspired by Antony's example, forming monasteries in Egypt were men live together fully devoted to God. Ambrose has even fostered a monastery here, just outside the city."

"A monastery in Milan?" said Augustine. "I have not heard of it."

"Seems that there is a great deal you have not heard. I myself sometimes desire such a life, free from the stresses of everyday life, especially from my job. Several years ago three friends and I were traveling with the Emperor's entourage. He noticed a circus and halted our trip to watch the races. While waiting for the games to end, my friends and I strolled through a large garden. We split into pairs. The other group wandered out of the park and happened by a house of Christians. While they waited for a drink of water, one picked up a copy of *Life of Anthony* and began reading. The text set him afire with longing for a better life. He turned to his friend and said, 'What can we hope to achieve with all our labors? What is our purpose in life? Why do we serve the state? Is not our position fragile, full of constant dangers? How many hazards must one risk to attain a position of even greater danger? I wish to become God's friend.' Then and there, he converted, walking away from all worldly ambition. As he talked to his friend, the other did so too. Shortly later when I and my companion found them, I suggested it was late and time to return. They told us about their decision to quit their jobs to devoutly serve God. I shared their longing but could not give up my job. Still, I do spend much time in prayer each evening, which has changed how I view my duties. No longer does the desire for ambition drive me, but every day I seek opportunities to aid others. I am a happier man for it."

Augustine felt shame as he listened to the stories, his conscience pricking him. Here were people who had found a truth they believed in so strongly they had given up luxurious lifestyles. "Do you have a copy of *Life of Anthony*?"

"I believe I loaned it to someone, but I will see if I can discover its location. Well, I must be off. Drop by my house when you can spare the time."

After Ponticianus left, Augustine was restless, battling with himself. The truth was staring Augustine directly in the face, and he was out of excuses for his blindness. He had long believed the traditional Roman gods were myths, fabricated stories spread by avaricious priests and embellished by poets longing for fame. The Platonists discussed the nature of God in depth but could not offer a path to the Creator. Mani claimed God could only be reached after decades or even lifetimes of purification. The Christians taught that God could be reached by faith and confession of sins. Then one must live a life patterned after Jesus.

All these recent stories of people who have given control of their lives to God were like boulders thundering against the stone wall Augustine had built around himself. Wealth, prestige, fame, pleasures of life. He clung to these, refusing to let go. Had he not worked hard, sacrificing much to climb to the position he now held? Why should he walk away from it all? Yet something tugged as his soul, gentle but persistent.

Holding Paul's rolled up letter, Augustine walked into the garden. Alypius followed close behind, concerned about his friend's anguish. Silently they wandered further from the buildings, finally sitting on a stone bench. Augustine's mental struggles became stronger, reaching a feverish pitch. Unconsciously, Augustine intertwined his fingers, clasped his knees, banged fists against his forehead, and even tore his hair. Nothing helped. No relief came to his tortured soul. He yearned to surrender to God, but his will desired fleshy pleasure.

Let it be now. Let it be now, he thought silently, but he could not let go of his familiar life. To make a public confession for Christ meant he could no longer teach rhetoric for it was unlawful for Christians to do so. Ambitions for a politics career would also need to be given up. Worst of all, he would have to forgo sex, the one thing which had held him back in becoming an Elect of the Manicheans. Even with the threat of losing the arranged marriage, he could not turn away from this addicted pleasure. To go the rest of his life without touching a woman again? Impossible. Many Christians married and had families, but deep in Augustine's soul he understood that for him to follow God meant complete surrender of that which he held strongest to. Like the hermit Antony, Augustine was being called to an ascetic life. But to give up sex forever?

In his mind's eye, his mental struggles personified into a beautiful woman, serene and cheerful. Lady Continence stretched out her devoted hands, revealing a huge multitude of people of all ages, men and women, children and youths, sober widows and elderly virgins. Each carried within them the spirit of continence, not miserable from a life of sacrifice but full of God's joy.

Lady Continence smiled encouragingly at Augustine. "Are you incapable of doing what these have done? Do you think them capable of achieving this by their own resources and not from God? Why are you relying on yourself, only to find yourself unreliable? Cast yourself upon him. Do not be afraid. Make the leap without anxiety. He will catch you and heal you."

Augustine brushed the image away, feeling the weight of his sins crashing down upon him. Needing to be alone, he arose and walked away from Alypius, leaving the scroll behind on the bench. Out of sight of his friend, Augustine dropped to his knees. Under the shade of a fig tree, he wept in agony from the arrogance and selfishness which kept him in bondage. The battle between will and spirit raged within him.

How long is this to be? whispered one voice in his mind.

Tomorrow, tomorrow, said the part of him which refused to yield.

Why not today? Why not put an end to my impure life this hour?

Slowly through his groaning and weeping, he dimly began to notice a child's voice chanting, "Pick up and read. Pick up and read." The voice came from a nearby house.

His crying stopped as puzzlement set in. Was this a line from a children's game he had never heard before? Then he remembered the story of Anthony, how one verse had changed his life. Walking back to Alypius, he picked up the scroll left on the bench and opened it, reading the first passage that randomly appeared. "Not in riots and drunken parties, not in eroticism and indecencies, not in strife and rivalry, but put on the Lord Jesus Christ and make no provisions for the flesh in its lusts."

The anxiety which had gripped Augustine's heart melted into peace. The God who had created the universe was taking time to speak directly to him through these holy words. Augustine smiled in delight, the depression which had plagued him for months vanished.

Alypius studied his friend intently. "There is a change in you."

"I have stopped fighting God, and he has filled me with joy such as I have never felt before in all my years of searching."

"I too feel this strange longing since Ponticianus spoke." Alypius looked away, uncertainty gripping him. "Why do I feel this way?"

161

"Look." Augustine pointed to the passage he had just read. "With perfect timing, God has given me this command."

Alypius read the verse, frowned, then read the next one below it. "Receive the person who is weak in faith." He closed his eyes, pondering. "That is me. So weak am I, changing my views like the wind. I crave substance, something real." When he opened his eyes again, determination filled him. "I too will follow God. We will walk this road together."

"You may not wish to travel where I will go. My job must be given up along with all earthly ambition. I will not marry or know any woman again."

The younger man said, "Lead, teacher, and I will follow. Giving up women is easy for me as I have none to give up. As for my career, I am sickened of bribed judges and twisted justice. I yearn for that which is pure and uncorrupted."

Smiling, the men rose and went into the house. Monnica looked up from her sewing. Carla walked in, munching of some fruit she had grabbed in the kitchen. She had just awoken, her long hair uncombed.

Augustine turned to his mother. "Your prayers have been answered. I have chosen to walk with God, now and forever more."

Monnica put down her mending and stood, studying his eyes. A smile slowly spread across her lips then she laughed joyfully. "God has heard the prayers of his handmaiden."

Carla looked between the mother and son, her eyes narrowing. "I thought you were already religious. You go to church."

"When did walls make Christians?" Augustine quoted Victorinus. Then his face became stern. "Now pack your things and leave. I will share my bed with no one again."

Carla frowned then shrugged. This had been the nicest house she had lived in, but it would be easy enough for her to find a new lover. She headed to the bedroom she had shared with Augustine and gathered her belongs.

Later when Nebridius returned home, he was caught off guard by the sudden changes. Carla had been kicked out. Augustine and Alypius were in deep discussion with Monnica, who they usually tried to avoid. His friends excitedly poured out the story of their conversion to Nebridius.

"Do not get me wrong. I am pleased you have finally found a religion which gives you happiness, but have you thought this out? You are both giving up your careers, just like that?" Nebridius stared at them in bewilderment. "How will you survive?"

"Who knows," responded Augustine, "but God will make a way. I will finish up this term and retire. The clinging illness affecting my throat has made public speaking difficult for me. I will have an acceptable excuse without going into details."

"Still, this is so sudden."

"Sudden? I have searched my whole life. When a person finds truth, he knows it. And he who knows it, knows eternity."

Nebridius shook his head. "Your words make no sense to me."

"They do to me," came the youthful voice of Adeodatus. The fourteen year old stood in the doorway, staring at his father. "The slaves tell me you sent Carla away."

"Yes, she is gone. No woman will share my bed again." Augustine studied his son who had grown into a young man. "I finally understand what you were talking about."

"I am glad." Adeodatus's voice remained flat.

"I...I am sorry about how I hurt you...and your mother. Can you forgive me?"

Pain flashed across the teenager's face. "God commands us to forgive others. I will do my duty and forgive you. Can you send for my mother to come back?"

"No, it would be best if we are not near each other again." Augustine stepped closer to his son. "Can you still bear to live with me or do you wish to return to Carthage to be with her?"

Adeodatus eyes flickered to his grandmother who smiled reassuringly at him. "I wish to remain near you, Father."

"And I wish to learn more about you, if you would let me."

The youth gave a brief nod. "I would like that."

Chapter Twenty-two

"Sir, is there something wrong with my argument? You keep staring at it."

Nebridius forced his mind to focus on the nervous student in front of him. "No, your work is fine, just fine."

He handed the wax tablet back and continued down the row of seated youths scribbling intensely. At the front of the room, Verecundus sat on a stool, listening to a student reciting a poem. The elderly man glanced at Nebridius, concern in his eyes.

In a strong voice Verecundus said to the class, "That is all for today. Make sure your declamation is finished by tomorrow. Do not take this assignment lightly for you will be delivering it in front of the whole class."

As the students filed out, Verecundus stood by the door, giving out praises and suggestions. Having inherited a large sum of money and several estates, Verecundus had no need to work, but his passion for sharing knowledge with the younger generation kept him in the class despite his hearing was starting to dim and he could not stand for long periods. After the last student had left, he joined Nebridius in straightening stools and stacking scrolls.

"You were distracted today. Has a new book stolen your attention?"

Nebridius grabbed a broom and began sweeping. "No, my roommates claim to have finally found truth and plan to walk away from their public lives to pursue it."

"Ah, they seek otium liberale, cultured retirement. Many serious minded senators and philosophers do so eventually. You can accomplish much without the consist demands from work and social obligations. Tried it twice myself, but each time after a year free of teaching, I came back. I had learned so much from my studies that I burst with the desire to pass the knowledge on to my students. But are not your roommates younger than you? Surely they are too unseasoned for retirement."

"Augustine's health is in decline, affecting his lungs." Nebridius paused in his sweeping. "Truth is, they wish to take a Christian otium. They have become fascinating by that religion and wish to study it more studiously."

"An honorable pursuit." Verecundus looked thoughtful, the wrinkles on his forehead deepening. "I find Ambrose's sermons intriguing and have considered become a catechumen myself. My wife has been a baptized believer for many years."

Nebridius's eyes widened. "I was not trying to sway you to Christianity."

The old man laughed. "It is not you who does the persuading but that irritating spirit they call the Holy Ghost. Not even Mercury, the messenger of Zeus, could be so accurate with his jabs at the heart." Verecundus sighed. "I think the only reason I have not publicly converted is because I would have to give up teaching, and I do love it. The life of an ascetic appeals to me, but my wife would have quite a lot to say if I took those vows." The man sighed. "My body grows so feeble that I will be unable to teach for much longer. Perhaps it is time for me to prepare my soul for the afterlife."

"Talk not of death. You have many years left."

"So speaks the young. You wish to think of life going on forever. But it does not. Death eventually comes to all of us, both peasants and emperors alike. Your friends will need a place to stay. Tell them I offer my country estate of Cassiciacum for their studies. It is a day's journey from here. Quite beautiful. I would join them myself but I have too much to do here."

Nebridius placed the broom in a corner. "I will pass on your message."

Verecundus stacked the last of the scrolls. "I think I will go to church this evening. It will please my wife."

Taking his time, Nebridius wandered through the crowded streets of Milan, pondering. He had qualms with his friends becoming Christians. He was happy that Augustine had finally shaken off that clinging depression. But for his friends to give up their careers? Augustine had always embraced his beliefs passionately, never satisfied until he fully understood everything, Alypius always following close behind. Their endless quest for wisdom and truth was the cement which bound the three friends together, even when the others followed paths that Nebridius saw as nonsense such as Mani and astrology. Surely Christianity would just be another phase in his friends' lives. Perhaps five years from now they would be bowing down to the beautiful statue of Iris, a popular Egyptian goddess. Or maybe becomes eunuchs for the goddess Tellus Mater. Imaging his friends dancing with other eunuchs in women's wigs made Nebridius laugh. If there was one thing he knew about Augustine, it was that his friend would not give up his manhood for any deity.

Parts of Christianity did appeal to Nebridius. A loving God who actually cares for humans, unlike most of the Roman gods who manipulate humans, leaving a wake of destruction from their endless wars and jealousies. But could a real god take on human flesh and walk among humans? Nebridius had grown up hearing stories about demigods such as Hercules and Jason, half-gods who supposedly lived on earth. He had never believed such fanciful stories as being real. Jesus was so different than them, strikingly so. He went on no quests after magical artifacts, never raged against a deity father who had abandoned him, never even trained as a swordsman. What demigod did not know how to fight? Jesus's teachings were peculiar like "love your enemy" and "forgive seven times seventy." Other demigods struck down their enemies or died trying. The sayings of Jesus rang loudly with wisdom, and Nebridius found himself wishing that Jesus could be real. But how could that be possible? No virgin could give birth. People did not walk on water.

When Nebridius finally reached the villa, he found it empty, even of slaves for everyone had left to attend the evening service. Monnica had a knack for Christianizing anyone who spent much time around her, even household slaves. She reached out to all, caring not what class someone was born into. After his friends returned, Nebridius shared the invitation of Verecundus which they quickly accepted.

A few days later near the end of class, Augustine announced to his students that he would not be returning as their teacher in the fall due to health reasons. Many students expressed disappointment in him leaving them. Others wished him well. After all the students had left, Augustine stood at the front of the classroom, lost in thought, barely noticing when the aide and the veil guard went home. Since he had been nineteen years old, he had always taught, sometimes with eagerness and passion, other times with apathy as his focus turned to other matters. Still, it was thirteen years of his life. Instructing others was engrained within him. He was eager to begin his new life, yet felt bittersweet about leaving his students.

Hearing footsteps, he looked towards the veil covering the hallway. The curtain was pushed back and four students entered, all from his hometown.

"Did you forget something?"

The four glanced at each other then Licentius spoke. "Sir, my cousin Alypius has told us the real reason why you and he are leaving. We wish to go with you."

"Your fathers sent you here for a proper education. The emperor will have another professor appointed to my position who may not accept you as pupils, but I will help you find a new rhetor teacher within the city. Perhaps Verecundus if he is teaching next year."

"We want only the best—you," Rusticus burst out. "And I do not say that just because you are my cousin." His brother Lastidianus nodded in agreement.

"You warm my heart, but I am to become a student myself, studying holy scripture. I will never again teach others to speak flattery lies. I am done with the business of rhetoric."

Licentius said, "Alypius speaks animatedly of Christianity, how he has searched for a lifetime but only now has found the truth. Why should we waste years of our lives studying what is false? Teach us about truth."

"Are we not bright pupils?" asked Trygetius, backing up his best friend. "You have told us so many times."

Augustine smiled in defeat. "Romanianus will be arriving soon to Milan. If you can gain his permission, then you may join Alypius and me."

The youths grinned in delight, certain of victory.

When Romanianus, along with Navigius, reached Milan several weeks later, they were caught off guard with the news of Alypius and Augustine's conversions. Navigius was happy for his older brother and relieved that their mother's many nights of prayful tears were finally answered. Thanks to long discussions with Monnica several years ago, Romanianus had already become a catechumen but he was not eager to deepen his faith. He had come to the imperial city because of an argument with a neighbor over land. The local judge had ruled in the neighbor's favor and now Romanianus sought for an audience with the emperor, a difficult task to accomplish. Romanianus was the richest and most powerful man in Thagaste, but in Milan he was just another highborn African seeking the emperor's favor. Much wining and dining would be needed for Romanianus to gain influential friends who could slip his name to the emperor.

His son and the other three youths carefully presented their arguments about why they should be allowed to pursue their studies with Augustine. Romanianus was at first reluctant, but after seeing his son's sincerity, he gave his blessing. Better to have Licenius and the other youths under the careful supervision of Augustine and Alypius than them running rampant in the city, getting into mischief.

When the summer break began, a group of nine journeyed to Cassiciacum, leaving Romanianus and Nebridius at Milan. As the only female and most mature Christian in the group, Monnica was treated reverently by the others. Once they reached the estate, she took charge of running the household. Adeodatus befriended the older teenagers, joining their joviality discussions. Navigius spent much time alone in the gardens, thinking of his wife and daughters. He had planned to only stay a few months in Milan then return home, hopefully with a victorious Romanianus. But now it looked as if his visit would be much longer. While Augustine and Alypius led lively debates, Navigius held back, rarely speaking.

Cassiciacum was indeed beautiful with lush fields and orchards. In the distance rose the lofty Alps with dense pine forests and snow-tipped summits. Once the group had settled into the opulent villa, Augustine began taking long walks alone, bringing a copy of Psalms with him. He would sit on a rock or kneel on the grass, memorizing the verses while admiring the vistas of soaring mountains stretching upward towards the heavens. Often he prayed, slowly learning how to turn verses into songs of worship which flowed from his heart. Sometimes he imagined speaking to the Manicheans, raging at them for binding him in lies for nearly a decade. Other times he felt pity for them and prayed they could see through their own deceits.

As Augustine studied the holy scriptures with his friends, the way he viewed the world slowly changed. The more he understood about Jesus, the greater he saw the ugliness of his own sins, of his pride. In flower-filled meadows away from the others, Augustine wept, feeling the weight of his past life, of the people he had hurt. Once he had been arrogant and ambitious, believing life centered upon him. Now he saw himself minuscule when compared to God. He had no more worth than a tiny pebble in a brook flowing beside an almighty mountain. When thinking about his past life, he felt anger at himself. How idiotic he had been to be ensnared by the foolish lies of the Manicheans. Even when he had doubts, it was his pride that kept him eating at their tables, spreading their propaganda. How many had listened to him and where now on the path to hell because of him? It had been only the mercy of God which had pulled Didius from such a road. Guilt crushed Augustine. And hope lifted him up again. Among the gentle flower-covered hills, the psalms came to life, giving Augustine deep understanding of mercy and love.

Away from the stresses which had hounded him, his lungs began to mend allowing him to talk for long periods without breaking into wheezing. He turned everyday events into lessons for the five youths. A centipede found crawling across a writing tablet was turned into a discussion about the Platonic belief of the immaterial nature of the soul. The youths were given assignments, often developing ideas alone then coming together for debates. Three of the discussions were recorded in shorthand. Then Augustine edited them into publishable works. Topics varied, from the nature of God, purpose of liberal arts, to the meaning of evil. The youths often used quotes from Cicero and Virgil when attempting to prove their points.

Monnica would listen quietly while mending, absorbing the arguments. Then with just a few words she would cut into the heart of a philosophy, leaving the others stunned with her insight. Still, she felt inadequate around the highly educated men. When she finally commented on her feelings, Augustine quickly reassured his mother that women could become philosophers equal to men. While the others remained impressed by Augustine, Navigius refused to see any point in the abstract discussions, preferring real life problems like how many seeds to plant or the trade value of an amphora filled with olive oil.

Augustine missed friends who had stayed behind in Milan. For Romanianus he wrote *In Philosophy*, a short piece warning against the Academics. Knowing Nebridius was considering converting to Christianity, Augustine corresponded with his friend through letters. Augustine also began a series of handbooks, each devoted to a different subject such as grammar, dialectic, or music. Not stopping there, he went beyond anything done before in literature, inventing a new writing style.

"This is the most profound, yet confusing work you have yet done." Alypius sat the scroll down on the table beside his friend.

Augustine looked up from his ink and parchment. "What has bewildered you?"

"Well, the entire format. It is a dialog with yourself instead of with a friend. And the name *Soliloquies*. I have never heard the term before."

"It is a new word I created for the title. I choose to have a dialog with Reason instead of a friend so as not to offend tender emotions. As you may have noticed, I criticize myself quite harshly a few times. Perhaps I will write a pamphlet to explain the book better."

"Knowing you, the pamphlet will be more ambiguous than the original." Seeing Augustine wince, Alypius added, "Then again it may be brilliant."

"It is not my feelings that hurt but my tooth."

"You still have that toothache? It has been over a week. Perhaps a paste made from willow bark will help."

"I have tried that the last three days, but the pain grows worse."

Monnica's voice rang out from another room, "Dinner time. No scrolls at the table, Licentius."

"But I am in the middle of writing a poem using picturesque imagery beyond anything you have dreamed."

"My eldest tried that line on me when he was ten. Move it off the table, now."

Alypius and Augustine joined the others in the large dining room decorated with murals of lush fields waiting to be harvested. Augustine only made it through three bites before he winced in pain. His mother looked at him in concern. He smiled reassuringly and continued eating slowly.

Over the next few days his gums became inflamed, his tooth throbbing. He tried ignoring the pain as he took his morning walks and wrote a new pamphlet, but the pain became excruciating. Unable to talk, he finally wrote on a wax tablet asking for the others to pray for him. Monnica immediately took charge, forming everyone into a kneeling circle. Augustine joined them on the floor, begging God for relieve from the mind-numbing agony. Around him most prayed silently, stiffly. Adeodatus held his hand, the youth's voice whispering a petition. Monnica spoke warmly to God as though chatting to a close friend.

Suddenly the pain in Augustine's mouth vanished. Though he had hoped it would happen, the reality caused him terror. Such horrifying pain then…nothing. Augustine had never experienced anything like it before, and he was caught off guard. The God who had created the universe had taken the time to heal him, a prideful sinner. Augustine ran his tongue over his gums. The swelling was gone, the tooth placid.

Awe filled him as he raised his voice loudly in thanksgiving.

Chapter Twenty-three

Voices rose and fell in harmony, the Latin chants embodying mystery and reverence for the Creator. The singers were all ages, dedicated to an all-night vigil at the basilica in Milan. As the moon began its decent in the wee hours of the morning, the singing continued with renewed vigor. The most sacred day of the year had arrived—Easter. Every nook and canny was well lit with lamps, bathing the church in light. Some of the children fell asleep, lying on the tiled floor near the walls out of the way of feet. The only place to sit was the stone bench at the front where presbyters and the bishop could rest. The congregation stood or kneeled on the hard floor.

Ambrose walked to the wooded lectern and spoke about the rite of baptism. As the sermon reached its end, Augustine eagerly rose to his feet along with other candidates who had submitted their names months ago. The group of twenty-two was a mixture of ages from both sexes. All had undergone the rigorous ascetical regimen during Lent. Daily they fasted, prayed, gave alms, and did not bath. Married couples refrained from sex. On Holy Thursday they had broken their long fast by visiting the public baths.

One by one, Ambrose called each of the candidates forward to recite the Christian creed in front of the whole church. Even the youngest, a child of eight, recited the lines from memory. Warmth filled Augustine when both Adeodatus and Alypius spoke. Then his turn came. He walked to the front and spoke in a firm voice. The creed was slightly different than the one he had heard growing up in Africa, but he was unconcerned tonight about technicalities. He burned with passion to publicly declare his beliefs.

> I believe in the Father almighty
> And in Christ Jesus, his only Son, our Lord
> Who was born of the Holy Spirit and the Virgin Mary
> Who was crucified under Pontius Pilate and was buried
> And the third day rose from the dead
> Who ascended into heaven
> And sits on the right hand of the Father

Where he comes to judge the living and the dead.
And in the Holy Spirit
The holy church
The remission of sins
The resurrection of the flesh.

When the last candidate finished the recital, Ambrose led them through a separate chamber, an eight-sided baptistery. A closed door separated the catechumen from the congregation which began singing Psalms 41. Augustine stood near his son, feeling at peace with himself and God. The anger and hurt which once existed between father and son had melted away, replaced by forgiveness and love. Ambrose consecrated the water in the pool by prayer and making the sign of the cross in the air. While facing west, the candidates renounced the devil. Then they turned to the east and proclaimed their allegiance to Christ.

Next they stripped off their clothes. None felt shame or embarrassment for all were used to public bathing. When Augustine's name was called, he descended into the pool of cold water to stand by Ambrose dressed in a drenched robe.

The bishop asked, "Do you believe in God the Father almighty?"

"I do believe."

Ambrose dunked Augustine under the water then helped him stand. Then he repeated the question, "Do you believe in God the Father almighty?"

"I do believe," said Augustine. Under the water he went again.

The question and answer was repeated a third time. After Augustine's final dunking, he walked out of the pool where a priest handed him a clean white robe to wear.

Turning to his dripping son, Augustine hugged him. "Now we are equals, both newly born."

"We will age together, Father," said Adeodatus, referring to the Christian habit of counting their age from the day of their baptism.

Alypius shook water from his dripping hair. "Teacher, student, and son—all the same age. Only God could work such a miracle." Around him, people laughed joyfully. Then some began singing the psalm that the congregation was chanting in the next room.

When the last person was baptized, Ambrose stepped out of the pool and anointed each candidate with the chrism, a consecrated oil made from balsam. Next, he washed the feet of each person, a custom unique for Milan during baptisms. A final prayer was given where the bishop invoked the Holy Spirit to give the seven gifts mentioned in Isaiah to the new believers. Each was signed with the cross then they walked back into the sanctuary.

The congregation burst into cheers as the white-clad initiates entered and stood in the railed section usually reserved for deacons and presbyters. Sleepy children awoke and looked about for the cause of the excitement. The sky turned a rosy pink as cheerful chanting rose heavenward. Time for the Eucharist, Ambrose asked all non-baptized to leave. A third of the congregation left, heading off for much needed sleep. The rest remained to partake in communion.

Augustine stood by his son and Alypius, feeling awe towards God. He caught his mother's eye in the audience and smiled at her. For the first time he was truly part of the body of Christ. The heavy weight of his many sins had been removed forever. Today was a new beginning. He was uncertain where God would lead him, only that he desired with his entire essence to follow, even if the cost was ultimately his life.

For the next eight days, the newly baptized attended special classes where Ambrose explained the mystagogy, giving detailed explanations of the deep mysteries of the Holy Scripture. Augustine drank in every word, eager to understand. Phrases he had heard since a child took on a new meanings. The way he perceived life had changed. No longer did he judge people by their education and wealth but realized each was precious because they were made in God's image. A beggar on the street was as important as the emperor. The beautiful chants at church deeply moved Augustine, distilling in his heart deep emotions of devotion that spilled over into tears during worship.

After the baptism, Augustine and his family returned to living in the villa in Milan that had been loaned to him. Nebridius listened to his friends chatter about their new faith. He questioned them about theological matters, especially about how Jesus could be both God and man. Augustine's understanding was limited, but he continued to read and study, broadening his knowledge. During the five months he had spent at Cassiciacum, he had written Ambrose, asking which books he should read. The bishop had suggested Isaiah, but when Augustine had tried reading it, he found its imagery confusing. He had put the book away for the day he would reach a deeper understanding of the scriptures. After his baptism, the tough questions began to attract him.

One day Nebridius was in deep debate with his friends when Monnica answered the door and announced they had a visitor from Thagaste. Nebridius stood, wincing as his feet had been bothering him lately. Augustine and Alypius greeted the tall Berber who was a stranger to them.

The handsome man smiled cheerfully. "What a surprise this Easter when I saw two of the most outspoken Manicheans from our small town baptized as Christians. God is miraculous indeed."

"Who are you?" asked Augustine politely.

"Evodius. No wonder you cannot recognize me. I was but a youth myself when you left Thagaste to teach in Carthage. We have a common friend in Milan—Ponticianus, a government inspector."

"Ah, yes, a good man who introduced us to the writings about Saint Anthony. He told us how several of his friends read the book and forsake their jobs to follow God."

"I am one of those he spoke about. I had climbed high up in my position as a secret police, hoping for a promotion to provincial governorship. Following Saint Anthony's example, I forsake all to follow God. That was over three years ago."

Nebridius leaned forward on his couch. "For three years you have had no job or income?"

"None. What need do I have for money? I live in the monastery outside town, studying God's holy scriptures and offering my skills to any in need. I am at peace for the first time in my life."

Augustine said, "Before converting, we three dreamed of forming our own little commune of friends sharing a household. We would put our money in one common coffer. Each year we would rotate so two would be in charge of dealing with household expenses in order to free the others for their studies."

"Why did you not go through with your plans?"

"Because the wives of several of our friends protested."

Alypius cut in with a laugh. "Especially Romanianus's wife. A pity, as he was the riches one of us all. With him in our group, we could have lived decades on his wealth alone."

Evodius chuckled with the others then sobered. "Monastery life consists of more than sitting around reading books all day. We spend hours communing with God, tending our garden, and helping those who seek our aid. It is a busy but rewarding life—at least to me. When I go to bed at night, I sleep peacefully knowing I have made a difference. I never felt that way working for the government."

Fascinated, Augustine and Alypius quizzed Evodius for several hours about monastery life. Nebridius listened quietly, his soul disturbed.

Finally Evodius stood to leave. "Come out and visit the monastery anytime. We welcome all men who quest after God."

After Evodius left, the friends discussed the conversation. Deep in thought, Nebridius rubbed the palm of one hand.

"Your fingers bothering you again?" asked Augustine.

"What? Yes, they still burn strangely. But that is not what bothers me. This Evodius is truly happy, though he owns almost nothing. He believes he found what I have sought for all my life—truth. How can any man know for certain when he has found it? You two also claim Christianity is the way to God. I grant that its version of a loving God who cares for humans is the most attractive religion I have studied. But how do you know it is true?"

Augustine placed a fist over his chest. "Because for the first time my soul sings. In all the years I was a Manichean, I was miserable, constantly trying to earn God's attention by being pure. But always was the heavily guilt of knowing I was never good enough, no matter how hard I tried. Now I have accepted that I will never be pure on my own, but through Jesus's death and resurrection, he paid the costly price for me. By his sacrifice, I can experience true love for the first time. It changes a man's entire outlook."

Nebridius sighed. "I was there when you began your teaching career and when your son was born. The pursuit of wisdom was the bond of our friendship. I know you as closely as any man can. The passion for Mani, deep depression when you realized it was false, ambition which dulled your kindness. Nine months ago you converted to yet another religion and changed again. This new you is kinder, more considerate of others. Now that is a miracle."

"Thanks…I think."

"I desire to know God the way you do. Starting this evening, I will attend church with you regularly, beginning my training as a catechumen."

Delighted, Alypius and Augustine introduced Nebridius to their friends at church and instructed him in the Christian faith. Several days later, they traveled outside the city wall to the monastery where Evodius gave them a tour. Evodius was well read and challenged them on several philosophical points, giving them much to think about.

For several weeks, Nebridius was truly happy, content he had finally found his lifelong goal. The strange sickness which had been slowly seeping his strength had been forgotten. Until one day when they were returning home after shopping for books in the market. A sudden storm hit and they ran the final distance home to protect their scrolls. Within minutes of arriving home, Nebridius whole body trembled, his hands visually shaking. A change of clothes and hot soup relaxed him, but as the days slipped by his health deteriorated rapidly. He lost weight and was lethargic, his mind struggling to remember profound text he had just read.

His feet and hands felt like pins were sticking in them. One day while waiting for supper to be served, he became sweaty then passed out.

Several doctors visited, diagnosing him with an imbalance of the humors. The cure, they declared, was that excess fluid needed to be drained. After each bloodletting, Nebridius was left feeling worse than before, barely able to rise from his bed for days. When awake, Nebridius passed the time in prayer and listening to his friends reading to him. Concerned he may die unbaptized, Nebridius sent a letter to Ambrose asking for a quick baptism. The request was granted. Surrounded by friends and a few priests, Nebridius was carefully helped into the pool where he was dunked three times. Though weak and cold, Nebridius smiled happily. He was ready for death.

One day as Alypius read the parable of the lost son, Nebridius sat up in bed, a faraway look in his eyes. "That is what God is asking of me. I must return home to tell my family about him."

"Return to Carthage? You are in no condition to travel."

"Then pray that God will grant improved health so I may tell my father in person I have finally found my heart's desire. That we can share that joy together."

Determined he must return home, Nebridius took short walks twice a day and ate many small snacks throughout the day. Over time he became stronger. Arrangements were made for Nebridius to travel with acquaintances back to Carthage. The parting was sad, as there was uncertainty if the friends would see each other again in this life. For Augustine, life in Milan without Nebridius seemed lackluster. His discussions with Evodius invoked a desire in both to return to their hometown. His brother Nebridius was also eager to return to his wife and kids. He had only delayed this long for he waited with Romanianus for a final decision about the land dispute. Alypius was content to follow Augustine, leaving his relatives behind in Milan.

Plans were made and final partings said. The teenagers Lastidianus and Rusticus would travel back with their cousins to Thagaste, but the other two youths would stay with Romanianus in Milan. Augustine felt concern about Trygetius and Licentius. While under his tutorage, they had learned much about God, but Romanianus was pushing his son towards seeking a public office. Already the glint for fame had begun to burn in Licentius, and he spent less time writing poetry and more time at the forums listening to political speeches.

The journey south was long and tedious. Concerned about his mother, Augustine did not push the horses too fast. At fifty-six, Monnica stayed active, seeing that everyone in their group had good meals. While riding in the wagon, she mended ripped clothes. They stopped in the ancient port city of Ostia located by the river Tiber. Once it had been the most important coastal city in Italy, reaching a population of seventy-five thousands, but naval activates had begun to focus elsewhere and city was slowly declining. Still the theatre and bathhouses were visited by thousands every day, and the warehouses stocked with products being shipped across the empire.

When they reached Ostia in late summer, they found the harbor closed. A usurper general was challenging the authority of Emperor Theodosius of the East Empire. To show off his power, the general had blockaded the harbors of Rome. Unable to sail, the African friends settled at an inn to rest from their journey. When several friendly people at a local church heard about their situation, they opened up their homes to the travelers.

Several days later, while the others were out exploring the city, Augustine propped on the sill of a window overlooking a garden below. Flowers were in full bloom, and bees buzzed about collecting nectar to take back to their man-made hives of wicker. Monnica walked up and leaned out the window, admiring the view. Mother and son chatted easily, the past where Augustine was quick to flee her presence was forgotten.

The beautiful view inspired them to wonder what Heaven was like. As they pondered the reality of the next life, their hearts became attuned as the world around them faded. To be constantly in the presence of their Creator, to see and walk in a perfect, untarnished world. To no longer battle against temptations or suffer pain. Deep yearning uniting them, and time itself seemed to freeze as they glimpsed beyond their world into the next. Too soon the brief moment passed. In the distance a dog barked. Sounds of traffic in the streets returned as wheels bumped along flagstone.

Monnica sighed. "Son, as for myself, I now find no pleasure in this life. What is left for me to do? Why am I still here? I know not. My hope in this world is already filled. The one reason I wanted to stay longer in this life was to see you a Catholic Christian before I died. My God has granted this in a way better than I had hoped. For I see you despising this world's success to become his servant. What have I to do here?"

Augustine looked at the garden, unable to reply. He spotted his son walking among the flowery path with his two cousins. "Adeodatus needs you."

"His heart shines pure like all my grandchildren. The temptations of this world will not cause them to forget their love for God."

Adeodatus spotted his father and grandmother. He waved at them, grinning about an amusing incident which had taken place with his cousins as they had walked near the river. Augustine walked downstairs to listen, silently reflecting on the conversation with his mother.

The days passed pleasantly in Ostia. The house they stayed at was on the outskirts of the city, away from loud traffic. Monnica came down with a fever, but she still kept busy, helping the wife of their host with chores. As she sat the table for supper, she suddenly collapsed. Augustine and Navigius saw her fall and ran to her side.

Slowly she awoke and looked about dazed. "Where am I?"

"In Ostia, Mother," said Navigius. "By the sea."

"Oh." For a moment she looked confused. Seeing the worried faces of her sons, she said, "Bury me here."

Grief filled Augustine as he fought against tears. Navigius tried to cheer her up as he carried her to a bed where she could rest.

"You cannot die here on foreign shores away from our beloved Africa. We have a grave already made for you beside Father."

Monnica looked at Navigius with reproach then glanced at Augustine. "See what he says?" She winced as pain filled her. When it faded, she was again the peacemaker. "Bury my body anywhere you like. Let no anxiety about that disturb you. I have only one request to make, that you remember me at the altar of the Lord, wherever you may be."

"Of course, Mother."

For over a week Monnica's body was ravished by illness. She spoke encouraging words to family members, trying to sooth their grief while her own feverish body contorted in pain. On the ninth day, Augustine held her limp hand as she whispered her final words.

"Ah, Augustine, my devoted son. I cannot recall you ever saying a single harsh or bitter word."

Augustine's lips trembled and he looked away, remembering the many times he had wounded her. She had forgiven him every time, even when he had abandoned her in Carthage so far away from her family.

"Navigius, you have your father's looks but my heart. Remember to give your daughters the gifts I bought for them."

"They will love the dolls. But not as much as they love you." Navigius's voice trembled.

"Tell your sister that I wished I could have seen her one last time. If God will allow it, I will be the first to greet her when she comes to my new home. Adeodatus, where are you?"

"Here, Grandmother." The teenager reached out and took her hand.

She squeezed it. "My beloved grandson. Never forget the one who gave you life."

"I promise not to. We will see each other again."

"I know." Her eyes closed. Shortly later, she breathed her last.

Augustine reached over and closed her eyes, grief overwhelming him. She had supported him all his life, even when he did not want it, and now he felt as if his life was torn into pieces. While he wrestled to control his emotions, his son wailed in grief, his whole body trembling as he hugged his grandmother. Adeodatus's loud cries continued while friends gently pulled him away from Monnica. Evodius picked up a psalter and began chanting a song from it. Others joined in.

Word of Monnica's death quickly spread to church members who came to pay their respects. While others cried, Augustine went to a room further away and chatted politely with visitors, hiding his deep pain so much that many thought he was cold-hearted. That evening Monnica's body was taken to the grave for burial. Throughout the funeral and even when they returned to the house, Augustine remained stoic on the outside. The pain he felt inwardly was far beyond words. He begged silently for God to remove the grief, but it remained. He went to the bathhouse, hoping for relieve, but he was followed by people concerned about him. He returned to the house, still miserable, finally falling asleep in a quiet bedroom.

He awoke before dawn and lay pondering. The grief from the day before felt lighter. He allowed himself to think about her gentle disposition, her deep faith which had led both her unfaithful husband and her wandering son to God. A tear slid down Augustine's cheek. She had never given up on him, even when he had mocked her beliefs and ran away from her twice. Her devotion and prayers had been the balm which helped lead him back to his Creator. Augustine began to cry in earnest, letting grief run its course.

Beyond the sorrow which he must endure lay hope. One day, he was certain he would be with her again.

Chapter Twenty-four

With the harbor still blocked, Augustine and his group returned to Rome to await the end of the civil war. The weeks dragged into months. With his friends, Augustine visited various monasteries scattered around central Italy, learning all he could about their lifestyle. Over the winter, they heard that Verecundus, who had invited them to the country estate of Cassiciacum, had died. They comforted each other with the knowledge that Verecundus had died after his recent baptism. The following spring, the eastern war finally ended and ships began sailing across the Mediterranean again. The friends boarded a merchant vessel sailing to Carthage. Seeing the first glimpse of the African shores stirred Augustine's heart, renewing his eagerness to return home to tell old acquaintances about his new faith.

They stayed in Carthage a few weeks, visiting friends, though Augustine avoided coming into contact with Galla or her family. He visited Nebridius at his father's country villa, staying for several days. Nebridius was weak, but cheerful, eager to discuss religion. Adeodatus stayed a week with his mother who now lived in her brother's household. She spoke little about Augustine but bathed her son in attention, cooking his favorite foods, ambling with him through their favorite parts of the city.

Too soon, it was time to return home. The travelers secured horses, riding the two hundred miles westward. When they finally climbed over the last hill and saw buildings stretched out across the rolling plains, Augustine felt warmth spread through him. Thagaste—his birthplace. Twelve years before he had sneaked out of the small town by starlight, fleeing both his mother and the memories of Didius. Back then he had seen himself as a rebel, standing up boldly against false beliefs, one of the few who knew Truth. Now he returned surrounded by comrades, embracing the very religion he had mocked before. He rode into town feeling like the prodigal son. Around him people waved in recognition, others pointing fingers and whispering. As the travelers reached the center of Thagaste, the church bell rung, announcing the beginning of evening service.

Evodius halted his horse. "We cannot pass up prayers."

Smiling, Alypius leaped off his mount. "Time to shock my family—again."

Augustine turned to his son who had already dismounted. "Ready?"

"Always, Father."

The group of seven entered the sanctuary. They were noticed immediately in the small church. Singers halted in the middle of their first song to stare at the newcomers. Suddenly a young woman yelled joyfully and rushed towards them, followed by two girls. Navigius hugged his family, not caring that he wept as much as his wife at the homecoming. The parents of Lastidianus and Rusticus moved through the crowd to greet their sons. Sheepish Alypius was embraced by his sobbing mother who kept repeating his name over and over. Evodius was pulled away from the group by his own relatives, leaving Augustine and Adeodatus alone. They stared straight ahead, singing as if they were regulars, yet sharing a secret smile. The bishop tried to refocus his congregation back on worship, but eyes kept constantly straying towards the returnees.

When it was time for communion, many glanced at Augustine, expecting him to leave. When he stayed, excited whispers broke out. Had the outspoken Manichean really become a true Christian? When the final prayer ended, Augustine and his friends where surrounded by curious people peppering them with questions.

"Where is Monnica? Has Romanianus also returned? Who baptized you? Did you meet the Emperor? Are you here to stay? Is this really your son? He has grown so much. Looks more like his mother. Where is she?"

Augustine answered their questions patiently, going into detail about his mother's death for she was highly respected by the townspeople. As the crowd began to thin, the priest invited Augustine for supper to learn what had brought about this spiritual change. Augustine declined as he had yet not unpack but promised to dine with him tomorrow. Then he traveled out of town, soon arriving at the house of his birth. The small villa looked the same as the day he left—tidy with chickens scratching in the yard. The slave Ruso, now gray-hair and using a cane to aid with walking, greeted Augustine warmly like an affectionate uncle. The other slaves had died over the years, and Navigius had bought no new ones. His wife and daughters kept the house in order. When not traveling Navigius worked the land alongside his tenants.

For a few weeks, Augustine rested, visiting with the bishop and friends. Leaving the house as his brother's inheritance, Augustine chose a small tenant house on the outskirts of his land as his new home. It was surrounded by a few olive trees and a garden. With the help of Alypius and Evodius, Augustine and his son turned the small hut into a decent house with plain bedrooms for each person, a study to hold their growing collection of books, and a small kitchen. When the roof was completed, the four moved in. They spent their days peacefully tending the vegetable garden, attending church services twice a day, and reading. Almost daily came visitors, many wanting to hear tales of their travels, others curious about their ascetic lifestyle. Augustine burst with passion to share his new understanding about God, talking to any who listened, even giving speeches in the forum. The few Manicheans who publicly challenged him where quickly thwarted. None, not even the local priest or city council members, could speak as eloquently as he. As Augustine's reputation grew, men walked for miles across the vast countryside to visit. Some came seeking solitude for a short time, needing spiritual healing before facing the difficult world again. A few took vows of celibacy and poverty, selling all they had and moving into the tiny, makeshift monastery. New rooms were built and the garden expanded.

Augustine was content, surrounded by a strong bond of friends sharing similar beliefs, spending late nights discussing literature and religion. He continued to write, starting with a pamphlet which methodically confronted the Manichean view about Genesis. His friends handwrote copies of the pamphlet as he read it aloud. Then the copies were sent to known Manicheans in the surrounding area.

Adeodatus worked alongside his father, showing maturity far older than his age. For hours at a time father and son discussed intriguing topics. Adeodatus was especially interested in education, seeing the teacher's role as a guide to inspire learning.

"All those disciplines that teachers claim to teach, even those of virtue and wisdom, are explained in words. Students must consider within themselves whether what was said is true, each consulting that inner truth according to his own ability. Thus a student learns."

Augustine found his own ideas changed by their conversations. "So you say that a student knows the matter of which I speak because of his own contemplation, not by the actual words I speak."

"Yes. You may speak what is true and the student hears it. But he is not taught by words, but by the realities themselves made manifest to him directly by God revealing them to his inner self."

"You are wiser my son, than I was at your age."

Adeodatus beamed. "What gifts I have were bestowed by you, Father."

"Not I, but by our heavenly Father."

Augustine recorded their dialogs by editing them into a book he called *The Teacher*. Privately he was proud of the deep faith Adeodatus had inherited from Galla and Monnica. Augustine had been too wrapped up in his own ambitions to give Adeodatus much attention as a child. Perhaps that was a good thing for Adeodatus was spared from developing his father's arrogance and cold-heartedness.

Nebridius corresponded regularly with Augustine, expressing disappointment that his friend had not visited again. He gave few details about his illness which continued to linger. Some days he felt almost completely well, then another setback would keep him in bed for days. The two friends mainly wrote about philosophy and religion, debating such questions as, "Can celestial powers influence human thoughts?" Augustine encouraged his friend to enjoy the forced retirement which gave him more time to grow Christ-like.

One day a merchant traveling from Carthage brought two letters. Augustine glanced at the first one and noticed Nebridius's handwriting. Settling under a shade tree near his house, Augustine opened it.

> Greetings my brother in Christ. As my illness progresses, your letters give me great pleasure to behold. While weakness cripples my body, your words free my soul. Such topics we discuss of Christ, of Plato. How I wish you could visit me in person. If God sees fit to restore my health, I will join your latest venture. Life as a *servus Dei* appeals strongly to me.
>
> Still, I am blessed, even in sickness. By coming home, God has used me as a witness to my family, allowing me to share my insight into Wisdom. My mother is delighted that I have finally found what I sought all these years. She had been curious about what Christians believed, having been impressed by several who helped her over the years. When I explained to her how Jesus is different from every other religion, she began attending church with my sisters. Now they have become catechumen and plan to be baptized this coming Easter.
>
> My father was pleased to have me home but disappointed I achieved nothing significant such as earning a government position while in Milan. Still, he has always supported me as a philosopher. He has listened to my discussions about Christianity but holds little interest in religious matters, preferring to build his own personal kingdom in this

world. When my mother and sisters began attending church, he said little. But when my oldest sister Lania declared God had called her to become a nun, he became furious. Already he has finalized her engagement with a rich family which holds government positions. She has pleaded with Father to release her, but he sees it as her duty to bring honor to our family. The shame of being a slave still burns within him after all these years. To be connected to a patrician family would allow him to gloat over his enemies. So blind he is to understanding that his true enemies are not human.

My mother, sisters, and I are praying and fasting, asking God to somehow change Father's mind. Hopefully my next letter will bring better news.

Living in his mercy,

Nebridius

Augustine read the letter twice then bowed his head, praying for Lania. The last time he had seen her, she had been a carefree girl, laughing and joyful despite knowing that her father had already began planning her marriage. Still, Augustine was uncertain how to pray. Did the girl seek an ascetic life in order to rebel against her father or because she believed God had really called her? Augustine prayed neutrally, asking God to guide the girl in the direction he thought best. Setting the letter aside, Augustine picked up the next one. To his surprise, it was written by Nebridius's father. Feeling apprehensive, he began reading.

You have been a close friend and companion to my son. If grieves me deeply to inform you that Nebridius has died. He went on a hunger fast which his weaken body could not handle. My hand shakes as I write. As both my son and my family hold you in high regard, you deserve to know the details. I know not what he wrote in his letter which accompanies this one. I have not the heart to break its seal. Already I have brought my son enough disappointment.

He begged that I allow his sister to become a nun but I refused. I had planned her marriage since birth. After serving my master faithfully all those years, now was the time for me to rise above all who despise wealthy freemen. Born as a Roman citizen, you know not the fear of a slave with no rights or the frustrations of a freeman who lingers on the edge of society. Still, you have always shown respect to my son and family, something I deeply appreciate. I had hoped that by my son living with you, he would become more ambitious like you, earning a reputable government position. Instead he came back to us weak in body but inflamed in spirit, already with one foot in another world.

Oh, my son. Why would I not listen! You told me God had a special plan for Lania and I must let her go. If I did not, I would make God my enemy. But I was stubborn and prideful. God has cursed me, taking you from me forever. Will I ever know peace again?

I rumble on, a foolish old man. Already I have told the bishop that Lania has my blessing. My youngest also expresses the wish to follow her sister's path. Is there nothing worse than having God's wrath against you? I have lost all hope of having grandchildren. Who will inherit my lands? My fine estate? The bishop tells me that it is more important to lay up treasures in heaven than here on earth. My wife wishes to start a charity in honor of Nebridius, giving money to the poor. She believes that by helping others I will find peace. I know not if that is true, but for my son's sake I will try.

I am seeking to learn how to please God. I can take no more pain. With the rest of my household, we will be baptized this Easter.

Sincerely,

Dacien

Augustine sat under the tree, not noticing a bee buzzing nearby. Overcome with grief, he stared at the dusty road disappearing over a hill. Nebridius dead? The illness had lasted so long that it seemed that his friend would be around for many years yet. Regret filled Augustine. Why had he not traveled to Carthage for a visit? There had always been tasks needing completed. Now it was too late.

Never would he see Nebridius again. He sighed, forcing himself to relax. His friend had died a believer. They would meet again in the next life.

Alypius walked along the path with several others carrying baskets of vegetables. Seeing Augustine's troubled face, he asked, "What has happened?"

"Nebridius has gone to see God before us."

Augustine passed the letters to Alypius. Then he walked away, needing to be alone. He wandered through ripen fields and olive groves, pausing to watch harvesters pick the fruit, but he did not really see them. Instead, he thought of jokes shared with Nebridius, their many debates, Nebridius sampling Galla's fine cooking. Both joy and pain resounded in the memories.

The sun was beginning to set when Augustine finally turned towards home. The monastery was still out of sight when he spotted his son walking towards him.

"Father, you missed evening prayers."

"I prayed alone tonight."

The youth fell in step beside his father. For a while they walked in silence. Finally Adeodatus said, "Nebridius has it better than us now. No more sickness. The best foods. And he can ask God directly all those questions he has been pondering."

Augustine laughed, imagining Nebridius sitting at the foot of God's throne, asking philosophical questions, his face enraptured in delight. "Yes, Nebridius is indeed in Heaven."

The harvest days of autumn kept Augustine busy, giving him little time for private grieving. Surrounded by the peaceful African countryside with its far vistas of rolling hills and distant mountains, Augustine felt peace when he took long walks alone. At times God seemed so near, the deity's presence real and inviting. Farm work, which he had avoided as much as possible growing up, now brought pleasure. He appreciated meals more when he was one of the workers who planted the seed, cared for it as it grew into a mature plant, then plucked its ripen fruit. He saw miracles in everyday events like a chick hatching from an egg, the fields bathed in sunbeams peeking through thick clouds, a rabbit outwitting the pursing dog with its quick zigzag leaps. Nature was filled with intricate designs made by the Creator. If God had taken the effort to put so much detail into a wildflower, how much more he cared for humans who he had made in his image.

When news arrived that Romanianus had finally returned from Italy, Augustine and Alypius walked to his villa. Romanianus greeted them warmly, but his face was haggard from the long trip. The petition had not gone his way, and he still felt chaff. The friends tried to cheer him up as much as possible before heading home. As they walked along a dirt lane, the clouds darkened and the cold wind cut into their skin.

"Looks like the first winter storm has arrived," said Alypius, increasing his speed. A sharp stone cut into his foot, causing him to wince.

"Do you still plan to go barefoot this winter?" Augustine's breath formed a fog.

"I have lived through two Italian winters, and they are far harsher than ours."

"You take the idea of ascetics too far. The body needs not to be punished, only refrained from sin."

"In Italy we met numerous Christians who go barefoot as I do."

"Yes, and some who took far too much pride in dressing in rags when they could afford better. I believe there is equal danger of those who dress ostentatiously for attention and those who brag about their rags, seeing themselves as more holy because of self-depravity. A person should dress modestly for their station, without putting on a show either way."

"You think I am too prideful?"

"Only your heart attune to God can tell you if that is so. I only know cold feet are uncomfortable. Ah, looks like it has begun to rain."

They ran the final half-mile, turning it into a race. Alypius reached the monastery first, panting under the dripping eve, watching his wet friend arrive.

Alypius smiled in victory. "Harden feet make for fast running. Are you sure you wish to wear shoes in mud?"

As they entered, Evodius was kindling coals in the hearth. He added wooden shavings, blowing on the red chars left from lunch. Flames leaped up, encircling the dry wood. Adeodatus walked passed with a kettle for boiling water. Other men went about their chores, chatting or humming softly. Augustine changed into a dry tunic then went to the kitchen to cook. Adeodatus was already cutting up cabbage while Evodius poured water into the kettle.

"Is it not my turn to cook?" said Augustine. Chores were rotated regularly.

Adeodatus and Evodius glanced at Alypius who was just entering. All three shared a skittish look. Evodius cleared his throat. "We have already started, so you can go ahead and relax."

"You have worked all day as I have." Augustine reached for the radishes.

Alypius side-stepped, blocking his friend's path. "What no one wants to tell you is that we prefer you stayed out of the kitchen. Save the cooking for others."

"All must do their part here."

"Yes, but some have strengths which better suit them for other chores."

"Is my cooking that terrible?"

187

"As we are supposed to be honest, I can say that…." He faltered.

Evodius took up the task. "The truth is you are the worst cook any of us have ever met. You scorched the porridge we had for breakfast yesterday."

"Burnt the leeks last week," added Alypius. "Was like crunching on insects."

"Somehow you even manage to turn boiled water into a muddy mess."

Adeodatus said, "You would think living with my mother all those years, you would have picked up a few cooking tips from her."

Inwardly amused, Augustine held his hands up in surrender. "I will bend to your collective wisdom. If you think my talents lay elsewhere, I will leave the kitchen to you."

The others sighed in relief. Adeodatus went back to chopping. "Pass the honey. I would like to try out a recipe Mother taught me."

Winter brought more time for reading and visitations. An occasional snowstorm kept the men housebound for a day or two, but the weather quickly cleared. As *servus Dei*, they felt it their duty to help the local church with various projects which included tending the sick and repairing crumbling homes of the poor. Travelers sometimes stayed overnight, feeling safer in the monastery than the inn. The monks attended services twice a day when the weather allowed. Much time was spent in prayer and reflection. Evenings often found the men enjoying discussions on intriguing topics.

Just before spring began, another illness made its rounds through the town. The monks visited the sick, helping in any capacity they could. Several caught the illness themselves and became bed-ridden. Eventually all recovered but Adeodatus. His temperature remained dangerously high for days before he slipped into a coma from which he never awoke.

Augustine sat at the edge of his son's bed, staring at the peaceful youth. The seventeen year old was in fit condition, used to working both the land and the inkwell. He looked as if any moment he would awake, ready to challenge anyone in a debate. Alypius led Augustine away so the body could be prepared for burial. The father shed no tears but his shoulders shook with the effect of keeping his grief hidden. When word spread of the death, many came to pay their consolations. Navigius cried silently as his nephew was placed in the ground, his daughters weeping loudly. They had grown close to their cousin over the last year.

After the bishop said a final prayer, Augustine looked down at the wooden box which contained his beloved son. "No words I can say will ease the pain of separation. Surely what Cicero wrote comes straight from the heart of all fathers. 'You are the only man of all men who I would wish to surpass me in all things.'

Now you delight in the presence of God. What more could a father wish for his son?"

He endured more well-wishers, finding solitude only when he went to bed. Sleep brought no relief unlike it did with his mother's death. The next day he went about his daily routine, always keeping busy. The other monks watched him closely, ready to comfort, but Augustine kept his grief buried. As he washed the supper dishes, he passed a clean bowl to his left, expecting Adeodatus to take it. The clay bowl fell onto the floor, breaking into pieces. Augustine stared at the fragments, his body trembling.

"Are you alright?" asked Alypius.

"Yes, I just…will finish these later."

Augustine left the house, ignoring the questioning looks directed his way by worried friends. He needed to talk to God alone. He walked into the gathering dusk until the monastery was no longer visible. Still he marched. The stars came out, their brilliant lights beautifying the ebony sky.

Augustine looked up, only seeing darkness. "Why, God? I attempt to trust your decisions. You took Didius from me to protect him from my foolishness. My mother had fulfilled her purpose and was ready to embrace you. Through Nebridius's death, his whole family has come to know your love. But why my son now?" Tears streamed down Augustine's cheeks. "He was a better person than I. You should have kept him here and taken me."

Slowly he dropped to his kneels on the cold ground, weeping, body shaking. He poured out his grief and broken heart to God. Finally, when he could cry no more, he laid on the grass, listening to night insects, the tightness of his heart fading. A shooting star zoomed across the heavens, bright for a moment then fading into nothingness.

"Like my son. Brilliantly magnificent for only a brief moment. God, do you see all of us this way? You exist outside of time. We are but tiny insects compared to you. Here for only a moment. How small and fragile we must look to you."

He lay quietly, listening to the musical sounds of the night. The stars loomed overhead, seeming so close he could touch them. Peace slowly swirled into his soul, damping but not erasing grief. Augustine did not understand why he was alive, but accepted that God still had a purpose for him yet to fulfill.

Chapter Twenty-five

Tired from a busy day of weeding in the morning then helping mend a roof after lunch, Augustine paused outside the church. Evening liturgy was still an hour away, but he considered going inside to pray. Pedestrians passed, carrying purchases from the market or laden pails of water from the well.

"Augustine?"

A gentle, familiar voice from behind caused him to turn. Even before he saw her face, he knew it was Galla. She stood quietly in the shadows cast by the church's roof. As she stepped forward, the hood formed by her palla dropped to her shoulders, revealing soft blond hair. She was as beautiful as ever, causing Augustine's heartbeat to quicken in response. As she neared, he stared into her eyes heavy with sorrow.

For a long moment neither spoke, the pain of their souls too great for words. Finally Augustine said, "Did you just arrive?"

Galla glanced over her shoulder down the street to where her brother watered two horses. "A short time ago. I expected to find you at the church. We came as soon as I found someone who could read the letter you sent."

"I have hoped you would have arrived in time for his requiem."

"Seven days is not enough time." Her lips began to tremble. "No time is enough."

He instinctively took a step forward to comfort her but froze. He dared not touch her again. "I...I am sorry...you missed the rite. It was well attended. Adeodatus was loved by many, though he lived here only a short time."

Galla nodded. "He was such a sweet youth." She glanced away, fighting tears.

Augustine struggled to find words to ease her pain. "He is at peace now, enjoying the bliss of being in the presence of God."

Galla reminded silent, brushing away tears which were quickly replaced by new drops. Augustine felt wretched, wanting to hold her, to kiss away her pain, or at least ease it. But he could only stand with hands by his side. The yard separating them might as well be a chasm.

He gave the only gift he had left. "I was wrong in the way I treated you. Forgive me."

She studied him for a long moment. "My path has been long and dark. How at times I hated both you and your mother. You for deserting me and her for being the knife that cut us apart. But she was right, in the end. I eventually passed out of the darkness and found not you, but Jesus, waiting for me. A man may turn against his lover, but Jesus never abandons us. He has showed me how to use my talent for cooking to bring happiness to those who hunger." Seeing Augustine's tormented face, she gave a bittersweet smile. "I forgave you long ago. And I rejoiced when I learned that you had abandoned your pursuit of marriage for the pursuit of heaven. It rest easier on my mind to know that it is not another woman that separates us but God himself."

"I wish it was not under these circumstances that we meet again."

"I too." Her face contorted in feelings she could not express. With effort, she wrestled her emotions back under control. "I go now to mourn my son." Galla pulled the hood back over her head, casting her face into shadow. "Peace be with you."

"And to you."

Galla walked away, her footsteps heavy. Her brother met her with a comforting hug. Augustine watched until they disappeared down the street in the direction of the cemetery. In his heart, he knew he would never see Galla again, at least not in this lifetime. He turned towards the church and entered its quiet sanctuary, seeking solitude.

Restlessness haunted Augustine throughout the spring, the void of missing companions left him with an oppressive hollowness. He continually looked for new projects to concentrate on, but nothing held his attention for long. Just like when Didius died so long ago, Augustine kept seeing constant reminders of people he had lost. A mother leading her children into church was an echo of Monnica. When hearing speeches at the forum, Augustine would imagine the comments Nebridius might have spoken. The last sunbeams peeking through clouds at dusk would bring him to tears as he remembered Adeodatus admiring a similar scene.

He began traveling to other towns, privately seeking a place to build a proper monastery for the growing population of men who had followed him in taking ascetic vows. Only Alypius and Evodius knew his true purpose. Augustine usually traveled alone, passing the journey in prayer as he rode across the wide open plains between towns. Remembering the story of Ambrose being forced into the role of cleric, Augustine avoided visiting cities where their bishops had recently died. Evodius received a letter from a former co-worker who sought advice on religious matters. Evodius was in the midst of a project so he asked Augustine to visit his friend. Augustine saddled his horse and rode the fifty miles to the coastal city of Hippo Regius.

Though not as large as Carthage, Hippo Regius was a thriving seaport sitting at the mouth of the Ubus River and surrounded by vast, fertile plains. To the northwest rose the high mountain ridge of Djebel Edough. During the summer months, darkness fell quickly due to the sun's final rays cut off by the lofty ridge. The city was built long before the Romans had invaded the land and reflected Punic design with curved streets which followed the shape of the land instead of the area being reshaped to follow an architect's master plan. The ancient Numidian kings had built a strong city wall and large palace. Once Rome took control of the region, public buildings had been added to bring the city up to their standards. The circus, amphitheater, and public baths were visited daily by thousands. The city was connected to Carthage by a long paved road which wound for hundreds of miles along the mountainous African coast, making travel slow. By ship, the trip could be made much quicker, and warehouses at both cities were stocked with imports from each other.

Augustine sought out Polus who welcomed him courteously. They discussed religion for hours. Polus was a recently baptized Christian intrigued with the ascetic life, but he was not willing to walk away from his career, unlike his friend Evodius. He invited Augustine to stay for a few days at his home. The next morning Augustine went to morning prayers at the Catholic church located in the heart of the city.

Directly across the street from the church was a basilica belonging to the Donatist, a sect which had branched off from Catholicism over a century ago. Donatists could be found across North Africa and disagreed with a number of Catholic doctrines. At times angry arguments and even riots broke out, usually started by the Donatists. Eighty years ago, one dispute became so heated that Emperor Constantine stepped in by calling for the Council of Arles where he listened carefully to both views. When he sided with the Catholics, the Donatist refused to accept the council's decision and called the Emperor the Devil. Things had only gone downhill from there. From out of the Donatists' ranks came the Circumcellion, bands of extremists who used violence against pagans in order to seek martyrdom. They attacked random travelers while shouting out "Praise God!" They hoped to provoke victims into killing them, wanting to be labeled as martyrs by their violent deaths. Many Donatists were ashamed of the

Circumcellion, but some priests supported them in sermons, even asking for their congregations to use violence against Catholics when a new dispute broke out.

Augustine paused to study the Donatist church across the street. It was larger than its Catholic neighbor, but not as grandly constructed. Twice as many people were entering it. He turned his back to the structure and walked into the Catholic basilica which was surrounded on the outside by a graceful colonnade. What had once started out as a house converted into a church had become a large three-nave structure, its floor decorated with colorful mosaics covering tombs underneath. Augustine stood beside other worshipers, singing heartily. The congregation was made up of people from all social classes, many from the poorer sections of the city.

After communion, Augustine politely introduced himself to the bishop, an elder Greek born in southern Italy. Valerius spoke Latin brokenly, but made up for that fault with his friendliness and generosity. He had read several of Augustine's tracks which dealt with Manichean teachings, and he eagerly invited Augustine for lunch. While eating a simple meal of vegetables and bread, Valerius chatted cheerfully with his guest about the latest news from the pope, various interpretations of their favorite scripture, and life at Augustine's monastery. Valerius was impressed by Augustine's eloquent speech and depth of knowledge. His own sentences were filled with pauses as he searched for correct pronunciations.

"You silver tongue is well needed here. I do my best disputing heresies, but Latin does not come easily to me. I am mocked as a foreigner, jeered when I act as arbitrary for church member facing lawsuits. I have yet to win one public debate."

"I have seen you are well loved by your congregation."

"Yes, those who hold the true faith forgive my unpolished words and see the genuineness of my heart. But I cannot understand the Punic dialect of the country-folk outside town where the Donatist hold much sway. Recently their bishop has forbidden the bakers of the city to sell bread to Catholics. My people are demoralized, some turning away to Manichean. Their priest Faustus is a polished orator who draws large crowds when he speaks at the baths."

"Faustus is here?" Augustine had not seen the Manichean Elder since he left Carthage for Rome.

"You know Faustus?"

"Long ago when I was blinded by the lies of the Manichean I would discuss books with him. Many times I stood with mesmerized crowds listening to his eloquent speeches, but never could he explain to me why natural phenomenon such as eclipses can be predicted. Because of this, I began to see Mani's sacred stories as only myths."

Valerius nodded thoughtfully. "Many are they who are awed by Faustus's stately words but few are they who understand enough to see the faults which lie hidden within."

Augustine spent several more days in Hippo Regius, enjoying the amity of Polus. His hope that Polus would become another of the brethren had ended, but they remained friends. On his last day in the city, he attended the morning Sunday service with him.

Valerius preached about the growing needs of his church, the many demands of ecclesiastical duty. "As I grow older, I lack the time to aid you as you deserve. We need another presbyter, young and energetic, skilled with words, someone bold enough to publicly challenge the enemies who surround us."

The congregation listened intensely, many whispering to each other while glancing over their shoulders. Augustine stood in the nave where he had been enjoying the engrossing sermon, but now he began to feel worried. People were staring at him, some even pointing. How many of them had read his writings, knew his pubic stand against the Manichean? He wanted to flee from the church, but he was trapped within the crowd.

The sermon was cut off as someone shouted, "Here is the one we need! Augustine!"

"Yes, Augustine!" yelled others. "He can stand against the Manichean."

"No, not I." Augustine shook his head. "You need someone else. I have a monastery to attend." But his words were drowned out by the crowd chanting his name.

From the front, Valerius said, "Bring forth the candidate."

Augustine tried to resist, but eager hands seized him, pulling him through the excited crowd yelling his name. He was brought to a halt in front of Valerius standing on the raised apse. Surrounding the bishop was half a dozen elderly presbyters, all staring sternly at him.

Valerius raised his hands for silence and immediately the chanting stopped. "Augustine of Thagaste, the people desire you for the office of presbyter. I myself have examined you and found that you are well qualified to handle the many heavy duties of a cleric. Do you accept this responsibility as an ordained priest of God?"

"I am unworthy of such a position. I am but a simple monk."

The crowd began chatting Augustine's name, becoming louder and louder. Trapped, Augustine lowered his head and cried. What punishment had God now condemned him to? All he desired was a quiet abode where he could live with his brethren, united in friendship and joy, worshiping and studying God's word. Did God now laugh him into scorn, punishing him for all those times in his youth when he had mocked clergymen and their congregations? Feeling his dreams ripped from him, he wept loudly. Some of those watching thought he cried from disappointment of being promoted to only a presbyter instead of a bishop.

"Do you accept?" asked Valerius patiently.

Remembering Ambrose's forced priesthood, Augustine yielded to the fate God had given him. "Yes, I will fulfill the duties God has appointed unto me."

The congregation jubilantly cheered, many coming forward to congratulate him. The presbyters greeted him with smiles, having been in on the plot to draft him. It was some time before the people left and Augustine could confront Valerius alone.

"This is not what I wanted." Augustine did not try to hide his frustration.

"What we want and what God wants is not always the same thing." Valerius walked into a side room and laid his tall, white cap on a shelf.

"Who are you to decide what God desires for me? I have spent the last three years as a faithful Servus Dei. There is still much I can do for him in Thagaste."

"Did you not tell me you had been restless?" The elderly man took off his outer cloak and hung it on a peg. "Augustine, you were never destined to live an isolated life in Thagaste. You have been in the Emperor's court, spoken with some of the most influential men of the empire."

"And I walked willingly away from that life. I no longer seek worldly ambition or the praises of men."

"Which is why you are needed here. God has prepared you for this moment, this purpose. I have already told my presbyters that I have chosen you as my successor. They agree unanimously with my decision. You are under no illusion that the job of a cleric can be lonely and dangerous. Bones of our martyrs rest under this sanctuary. Like Jesus, we are hated and despised by many. But I see within you the passion for truth. You will not be silent when your life is threatened."

"What about my monastery?"

"Build it here." Valerius walked out of the side door and led Augustine behind the church to a large garden. Beyond the field was parkland separating the villas of the richest residences in the city from the business district. "The garden I give to you. Build your monastery there."

Augustine felt his last argument conquered. There would be ample space for both the monastery and a garden for his monks to grow food. "I will abide by your wisdom."

The trip back to Thagaste weighed heavily on Augustine. He had wanted a new, larger location for the monastery, but it came with the price of becoming an ecclesiastic. As a church official, he would be expected to council those seeking advice, tend the sick, advocate for church members facing court cases, speak out against corrupt public policies. If he was promoted to bishop, then there would be sermons to preach, services to plan, various churches in the diocese to visit. When would he find time to read for pleasure or write new books? The simple life of a monk living in constant worship to God was now snatched forever from him.

Back at Thagaste, his friends received the news joyfully. "Think what great accomplishments God can do through you," said Alypius.

"He will give you the strength you need when you need it." Evodius smiled. "Augustine, the presbyter."

Resided to his fate, Augustine began putting his affairs in order, selling the few acres of land he had not given to his brother. He made one final trip to see his sister who lived several villages away. He found her depressed as she dealt with the lingering illness of her husband, now in his early forties. Isauricus had awoken one day to find the right side of his body frozen, his speech impaired, his thoughts muddled. The doctors knew no cure. Perpetua tenderly attended to her husband's needs, feeding him when his hands shook too badly to hold food, leaning in closely to listen to his muttering then interrupting it for others. She oversaw the daily running of the estate. In the evenings they would set on the terrace, Perpetua telling her husband about the day's events and patiently listening to his slow speech.

Augustine was pulled out of his own misery as he watched his sister deal with her heavy troubles. One afternoon they sat on the veranda as her husband dozed in a chair. Perpetua tucked a blanket around Isauricus then sat by Augustine, her eyes keeping close watch on her husband's occasional movements in his sleep.

She tried to keep the conversation light, but deep grief lined her face. "I am very proud of you, brother. A presbyter. And someday a bishop. God will do such wonders through you."

"I follow wherever he leads, though I had wished the path led to quieter pastures."

"You speak not like the Augustine I know, full of dreams and ambitions, travelling to far off places, meeting important dignitaries. How many of us living in small towns have dreamed of such adventures? You can help so many people while I sat here…and…and tend to one man. Sometimes I wished God had made me male so I could accomplish more."

"Speak not so, sister. Do you think I am better than you because I was educated? I wasted years of my life, chasing vanity while you, barren, devotedly raised two children you did not birth and was a helpmate for a husband you loved. I took my concubine for granted and ignored my son. I am the selfish dog and you the saint."

Perpetua reached over and took Augustine's hand. "You are too hard on yourself. I remember you as a loving brother who would tell me such wonderful stories. Perhaps, someday when Isauricus recovers, we can visit Hippi."

"I would like that."

For a while they sat in silence, each lost in their own thoughts. Sorrow became too heavy for Perpetua as she watched her husband sleep. "The doctor says he will never get better, lingering like this for months or years until…until…" Her voice broke. "I cannot survive as a widow. Isauricus is my life."

Now it was Augustine's turn to comfort. "Perhaps, like me, God has another plan waiting for you. Did widowhood ever stop our mother? She accomplished far more single than married, traveling across the empire to aid a wayward son. Living such an exemplary life of service that even Bishop Ambrose praised her. I am certain God has something extraordinary waiting for you."

Perpetua dried her tears. "As he does for you, brother."

Augustine felt uplifted as he travelled back to Thagaste. A new life with tantalizing adventures beckoned. Grief of lost friends and family was replaced with dreams of noble service for God. A proper monastery needed to be built, not a house with a few added rooms. The heretics of the Donatists needed to be opposed. But first, Augustine had to face his past.

Within a short time of moving to Hippo Regius, both strangers and friends began suggesting that Augustine challenge Faustus to a public debate. One day as Augustine and his monks rolled heavy stones into a pile to be used for their new monastery, several Donatist leaders walked over from their church. They frowned as they watched the foundations for the structure being laid but chatted cordially with Augustine.

"We have heard it said you are a reputable speaker," said the eldest. "If so, you should match your skills against Faustus, the best orator in the city. Not even our bishop can outwit this Manichean presbyter. His words are like liquid silver, attracting many away from the Christian faith, burning their souls with his flattering lies."

Augustine set another large rock into place. "If Faustus is willing, so am I. As the Holy Word says, 'Be ready to give a defense to everyone who asks you a reason that he may be able, by sound doctrine, both to exhort and convict the gainsayers.'"

"An interesting combination of quotes from both Peter and Paul. You know your scriptures well. But that will not be enough to beat Faustus. His elongate discourses make the Manichean myths sound like truth to the untrained ear."

The new presbyter smiled. "I too have deep insight and can recognize truth. Tell Faustus that if he is willing, I will debate him at the Baths of Sossius at his customary spot."

The Donatists departed and sought out Faustus, who was reluctant to accept the challenge, remembering all too well the restless, probing questions of a young Augustine. Other Manicheans quickly took up the cry, demanding that their leader face off against the new upstart. Faustus hesitantly agreed.

A few days later, on August 28, hundreds of people gathered in the great hall at the baths. Faustus was surrounded by his supports, while the Catholics gathered in groups near Augustine. Among the crowd moved the Donatists, hoping Faustus would be routed, but wishing Augustine ill at the same time. Any weakness they saw in Augustine would be used later against him. Many spectators came out of curiosity, some Jewish, others pagan, a few with no faith. The debate was the talk of the city for Faustus was well-known.

The combatants stood on a dais above the crowd, both looking confident. Stenographers sat close to the stage, ink and parchment in hand, ready to write down every spoken word. As Augustine had given the challenge, he spoke first. He had spent the day before in fasting and prayer, reflecting on what to say. Today would be one of the most important speeches of his life, for greater than when he spoke in front of the emperor. Then he had spoken lies to flatter men. Today he spoke truth to free souls. His concern was not just for Faustus, but for all who listened today and others who would read the words of the transcribers. Most of all, he wanted to honor his God, so others may feel the love and freedom he now knew.

He began by graciously thanking Faustus for accepting the invitation. The Manichean smiled and politely returned greetings. Then both became serious, slowly feeling each other out as they dived deeply into doctrine. Faustus knew how to work the crowd, to use humor and emotional appeal. Even when many could not gasp complex Manichean concepts, they cheered for his moving anecdotes. For anyone lesser trained, his words seemed like golden wisdom, but Augustine was not fooled. He used logical reason to cut through the lies, carefully restating his opponent's stance in simple terms then slashing it apart with facts. Using his vast knowledge of literature, Augustine quoted from many sources the audience could relate to. A polish speaker, Faustus smoothly countered his rival.

For hours they debated as the boisterous crowd cheered well-spoken points or jeered lines which went against their particular view. As evening closed with no clear winner, both contenders agreed to a break till the next morning. Surrounded by friends, Augustine returned to Valerius's house where he was staying until the monastery was completed. His friends quoted their favorite lines from the debate and offered suggestions for tomorrow. After dinner, Augustine redrew from them, praying late into the night. The final words on his lips when sleep took him were, "Not for my glory but for yours, Father."

The next morning, Augustine was refreshed and confident. Faustus, on the other hand, seemed slightly frazzled. The words of his younger rival had haunted him throughout the night where there were no crowds to flatter as he lay in bed. There Faustus had looked directly into the arguments and trembled that he did not know the answers. The crowd was larger and more energetic than the day before. Faustus tried to portray his usual confidence, but he began faltering in his answers, unable to counterattack his opponent. Even his closest supports began to notice his uncertainty.

For several hours Augustine effortlessly swept away Faustus's every point. Finally Augustine asked, "Do you have any other proof that Mani founded his religious on truth? What concrete proof do you have that his books are not simply the works of a creative mind filled with well-wishing?"

Faustus stood before the crowd, his eyes showing doubt. "I..I thank my opponent for his insightful questions. I will consult with my superiors the arguments I was unable to refute. On the perchance they cannot give satisfactory answer on these matters, I will consult the welfare of my own soul."

With that, Faustus turned and left the dais. His departure was so abrupt, that the crowd was caught off guard. Several booed his leaving. After a moment of silence, friends of Augustine leaped on the stage to congratulate him, while Manicheans shamefully redrew from the crowd, disappointed and troubled that their greatest orator could not withstand Catholic teachings. Donatist leaders were also wary as they moved through the excited crowd. How many of their own followers would be attracted by this new presbyter's charismatic speech and turn away from them? Already they sensed doubt in their church attendees as they passed.

Augustine was embraced by the warmth of his friends.

Alypius grinned, "You left him so confused he will leave the city in shame."

"Now the supporters of Faustus will see that his honeyed words were only elegant falsehoods," exclaimed Evodius.

Elderly Valerius bounced with glee, looking like a school boy. "I knew, just knew you were the answer to my prayers. Who else could stand against Faustus?"

The joyfulness of the victory overwhelmed Augustine. "Not I, but God has conquered his mind and perhaps his heart one day."

Chapter Twenty-six

Triferus now had a busy life. Several days a week he and Possidius visited sick wards, helping where they could. Other days, Possidius worked in the library, attempting to organize and preserve the writing of Augustine. Triferus continued to practice reading, finding the words of Augustine filling not just his mind but also his soul. He was changing, feeling hope for the future again.

When he placed the last chapter of *Confessions* in its bin, Possidius said, "You have greatly improved your reading skills. You flew through the last section."

"I wanted to finish before...he left us."

The bishop nodded, sadness in his eyes. "Augustine has been a great friend and mentor to me."

"How did you first meet Augustine? You are not mentioned in his book."

"He wrote *Confessions* shortly after becoming bishop here, before we met. I was a county lad, much like you, who grew up in a village not far from here. From an early age I knew I wanted to serve God. I heard of a monastery established by a holy man of high reputation. I came, full of eager zeal. Little talent did I possess. No money, little education. But it did not matter. I freely offered my two hands for service. Many have come to this monastery. Some were dreamful youths like me. Others aged before their time with grief and disappointments from life, broken men needing mending. Then there were several educated nobles, great writers and speakers, ready to defend God's kingdom against all heathens, much like Augustine. There were also slaves given to the church by wealthy owners who thought doing so earned them God's favor. Augustine accepted all who came with a sincere heart, regardless of class. He believes everyone is equal in God's eyes. For five years I lived here, learning from the wisdom of my elders. Eventually I was asked to become bishop of Calama."

Triferus sat on a stool, rubbing his injured leg which throbbed from weeding the garden earlier today. "What happened to others in the book, like Augustine's family?"

"After Perpetua's husband died, she came here. With Augustine's help, she established the first nunnery in the region, serving as prioress until her death a few years ago. Navigius remained a farmer in Thagaste. His two daughters became nuns who still live here in the city."

"What about the family of Navigius?"

"His father became a Christian, earning a reputation for generosity to the poor. His sisters became nuns. They trained at the nunnery here for a few years before returning to Carthage to establish one of their own."

"Alypius?"

"He only lived here briefly before being drafted as bishop of Thagaste. He often visits here as a stopover when traveling to Rome to represent our providence to the pope or going to Milan to bring religious matters to the attendance of the Emperor. That is where he is right now, pleading for Valentinian III to remember his citizens of Africa."

"Will the Emperor send troops to help us?"

Possidius paused, looking wearily out the only window in the library. "Perhaps in the spring when the ice melts and shipping lanes open again."

"But it is August now and winter yet to come. We cannot last till spring."

"It takes time to move troops."

"The Vandals have been in Africa for over a year. How much time does the Emperor need?"

The bishop looked at the youth and spoke hard truth. "North Africa is not the main interest of the Emperor. Other providences are unstable. Just twenty years ago Rome itself was ransacked by Alaric, king of the Visigoths. His troops did not stay long, but many of our citizens lost confidence in the ability of our government to protect us."

Despair smothering the brief hope Triferus had begun to feel. "If the Emperor abandons us, we die."

"Place not your hope in emperors, but in God. Only he truly controls our fate."

The old anger returned to the youth. "Why does God allow this? If he is love, why does he allow evil to exist? Does he even care that we suffer?"

"Yes, did he not send his only son to share our pain?"

Triferus looked away. Yes, Jesus may have died a torturous death on the cross. But why did God not just end suffering? The youth closed his eyes, feeling the heaviness of the world on his shoulders as he remembered the faces of the dying he had met in the sick wards. His family being slaughtered before him. Only fifteen, he felt like an old man.

"Your questions, Triferus, are not easy to answer." Possidius rose stiffly from his stool and walked to another bin. "Many have asked them before, including

202

Marcellinus, an associate of Emperor Honorius. After the sacking of Rome, he wrote to Augustine, asking him to explain why God had allowed this to happen to a Christian nation." The bishop pointed to the bin filled to the brim with scrolls. "This was Augustine's answer. For eighteen years, he labored on *City of God*, only finishing it a few years ago. His greatest work, in my opinion."

The youth looked at the huge pile of scrolls. It has been difficult enough reading a short narrative. It might take a lifetime for him to struggle through such a weighty tome full of theological jargon. "Is there a way to sum it up, without the studying?"

"Yes. Trust God, even when you do not understand. That is the short answer. When you are ready for a deeper response, start here."

Possidius placed the first scroll in Triferus's hand. The youth tucked it away. He was in no mood for more reading.

Triferus left the library to work on chores, aiding several novices in sweeping the floor of the church. He then volunteered to carry Augustine's supper to him. Under the bishop's own orders, few were now allowed entrance into his cell. Sometimes when Triferus brought meals, he would stand at the door listening briefly to the holy man's prayers. Phrases he heard including appeals for the souls of Africa, psalms woven together in blissful worship, even pleads for the Vandals to find salvation. Augustine chatted with God as if conversing with a close friend.

Triferus felt guilty for eavesdropping. Today, he entered quietly, replacing the half-finished meal from lunch with a new bowl of hot soup. The bishop slept, allowing Triferus to study the wrinkled face of the seventy-six-year old. In sleep, Augustine looked peaceful, but his pillow was wet from weeping.

Triferus left, heading towards the kitchen. He was halfway down the hall when a strange man cradling an unconscious boy blocked his way.

"Where is Augustine? I must see him."

"He is not well and will receive no visitors."

"That is what the other monks said, but I must see him." The man glanced worriedly at the pale child. "My son dies."

Hearing noise, Possidius stepped out of the library. "You can take your son to the church for baptism."

"No, my son will not die if I can see Augustine. Please."

Possidius frowned. "I will check if he can see you." The bishop led the way to Augustine's cell and stepped inside alone. A moment later he beckoned the father in. Augustine was awake but too feeble to sit up.

The man knelt by Augustine's bed. "Please, sir, I implore you to place your hands on my son to heal him."

Augustine weakly looked at the sick child, pity in his eyes. "As you can see, I am dying myself. If I had the ability to heal, I would surely have used that power on myself first."

"But you must. Last night I saw in a vision God telling me to come to you, asking you what I had said. In the dream, my son recovered."

"If God has directed, then I will do so." Augustine reached out a thin, wrinkled hand and rested it on the boy's head.

Before the bishop even began to pray, the child opened his eyes and yawned. "Where am I, Father?"

The man broke down into tears. "With the holy bishop, my son."

Possidius touched the boy's forehead. "His fever has broken. Now Augustine must rest."

With many thanks, the father left with his son walking beside him. Possidius shut the cell door, leaving Augustine alone. Behind it Triferus could hear the hoarse voice of Augustine singing a psalm of praise. Triferus was filled with wonder and astonishment. In the midst of death and despair a miracle had taken place. If God could heal this young boy, why did he not just end the war? Bring peace and life everywhere? It was difficult to trust God when God seemed so distant and tragedy so close.

After supper, Triferus sought isolation, watching the sun disappear behind the trees beyond the garden. Here, surrounded by the final harvest before the brutal winter, Triferus pondered the meaning of the miracle. Had God healed the boy only for him to starve to death in a few months? Or would God protect the boy and his family for some greater purpose?

The words of a psalm drifting into Triferus's mind, *Be still and know I am God.* Triferus allowed himself to relax, breathing in the fragrance of late blooming flowers. The first frost would soon kill them. But for now, life was wondrous and mysterious. At least for this moment, this heartbeat, Triferus knew the joy of seeing a true miracle.

The next day Augustine left Hippo Regius for the last time. Triferus was the one who found the lifeless body when he brought breakfast. For a long moment he stood still, holding the tray of food, feeling sadness, but not deep grief like when he had lost his family. Triferus had seen death countless times now. Often it was terrible and cruel, but here, in the bishop's cell, it came gently and somehow beautifully. An otherworldly presence seemed to lingered, a sweetness Triferus could not explain. For the briefest of moments, the youth felt that windows of Heaven were open, shining light into the small chamber, filling his soul with yearning for a paradise which lay just beyond. Even as the emotion faded, its echo would stay with Triferus forever.

A simple service was held for Augustine that afternoon. Heraclius, who had been co-bishop of the city with Augustine for the last four year, spoke movingly of his friend. The sanctuary was packed with mourners, including General Boniface, city officials, and other nobles. They stood beside slaves, freed men, and tenants, all who came to pay homage to the holy man. Already, the people began calling Augustine a saint.

Sadness hung over the monastery for weeks. Triferus moved among the grieving bishops and presbyters, serving meals and cleaning tables. He listened to their many stories. How Augustine boldly stood against countless heretics, challenging them both in public debates and in writings.

"It is because of him, we Catholics can hold up our heads again in Africa. With him as our spokesman, we went from a persecuted minority to thriving majority."

"Remember the time when he was away visiting another city and we discovered that slavers were capturing Roman citizens from outlying villages and transporting them through our port to plantations in Italy. We used all the church's gold to buy their freedom, even selling the communion cup. We feared Augustine would be furious at us when he returned, but instead he praised us, wishing we could have saved more."

"Yes, he spoke out furiously against city officials turning a blind's eye to the illegal trading because their coffers had been filled with bribes. I remember how tenderly he spoke with that little girl we rescued, asking her about the home she had been kidnapped from. What a relief we could return her safely to her family."

On and on went the stories. It was from this monastery that many had trained, going out to other cities to build their own. How many churches still remained that the Vandals had not burned? The loss of Augustine amplified the priests' deep grief for their parishioners, for the destruction of quaint villages and mighty cities. Some pondered out loud if the wrath of God spoken of in Revelations was coming to pass now. Was it the end of the glorious Roman Empire? Perhaps the whole world?

Winter came, bringing starvation. What little food had been stored was soon gone. Across the city, people became desperate, eating livestock, even pets. Then they turned to vermin, catching the rats and roaches crawling through the drainage channels. The stench of death constantly hung over the city, plagues daily snatching away souls. Triferus was repeatedly sick, days going by when he could not rise from his bedroll, barely sipping the soup- flavored water given to him. When he had strength, he aided others sicker than himself.

Spring finally arrived. The monks planted their field, enlarging it to include the parkland which separated the church grounds from the villas of the rich. The wealthy had their own gardens and beehives. Servants had to be constantly on guard to defend against hungry looters. When fresh vegetables finally became part of Triferus's diet again, his mind cleared and his strength returned. He visited sick wards across the city, often alone, sometimes with Possidius or another monk with him.

His new duties did not go unnoticed. As a monk passed out clean laundry, he handed Triferus a black robe instead of the usual brown tunic. Triferus stared at the black cloth in his hands, understanding the heavy responsibilities which went with it. Only monks who had taken their vows or candidates contemplating such a life were permitted such clothing. Triferus had never stated he desired to be a cleric, yet he lived it every day. After a moment, Triferus nodded his thanks to the monk, and walked away with the robe. After his evening bath, he put it on.

People treated Triferus differently. Before, he could limp down a street unnoticed. Now strangers nodded to him cordially or moved out of his path so he would not be jostled. A traveler looking for an address or a child who had lost his way would call to him for help. But the robe also drew hatred. More than once a drunkard would strut up to him, cursing loudly both God and clerics. Random people, bitter and hungry, sometimes spat at him without warning. Each time Triferus simply walked on, ignoring those who mistreated him. He also was hungry and weary, knew too well the companions of grief and hate.

One day as Triferus was about to leave a sick ward, a soldier marched in, asking for a priest. Triferus stepped forward. "How can I serve you?"

The man frowned. "You are too young." He glanced about the many bedrolls of the dying, seeing no other clerics. "I guess you will do. Come."

Triferus followed the man towards the harbor where the military barracks were located. He was ushered into a room with a desk covered with parchments. A map of the city was tacked to the wall. General Boniface was studying it, his lips pressed into a deep scowl. He glanced at Triferus then said to the aid, "Could you not find one older?"

"Many of the oldest have died, sir. I brought who I could find."

Boniface dismissed the aid and sat down, his face fatigued. "I have met you before when visiting Augustine. Sit. I would offer you something to drink, but we have only water left."

"If you wish for a seasoned priest, you can visit a church." Before the Vandals arrived, Triferus would have been intimated to be in the presence of a general. After the death of his family he had felt hatred. Now he only felt weariness.

"As I am sure you have noticed, tensions are high in the city, and I am unpopular. No longer can I walk about the city without an armed escort. I thought it best to bring a priest here."

"What services are you seeking from a cleric, sir?"

"To hear my confessions."

"Then you should know that I have taken no vows though I wear the robe."

"Yet you do the duties of a monk." The general leaned back in his chair, for a moment letting the heavy load of his responsibilities slide away. "I once was in your position. After my wife died, I longed for the solitude of spending my days in prayer and studying the Holy Scripture. I even spent time in the monastery as a candidate."

"I did not know that. Why did you not become a monk, if you do not mine my asking?"

"Though you have not been consecrated, I trust you will keep what I say in confidence."

"Of course, sir."

"My pride. I went back to the army. Ambitious to prove myself great, I eventually earned my current position. One day I received a summons from Placidia, the Empress who governs for young Valentinian III. I did not know it then, but a rival of mine named Aetius had persuaded her to call me from Africa. Aetius whispered lies to me, saying she was going to executed me. In my pride I listened to his poisonous tale and rebelled against the Empress. I invited the Vandals here to Africa as an ally against her, having no idea what hideous savagery they were capable of."

Triferus's fingers tightened on the armrest. He knew firsthand what they could do.

"They secretly joined forces with the Moors and began plundering the land. Because of their hatred for Catholics, Donatist began supporting them." Anger lined the general's face. "By the time I learned of their actions, several cities had already fallen. Still I tried to seek a peaceful compromise. I met with their king, begging him to return to Spain. Genserik just laughed in my face. No longer could I control the forces I had unleashed. Augustine and Alypius traveled to me, despite their elderly age, asking me to engage Genserik in battle to protect our countrymen. But I kept tarring, hoping the Empresses would send reinforcements. I wrote her, explaining I had been tricked by Aetius, pleading for more troops. But from Milan only comes silence."

"The Roman government has abandoned us then?" Triferus kept his voice flat, hiding the stab of fear he felt.

"It would seem so." The general looked back at the map on the wall, his face haunted. "The destruction of the realm comes because of my pride. When I was a candidate, Augustine had warned me of my folly, that I had to let it go. I envy you. No dark deeds eat at your soul. You serve God while I have served myself. Oh, how I wished I had casted away pride and joined the brotherhood so long ago. Now it is too late. I will spend the rest of my life seeking to amend my mistakes, watching good men die for my vanity. That knowledge ravages me. Is that a good enough confession for you, young priest?"

"I too see good people suffer. I hear their prayers every day. See their tears." Triferus felt a stab of the old anger.

Boniface swallowed, his eyes troubled. "You smother me under more guilt."

"I know not what words to say to give you peace."

"I will know no true peace as long as Genserik and Aetius live. Go back to your holy church and find the peace I cannot. When God answers you, say a prayer for me. Ask him for my forgiveness."

"I am certain Bishop Augustine has already talked to God on your behave." Triferus stood. "But I too will pray for you, if I find peace."

The conversation haunted Triferus throughout the long walk back to the monastery. No longer could he hate the general after looking into the man's tormented eyes. Still, because of his mistakes, the entire providence lay in ruins. But Boniface's guilt was shared with others. King Genserik was the one ordering his troops to target Catholics, promoting rape and torture. Aetius thought only of ridding himself of a rival, caring nothing about the tens of thousands who would suffer as he manipulated Boniface. Unlike the others, Boniface sought redemption for his mistakes.

Entering the sanctuary of the basilicas, Triferus paused, watching several people kneeling in prayer near the front. He walked down the aisle and bent on the floor, praying silently for God to forgive his hatred against the general. He then found a broom and swept, cleaning the mosaics covering the bodies of saints. He paused near the lectern at the front of the church. Here, under the decorative marble floor lay the body of Augustine. Triferus felt pangs of grief as he continued to sweep.

Months drifted by slowly. Riots over food occasionally broke out. Those with gardens guarded their vegetables constantly, even the monks. The Vandals now rarely attacked the wall, simply waiting until the city was starved into submission. Then one day without warning, the siege was lifted. When dawn arrived, Romans on the wall looked out to see an empty, muddy plain where for fourteen long months had camped eighty thousands foes. Word quickly spread through the city and throngs of people climbed the steep stairs of the walls to see for themselves, including Triferus.

Around him people shouted in joy. Yet others doubted. A filthy man in rags danced up to Triferus and patted him on the shoulder. "God has answered our prayers, holy man!"

"How can you be sure?" asked a weary woman holding an infant. "What if it is a trick, like in Troy?"

"Have you not heard? General Boniface's scouts have already tracked them far to the east."

Triferus frowned. "It is only mid-morning. How have the scouts found the time to follow them so far?"

The man brushed away the youth's concerns. "The Emperor's troops must be marching from the east and the Vandals are setting out to meet them. We are saved!" The old man grabbed the woman and twirled her about in a dance on the massive wall.

She quickly pulled away, glancing at her infant which had just awoken. Still, she smiled. "I can return home now."

Many thought like her. Within hours, a massive exodus began as thousands of people poured out of the city, spreading out across the countryside. Triferus watched from the wall as the roads were crowded with hungry people eager to escape from the city which had become a death trap. Due to the lack of horses and oxen, groups of men heading to the same village pulled wagons together, their women and children walking beside them, carrying bags. Triferus glanced towards the empty east, hoping the Vandals did not return and catch the travelers unprepared.

He returned to the monastery, finding Possidius working in the library. "Are you returning to Calama? I see other priests already leaving."

Possidius put down the parchment he had been reading. "Calama is to the east in the path of the Vandals. Traveling will be very dangerous right now. Without food, honest citizens may resort to thievery. There will be many who lived through the siege only to loose their lives on the road home. Besides, there is much that still needs to be done here. I promised Augustine I would preserve the library. Our transcribers are nearly finishing copying his *On the Trinity*. I wish to bring a copy with me back to Calama. Are you returning home?"

"The village of my birth is no longer my home. There is nothing to go back to but painful memories."

Within days, Hippo Regius became a desolated, empty city. Even Boniface pulled out most of his troops and headed east after the Vandal army. Only a skeleton crew was left behind to defend the walls. Still, hundreds of citizens remained in the quiet city. Some were too sick or old for travel, others too afraid. Wealthy patricians hid in their beautiful villas whose stone walls protected precious gardens. Most of the bishops left, heading back to their sees. Triferus remained at the monastery, working in the fields beside the monks who chose to remain.

He enjoyed the feeling of warm sunshine on his back and the weight of a basket as it filled with produce he picked from green stalks. This had been his life before the Vandals came. A farmer tending crops. Simple, honest work. With better food, his cripple leg had mended, his limp not as pronounced, though it would stay with him the rest of his life.

Life. Was it really possible to have one now? At night, as Triferus lay on his bedroll in the cell, now with no roommates, grief for his lost family lured him into short bouts of depression. Bright sunshine and cheerful greetings of friendly monks pulled him back from it.

Triferus helped carry extra vegetables to needy patronages who had remained in the city. As he handed over a heavy basket to a young man who had stayed with an aged grandmother, they both noticed a panicked man running down the street.

The man screamed, "The Vandals have returned! The city burns! Run for your lives!"

Looking at the sky, Triferus spotted smoke rising in the north. Leaving the young man to aid his family, Triferus hurried towards the monastery, his crippled leg keeping him from a full sprint. Spotting a monk with an empty basket walking out of an apartment building, Triferus yelled out the news.

"The Vandals are in the city! We must warn everyone."

The other monk glanced at the skyline, his face showing horror. "I will tell the nuns, you go to the monastery."

Triferus ran, ignoring pain from his leg. Glancing behind him, he could see the sky darkening, blocking out the sun. His worst nightmare had come true. The barbarians had returned, easily overrunning the few city defenders. Now nothing remained in their way of slaughtering the people left. He passed through an empty market. Once there had been dozens of booths selling imports from across the empire. Now only a few merchants sold basic supplies. Triferus yelled out a warning and continued, his breath wheezing, terror keeping his feet moving.

He ran up the steps of the church and collapsed in front of Bishop Heraclius who had been counseling a patrician. "Vandals…here…in city."

The priest paled and immediately began issuing orders. While Triferus lay on the floor, regaining his breath, he watched visitors dashing out to warn families and monks running by with the gold communion cup and other valuables to hide. He rose and limped across the insula to the monastery, finding Possidius in the library, aides dashing by with documents to stash in the damp cellar.

Triferus stood still in the chaos, he mind screaming it was unfair. Just when he was beginning to feel alive again, hope had been snatched away from him. Why could he not have died during the winter when he had lain weak with hungry, unable to rise, mind too numb to care?

Seeing the youth's frighten face, Possidius said, "We will go to the sanctuary to pray."

"What good will it do? We are dead."

"Not yet, son. Perhaps God has plans for us yet."

Triferus followed the bishop back into the basilica, his body trembling. The breeze from the sea brought not the smell of salt but of smoke. The sanctuary was already filling with frighten people, parents holding children tightly, merchants who had abandoned their wares, bloody soldiers tired of running.

Staring at them, Triferus whispered, "Why are they here? Do they not know Vandals will target this church first?"

"They come for hope from the only one who can save us now."

People dropped to their knees, pleading to God for mercy, weeping desperately. Possidius knelt down with other clerics, his lips moving in prayer. Out the windows Triferus saw people running down the streets, some in a blind panic, others trying to drag belongings after them. What was the point? Everyone would die, if they fled or stayed. Triferus knelt on the floor with the others. The sky blackened as the smoke thickened. People began coughing, covering their mouths with cloth. The crying grew louder.

Looking at the floor, Triferus noticed he was near the lectern. There, under the cool marble tile lay Augustine, in peace while his world burned. Under other decorative murals lay bones of martyrs, heroes who had chosen to die for their faith.

Silently Triferus prayed, "Why, God? How do our deaths serve some great purpose? I do not understand."

In his mind whispered Possidius's comment from weeks ago, *Trust God, even when you do not understand.*

Trust. Even when the world was ending? When death was a certainty?

Someone began chanting a psalm. Others joined in, their voices growing stronger in unity. Triferus closed his eyes and thought of the peace he had felt when he had stood in Augustine's cell the day the saint had died. Soon he would also be with his family, the miseries of this world forgotten. He added his rough voice with the others, singing for the first time since his sister's death.

For hours the people prayed and sang, expecting death by fire or by sword at any moment. Night fell and neither came. Tidbits of food were passed around in the darkness. People slept on the cold floor, sharing blankets the monks had brought over from the monastery. Triferus woke at dawn, hearing several voices whispering in awe.

"It's a miracle, I tell you. I walked about outside, and the fire missed us completely. Come and see."

"But the Vandals?"

"I saw none. Perhaps the fire killed them too."

Triferus arose with others and stepped outside. The buildings near them were unharmed, but ash drifted down from other areas of the city still smothering. The fields which the monks kept well-watered had acted as a shield, protecting the church from the fire while the rich villas on the other side had been incinerated. People stared in shock, many saying prayers of thanks. But the danger was not yet over. The Vandal army lay somewhere nearby.

Some people went home. Others stayed at the church for they had nowhere to go. The waiting was intense. They have survived the fire, but next would come the sword. Midafternoon several armed Vandals walked passed, swords in hand, eyes alert for trouble. They gave no heed to the church or the people huddled inside.

Several hours later an excited merchant entered the church. "It is over. Finally. We can move about without fear."

"How do you know?" asked people crowding around him.

"Because a Vandal stopped at my booth, asking me why my shop was closed. He wished to buy something. Fearfully I told him he could have anything he wanted. He laughed and pulled out money. Told me the city was now under Vandal control and life would return to normal—as long as we obeyed their laws. He said to spread the word that they expected businesses to open because they wanted their taxes."

"What about the church?" asked Triferus. "They burnt the one in my village."

"They do not seem concerned about that right now. My cousin went up on the wall. He said the forces which attacked us are only a third of what used to be out there. He figures their main force is still moving east. Carthage will be their focus. Whoever controls that city controls all of North Africa."

Life began to return to the city. The Vandals set up headquarters in the Roman barracks, opening up the port for trading with other cities they had conquered. They needed a steady supply of food and equipment, which meant it was urgent to develop a thriving economy as quickly as possible. Those who survived the original attack of the city began putting their lives back together. Shops reopened. Homes began to be rebuilt.

Several weeks later, Possidius and several other monks left Hippo Regius to return to Calama. Triferus joined them. Beside the food in their bags, they also carried copies of the gospels, the letters of Paul, and several books of Augustine. They walked along the Roman road, passing through ruin towns and villages. The Vandals had left a wake of destruction in their path. Some settlements had been completed destroyed, the inhabitants vanished. Fields had been left unplowed, orchids unattended, pastured abandoned. Only burnt husk remained where Catholic churches once stood. At times grief overwhelmed the monks, and they feared what they would find at Calama.

Remembering his promise to the dying soldier in the warehouse, Triferus sought out the town where the man had once lived. Most of the town was intact, and a merchant pointed Triferus to a small villa on the outskirts of town.

An old, wary man answered the door, glancing in concern at the three monks still standing in the road. "What do you want?"

"I met your son in a ward. He asked me to give this to you after his...." Triferus held out the sealed parchment, unable to say more.

The man's eyes soften and his lips trembled. "I...thank you. Please, come in and refresh yourself."

"We must be going. We hope to reach Calama by nightfall."

"The city did not fare well, at least that is what I heard."

"Thanks for the warning."

As the sun faded that evening, they entered the remains of a broken city, its protective walls gone, churches, forum, and theaters burned. They walked down the main street, and people recognizing Possidius came out to greet him.

"They burnt our churches, Father. But they left the Donatist church."

"The priests who stayed were murdered, including my cousin. There is none left to give the Sacraments."

"My wife died without anyone to give last rites. Did she at least make it to purgatory?"

"They took my daughter. Have you seen her? She has her mother's blond hair."

The weight of their pleas broke Possidius. He stood in the middle of the road, surrounded by his people, tears streaming down his face. "I should have been here for you."

A disfigured man missing several fingers stepped forward. "You would only have been killed with the other priests. We are grateful you are here now. We have already begun to rebuild the church. Come and see."

They walked to the center of town where a small building stood with an half completed roof.

"Sorry, Father, that it is not as big as our other church."

"It will do. Tomorrow I will give the Eucharist to all who wish it."

"We will spread the word."

Triferus lay on his bedroll on the floor of the homely church, staring at the stars beyond the exposed beams of the unfinished roof. So much destruction and loss, yet still the people kept their faith. They had built a church though there was no priests. They hungered for reassurance in a chaotic world. For peace. For God.

The next morning the small building was packed with people eager to hear the bishop speak. After communion, many asked for special prayers, even as the red tiles of the roof were still being laid into place above their heads. Throughout the day others came, asking for baptism or to give alms. Triferus helped by joining a line of people passing clay tiles up to the roof. Later he fetched water. It felt good to help, to watch people begin to heal.

Several days later, after a long day of labor, Triferus sat on a hill overlooking the church and half burnt town. He gazed beyond to a mountain range covered in low clouds. The breeze brought the scent of rain. Triferus breathed deeply, feeling refreshed. He unwound a scroll, the first section of *City of God*. Believing the text would be full of theological jargon, he had put off reading it till now.

To his surprise, it began by describe the sacking of Rome twenty years before. Of torture and murder, rapes and enslavement. Yet in the midst of darkness, people had been saved. The invaders were apprehensive of the Christian God, giving sanctuary to any inside a church. Learning that, pagans had hidden with the Catholics, proclaiming a faith they did not believe.

Augustine wrote, "For this clemency our detractors ought rather to give thanks to God. They should have recourse to his name in all sincerity, so as to escape the penalty of everlasting fire, seeing that so many of them assumed his name dishonestly to escape the penalty of immediate destruction."

Triferus felt a stab of guilt. Why had he stayed for so long with the monks? They gave him food and shelter in time of crisis. He had repaid them by doing chores. But why did he still wear the robe? He had never even asked to be a candidate when he began wearing their black cloth. The battle front was now passed far to the east. Triferus had no more excuses. Either he should take the vows of a monk or become a layman. No longer could he continue to walk in between.

He looked out beyond the city to fertile fields which peasants tended. There were young maidens who had escaped the raids. Perhaps he could win the hand of a bride. Though he had a limp, he could still plow and hoe. Life as a farmer appealed to him. Had that not been what he wanted before the invasion? But now, after seeing so much despair, of seeing people rekindled with hope in God, a part of him wanted to continue serving. But to be a monk? Never to marry or have children? To live one's life in constant service, having no private funds or property? To be hated and persecuted by heretics? Was he willing to embrace a lifetime of sacrifice?

He glanced back at the text in his hand. "For God's providence constantly uses war to correct and chasten the corrupt morals of mankind, as it also uses such afflictions to train men in a righteous and laudable way of life, removing to a better state those whose life is approved, or else keeping them in this world for further service."

The words spoke to Triferus's heart. He had asked God repeatedly why he had lived while so many others had not. Was God protecting him, preparing him for the harsh life of a monk? Triferus felt himself unworthy. He could barely read, let alone speak before a crowd. But that did not matter. He had two hands in which to serve.

Rain gently began falling. Triferus tucked the scroll into his robe but did not hurry indoors. Instead, he looked up to the sky, letting cool water run down his face, baptizing him anew.

Afterword

The Vandals continued to advance against the Romans, finally agreeing to a halt in 435 AD. General Boniface returned to Rome and challenged his rival Aetius at the Battle of Ravenna. Boniface's forces won, but he died shortly afterwards from wounds received in the fight. Four years later King Gaiseric broke the truce, taking Carthage by surprise. The victory gave him access to a major shipyard and the galleys anchored there, putting him in the position to challenge Rome.

History only records three churches in the African providences escaping destruction: Hippo Regius, Carthage, and Cirta. After several years, persecution against Catholics increased again, forcing Possidius to flee his beloved homeland for Rome. He spent the rest of his life preserving religious text. Triferus journeyed with Possidius to Italy but soon grew restless. Believing the Holy Word should be shared with barbarians, he became a missionary, traveling north to the Goths where he established a monastery. Following the model of Augustine, he trained dedicated men who went out themselves to create new abbeys.

In 455, King Gaiseric sailed for Rome. Hearing of his coming, the citizens panicked, fleeing the city in vast numbers. Emperor Maximus, fearing he could not raise an army in time to protect the city, abandoned Rome. An angry crowd recognized him and stoned him to death. He had only reigned for seventy days. When King Gaiseric landed in Italy, he met no resistance. For two weeks the great city of Rome was plundered and countless riches were shipped away, leading to a new word entering the Latin language—vandalism.

Yearly the Vandals continues to sail along the coast, raiding cities and pirating ships. In an attempt to stop them, Emperor Leo launched the most expensive expedition in Roman history. Using stealth under the cover of night, King Gaiseric's fleet decimated the Roman ships. But it was a Gothic solider named Odoacer who took control of Italy in 476, marking the end to the Western Roman Empire.

Less than fifty years after Augustine's death, the world he had written about was gone. An entire culture collapsed, its advance knowledge of math, science, and technology slowly fading into obscurity. Countless books disappeared forever. Catholics continued to be persecuted in North Africa. Most were wiped out in the subsequence invasion of the Saracen. Yet Christianity persevered, spreading across Europe. Through the centuries of great darkness when few could read, monks continued to copy by hand the ancient books of beloved writers.

Thanks to their labors, over a hundred books, sermons, and letters written by Augustine can still be read sixteen hundred years later. Every document that Possidius listed in *Indiculus* has been preserved, including several lost pieces rediscovered in 1975 and 1990. *Confessions* had never been out of circulation from the time of its first publication in 397.

Augustine's many works have been highly influential in shaping Christian theology. Augustine was canonized by popular demand. In 1298, Augustine along with Ambrose, Jerome, and Pope Gregory I were recognized as the Great Doctors of the Western Church.

Monnica, the mother who refused to give up on a wayward son, is the patron saint of wives and abused victims. By order of the pope in 1430, her relics were brought to Rome and placed in the basilica construction in honor of her son.

Author's Note

Most characters, both major and minor, in this novel are based on real life people. Their fates in the story match what history records about them. Triferus, though, is a fictional character.

After reading Possidus's biography about his friend, I realize that Augustine's story was not about just one man but about an entire society facing heart-wrenching catastrophe. Triferus became a symbol of what the North African people endured as the Vandals raided their towns, mercilessly slaughtering and destroying. He also represented the rekindling of faith when there was little left to believe in. His fate is intertwined with the many monks who dedicated their lives to preserving precious texts and spreading God's love in a dark, uncertain world.

References

The following is a list of many, but not all sources, used in the research for this novel.

Angela, Alberto (2009). *A Day in the Life of Ancient Rome*. Translated by Gregory Conti. Europa Editions: Canada.

Brady, Jules, editor (2002). *Augustine for Everyone*. St. Paul: New York.

Brown, Peter (2000). *Augustine of Hippo: A Biography*. University of California Press: Berkeley.

Chadwick, Henry (2009). *Augustine of Hippo: A Life*. Oxford University Press: Oxford.

Fitezgerald, Allan, general editor (1999). *Augustine Through the Ages: An Encyclopedia*. WM B. Eerdmans Publishing Company: Grand Rapids, Michigan.

Possidius, Bishop of Calama (2008). *The Life of Saint Augustine*, a translation of *Sancti Augustini Vita*. Translated by Herbert T. Weiskotten. Christian Roman Empire Series, Vol. 6. Evolution Publishing: Merchantville, NJ.

Saint Augustine (2003). *City of God*. Translated by Henry Bettenson. Penguin Books: London.

Saint Augustine (2008). *Confessions*. Translated by Henry Chadwick. Oxford World's Classics. University Press: Oxford.

Saint Augustine (1996). *Enchiridion on Faith, Hope, and Love*. Translated by J. B. Shaw. Gateway Editions. Regency Publishing, Inc: Washington, D.C.

Shelton, Jo-Ann (1998). *As the Romans Did*, Second Edition. Oxford University Press: New York.

Virgil (2006). *The Aeneid*. Translated by Robert Fagles. Penguin Classics: America.

About the Author

Books have fascinated me since I was a small child sitting beside my mother, listening to her read books I had selected from the library. Soon I was reading on my own, and I never stopped. Over the years my interests have varied wildly from stories about animals to the classics to science fiction, and much in between.

In sixth grade my English teacher assigned us to write a short story. I got a tad carried away, writing a VERY long story about the adventures of a cat. Part of the way through the writing process, I realized this is what I wanted to do the rest of my life.

So I began writing short stories and eventually novels. I also became an English teacher because I wanted to share my love of literature with others. I later branched into teaching technology, another one of my passions.

The results you hold in your hands is from years of exploring my imagination and the intensive but exciting labor of writing.

I would appreciate, if you have a moment, giving my book a rating at Amazon, Goodreads, and other sites that interest you. In the limited free time I now have, the books I choose to read are usually recommended to me by friends, so I know the power of word-of-mouth.

I hope you enjoyed reading this book as much as I enjoyed writing it.

Sincerely,
Vista Townsend

Updates for new projects can be found at:
Website: vistatownsend.net
Facebook: Vista.townsend
Twitter: Vista_Townsend

www.ingramcontent.com/pod-product-compliance
Lightning Source LLC
Chambersburg PA
CBHW060913180626
46817CB00004B/1244